0

THE DAYS OF HAIRAWN MUHLY

A Novel by

Carol Ann Ross

1

DEDICATION

I dedicate THE DAYS OF HAIRAWN MUHLY to my brother John. Thank you for always being honest and telling me as you see it. Thank you too, for never being judgmental.

ACKNOWLEDGEMENTS

Putting a book together is a lot of fun, especially if you love what you're writing about. I tingle at the opportunity to learn the history of an area and am overwhelmed with gratitude that God has allowed me to experience the creative process. But there is work involved too when writing – that's the not much fun part. What makes it all worthwhile though, are the people who help you do the things that are not much fun. I marvel at their knowledge and their patience and stand very grateful for their help.

First, thank you so very much Rudy Batts. Your knowledge of the area is immense. I thank you not only for the historical information you imparted to me, but also for your and your lovely wife, Rosilee's hospitality. I have never walked into a home that exuded such friendliness and acceptance.

Secondly, I would like to thank Cathy Teoste, Patti and Bruce Blacknight, Debra McKnight, Amy Pretty and Kelly Lafar. You are all so talented – and you are computer savvy too!

Thank you all for your dedication and help.

INTRODUCTION

1933

In the dune valleys and flats of the banks a particular plant grows alongside the yucca, cactus and sand spurs. It is common to the sandy barrier island and in the winter months its long beige-gray stems stand dormant as it blends with the other sleeping beach grasses. But in summer it comes to life as the stems, seemingly caught in death's firm grip, burst forth with a haze of purple blooms. The Hairawn Muhly makes even the tall yucca, with its showy white bells, pale in comparison as it catches the eye with its lonesome beauty, swaying with the breezes off the Atlantic.

Pearl Scaggins loved the Hairawn Muhly. Its blooms were her favorite color and when she came with her family to the banks her parents knew that if she was nowhere to be seen, she was most certainly in a valley picking the plant.

During its season her bedroom would be ablaze with the beach flower as a dozen or so quart size canning jars, half filled with water, supported the sprays of what she called purple heather. With the sprays of muhly in her room and the shades pulled up letting the sun in, Pearl could see the dust like muhly fuzz float through the air.

She'd watch the dust like particles and laugh as they sparkled in the sunlight. Even in the evenings when she came from doing her chores, the room still sparkled with muted shades as the setting sun filtered into her room. And after winters of drab sameness, summer and the muhly added something different to her surroundings, making her feel brilliant and shiny herself.

The Scaggins family lived a short distance from the banks, across the broad sound and waterway that separated the island from the mainland. From their back porch the marshes of the island could be seen. The high sandy dunes and grass covered hills were visible as well and blocked the view of the ocean before it.

From the Scaggins home a slight downward slope of land led to a landing where a dory, skiff and flats boat were kept. The family often rowed the skiff to the island to picnic or pick wild kale and to fish. The dory was used for seine fishing and the flats boat was used for clamming and oystering.

Jess Scaggins had built all of his watercraft and was known in the area for building sturdy broad boats with high prows. He'd built several for other local farmers who frequented the banks and on each one he sculpted his personal insignia along the lines of the port side prow: *JES*, Jessie Erskine Scaggins. Flamboyantly he swirled the *s* of his last name around to end with a star. As he told his patrons, "It's a star to guide ya by."

Near the woods and to the south of his home Jess had built large wooden chocks for boat building, a barn for the horses and chickens and a lean-to shed for housing wooden materials. He'd built nearly everything on his land, including his home, a small two bedroom building with a breezeway between the kitchen and rest of the house. And since the family spent so much time outside, he'd built screened porches on both the front and back that were nearly as large as the house itself.

For access to the little landing where Jess kept his boats, he sank posts into the marshy ground and built a small dock. There his three boats, which he had tied to old steering wheels, swayed to and fro with the tide.

The small farm was home to cows, chickens and a few hogs that Jess kept for slaughter throughout the year. Twenty-five acres was set aside in the far west corner for raising tobacco. Pearl hated working that crop; it was truly hard work especially in the hot sun. But she did feel lucky since some of her classmates at school often missed the first month or so to help out on their families' farms. Pearl was glad her daddy didn't make her stay home since those children usually lagged behind and took nearly half of the school year to catch up.

The family grew nearly all their own food except for the flour, sugar and spices they bought at Amos Howard's general store in Virginia Creek. Amos had just about anything anyone could want and if he didn't he'd order it.

Twice a year the Scaggins family drove their wagon the thirty miles south to Wilmington to buy extras. Pearl dreaded the long journey by cart but was overwhelmed by the beauty of the port town once they reached Market Street. There grand pillared houses lined the cobblestone streets and giant oaks dripping Spanish moss, made an arbor across the roadway. While there, the family purchased tools for Jess and a dress or two that Lottie Scaggins preferred to shop for rather than buy sight unseen from catalogs.

Shoes were another item purchased in Wilmington. Lottie, always wanting the best for her daughter, insisted on Pearl trying on a pair of shoes before buying them. She saved all year for these special trips to Wilmington just to purchase Pearl's shoes. Pearl, though grateful, looked upon them with distain and if it had been up to her, she'd never wear the shoes at all. After school they came off immediately, the rest of the time she suffered through what she called – "the suffocation of my toes."

Pearl gathered eggs every morning, fed the chickens and carried the trash to the big barrel where it was burned once a week. During the season she picked and husked corn, picked and shelled peas and beans, gathered squash and okra and helped her mother with the canning of these vegetables. At hog killing time she helped Lottie make the sausage and cheese from all the spare parts left from the main cuts of pork.

She was a farmer's daughter and learned at an early age all the necessities that came with living as one. It was a prudent and practical lifestyle; Pearl was thus, a prudent and practical child. But not one of unhappiness or sullenness – rather, Pearl found happiness in almost everything she saw and did.

The barn was one of her favorite places. It smelled sweet, provided shade and breeze during the warm months and in the winter was warm and cozy. Many a night she spent there, tending to new born pups or kittens and then there had been times when she'd stood by her parents as they welcomed a new foal or calf into the world. Her mother was most proud of her birthing abilities with farm animals and had even been midwife for a neighbor once when the doctor could not make the trip in time.

Pearl spent hours brushing the four quarter horses used to move the cattle around from one small pasture of the Scaggins land, to another. Fifty head of cattle was not much compared to neighbors whose herds numbered in the hundreds, but it was enough for the Scaggins family.

During the winter the cattle were driven to the banks to feed on the natural grasses there. In spring they were rounded up and brought back from the island to roam the Scaggins land, ninety-seven acres of low lands, dense with pines.

Squatty water oaks abounded on their land, along with dogwood, hickory and cedar. It was good land, rarely flooded, and provided the Scaggins family with all the needs for healthy living.

Pearl worked the cattle alongside her mother and father. She'd been doing this for as long as she could remember and it was something she looked forward to. On their homeland the herding was easy, the cattle moved along as if they knew where to go – and they did – they traveled the same trail year after year with the cows following each other, slowly, ploddingly, as their tails swished the flies.

Taking cattle to the banks was much more exciting. There was more to see, there might even be a little excitement as the cows balked when a gator slid from the shore to the water rousing the waterfowl to take flight. Lottie Scaggins usually rode next to her husband Jess. Always giddy, she loved taking the cattle across, and was most keen on watching for gators, not because she was afraid of them, but because she loved the taste of gator tail. Each time they took the cows to the banks, Lottie could be heard to say, "I'm off to get me a new purse." A few minutes would pass – a rifle shot would be heard, and shortly thereafter, Lottie would be seen trotting her horse back to the herd with a gator tail strapped to the back of her saddle.

It seemed to Pearl that her parents had the same conversation every time they as they took the cattle across to the banks. *I'm off to get me a new purse,* her mother would say. Pearl's daddy would shake his head, *gators are just being gators, they ain't going to bother nobody.*

Pearl could nearly mouth the words; she had heard them so often. She'd laugh as she watched her mother trot back to join her husband, her hat resting against her back and the breezes blowing through her dark, curly hair. Moving her horse close, she'd laugh and wink – shaking her shoulders flirtatiously. Her husband, would wink in return, shake his head, and manage a slow guffaw as his wife explained that the meat would taste oh so good when she fried it up with the fish they would catch at the banks. It was the same banter between the two every year.

At first, on these cattle moves, Pearl sat with her father, holding on tightly to the saddle horn while they moved through the water – walking, wading or swimming, depending on how the tides had shifted the sands. But by the time she was six she was riding her own horse, a gentle and plodding gelding named Topsy. Pearl moved with the cattle, maneuvering as her father had taught her.

Jess Scaggins always crossed his cattle at Sears Landing, about a quarter mile from the banks and he always chose days that were calm. It made the crossing easier and as Jess put it, "no sense making things any harder than they have to be." There was no great trick to bringing the cattle across;

the job mainly consisted of making sure no cattle strayed away from the others and that the calves stayed with their mothers. The bulls, always slow and plodding, were the only sources of concern. Their naturally aggressive demeanor could be unpredictable, but Jess, with one of the neighboring men that usually went along on these trips, kept close watch as the bulls followed behind the cows, noses lifted high to smell the scent of what made their way before them.

Pearl had often heard her father talk about how the government was building a waterway all along the east coast of the country, from New Jersey to Florida. He'd even shown her on the map where it had already begun and where it was supposed to end. After every cattle drive he talked of it as the family gathered in the living room, recuperating from the days hard work.

"Just where they 'spect me to graze my cattle?" Pearl listened intently to the words, ambiguous feelings of impending change swirling in her mind. She watched as her mother usually chimed in, "Well, they didn't do it this year. Did they sweetheart?"

It seemed Pearl had heard this conversation for as long as she could remember too. Perhaps it would never happen, and then again if it did . . . what changes would it bring? The thought of never being able to take the cattle over again did not seem possible. As her mother had soothed her father, the repetition of their conversation made improbability more real than any waterway.

Still, Jess insisted that the work on the waterway had been in progress for several years, and that the only reason the banks had not changed was because it was not used regularly. "It is going to happen, gal. I heard just the other day from Carl Burns that it would not be long before the government would begin work here too. Then all the waters between the banks and the mainland will be deepened to the regulation forty feet."

This concerned Jess, since it wouldn't matter that the Sears Landing access was such a short distance; it would simply be too deep to cross. Barges and other big boats would start using the waterway more and more, just as they had already begun to do in places north of the banks, like Beaufort and Morehead.

"Till then, when they make their mind up to do it, we'll just go on doing like we've always done," Jess would shrug – disappointed, but resigned to impending change.

Change was something Jess was not real fond of. He wasn't afraid of it, just wary. Sometimes it was good and other times it wasn't. He liked the tried and true and felt comfortable with the way things had been for the last decade or so. Still he knew change was inevitable. He often thought of how things would be for Pearl - how she too would change in time and so he prayed a lot, prayed that it would be gentle for her.

Pearl perched close to her father, secure in the knowledge that this discussion about change was just another parental ploy to make her look at life more seriously. But she loved taking the cattle to the island, it was another world there — where all kinds of plants grew and the ocean, well, who would not be impressed and fall in love with such an entity. "This must be where God lives," she insisted one day at Sunday School when Miss June had insisted that God lived in the heavens above.

"You are a dreamer, child," Miss June had admonished. Then she smiled too because she had grown up going to the banks as well.

On days when cattle were herded to the banks and after the cattle had been led to where Jess deemed them best off, he and the other men who had come along for the drive would go hunting. The marshes were chock full of alligators, ducks and deer.

The alligators would make an easy mark as they basked in the sun and could be killed with one good shot to the head. The tail would be cut from the body, then skinned and salted down for the winter. The deer would be hung in the smoke house and the duck would be saved and savored for Thanksgiving and Christmas. While Jess hunted for meat, Lottie and Pearl gathered wild kale and searched for oysters, usually filling up at least two croaker sacks of the salty treat.

"Ya know gal, I named ya after one of them oysters." Pearl heard this too every time they went over to the banks with the cattle. She smiled, knowing her father and mother's deep love for her and was never bored with the comparison.

"But when yer hair's all messy like now and ya smell like a horse, guess I oughta call ya "oyster." He'd always chuckle and give her a hug, she leaning in to accept the squeeze from her father's strong arms. "I named ya Pearl 'cause yer a real gem. Outta poor ol' me and yer ma, just like an oyster – yer my Pearl." He may not have said it often, but it stayed with her all year until the next time she would hear it.

Some days, when all the work and chores were done, Jess rowed his family to the banks for a day of surf fishing and picnicking. Usually the West, Rosell or Burns families went with them, the wives bringing along their best covered dishes: slaw, deviled eggs, and fruit cobbler - to be consumed ravenously alongside the day's fresh catch. While the men fished the women scoured the sands for driftwood to make a fire. In her large cast iron skillet Lottie melted pork lard and the fish were fried, and when nearly done, she added batter for cornbread. Fried next to the fresh fish it tasted elegant. The fish tasted different too, so much better than the salted fish they ate at home. It was a picnic with a blanket laid in the sand as the families munched on cornbread cakes, fish, pickled beets and deviled eggs. After the meal, the men took turns belching and the women stretched and rolled up their pant legs, readying to take an after lunch walk. Pearl and the Rosell cousins, Ellie, Paul and Phil took their cue at these times – racing toward the dunes to play. Paul, it seemed was always tugging on her braids or chasing her into the water. Why, she did not know and she usually ended up by the end of the day wrestling him to the sand and rubbing his face in it. Or if she could find a way, she'd sneak off from the other children to find her favorite flower, purple heather.

During the fall months families from nearby communities like Holly Ridge and Sneads Ferry came to seine fish at the banks. It was a tradition – one might even say it was a family reunion of a type, since many did not even see each other except for these times. It was always a big to-do, much like a party as all joined in, lending a hand in whatever way they could.

Rawl West and his wife Frances, Carl and Bella Burns, Leo and Carla Weldon and the Rosell families, along with all the cousins, and second cousins were the regulars at the seine fishing conclave. All the families had been in the area for as long as anyone could remember. They all chipped in to help and all brought their children to learn the trade.

Out of all the families, Bud Rosell was probably the most successful – at least when it came to money. He was the area's largest tobacco farmer and spent most of his time cultivating that crop or traveling to Raleigh for business and to visit with his wife's family. He still loved fishing and spent much of his free time making crab traps and small cast nets despite the chiding from his wife Noreen, who detested anything to do with the gathering of seafood. During seine fishing season, she drove to Raleigh to stay with her parents, leaving her daughter Ellie to tag along with her father and cousins Phil and Paul who found it a great get away from their quarrelsome family.

Though thin and wiry, Bud was one of the strongest oarsmen of the bunch and when he and Carl Burns dipped theirs oars with the others, the boat seemed to pull ahead as if an outboard motor sat on the transom.

Rawl West was normally the spotter, the one who kept an eye out for the black cloud of fish that swam south. He'd wave his jacket about whenever he spied them, signaling the men to load the seine in the boat and take to the ocean. Leo Weldon, from the small community of Ottoway, just the other side of Holly Ridge, was considered the best seine maker in the area. The others were proud to have him and considered him their finest asset. He usually received a larger percentage of the catch.

The men did the strenuous part, carrying the boat to the water, loading the seine, rowing and snaring the fish. The women gathered driftwood for the fire, readied the barrels and laid out the food for the picnic that would ensue after the gathering of the fish. The kids helped the women, but when the boats came in and the seine needed pulling, all joined in.

Tons of fish were caught. And for the next few hours all were busy pulling, salting, packing, and anything else that needed to be done.

Jess took great pride in Pearl as she pulled on the seine with the grown-ups. He knew she liked it and that she found it a challenge to hold down the lead line to keep the flipping fish from jumping out. He bragged on her and her ability to gather the seine without bunching it and swore that his little gal was better than anyone. Lottie, on the other hand, dissuaded her daughter from pulling the seine, encouraging her to sit on the blanket with Ellie, who never helped at all.

Lottie argued with Jess every time fall seine fishing season came about. Pearl could nearly mouth the words to this argument too:

Pulling on something that heavy will make her barren, Lottie argued.

My maw did it all her life and here I am with four sisters. Jess would retort.

Although the seine pull argument seemed to get a little more heated than the others, Pearl always knew the outcome - a long kiss and long gazing into one another's eyes. The seine pull argument was usually at the dinner table the day after seine fishing, since to Pearl it seemed both parents were just too tired to argue on the day of it. It always started with Lottie saying, "I'm telling you Jess, that girl shouldn't be pulling all that much weight, gonna make her barren."

18

Then Jess would answer, "Four sisters, Lottie, four sisters."

Sometimes her daddy would wink as he argued with his wife and often Lottie would lean over to pat her daughter's shoulder, saying, "We love ya sweetie – just want what's best."

Pearl had never heard one raise their voice against the other, or seen a hand raised in anger. Unlike her friend Ellie, whose parents rarely spoke without anger in their voices or with biting remarks about the other's failings.

Ellie's home was much bigger than the Scaggins'. Her family's two - story home, complete with a modern kitchen and carpeting throughout, sat on the far northern acre of their two hundred acre spread. A yardman came twice a month to manicure the lawn and keep the flower beds looking just so. On one hundred and thirty acres of their land, Bud grew tobacco. The rest he rented out to locals for gardens. The Rosells owned a car and a truck that the hired yardman washed and waxed on the days he came to work on the lawn.

Mrs. Rosell, Miss Noreen, as Pearl called her, always wore pretty dresses and had her hair done up in a way that let you know she didn't work too hard. A cleaning woman came once a week to do the laundry and hard cleaning. It was evident that Noreen did little work with her hands since they always looked soft and pretty.

Ellie commented often about the great brick house her grandmother Portman in Raleigh lived in - about the white pillars, the dining room, glorious sunroom, five bedrooms and the three big bathrooms. Each had a bathtub big enough for her to stretch all the way out.

She bragged about how the front yard was manicured with green grass, pink azaleas and an assortment of gladiolas and other colorful flowers - that it was prettier and fancier than even her own home's flower garden and that of either Miss Bella or Miss Francis, both of whom were considered to have the best gardens within a twenty mile radius of the banks. But to Ellie there was simply no comparison. Nothing could measure up to Meemaw Portman's and her backyard with the white gazebo and water flowing fountain.

"Meemaw's got a colored woman that comes in three days a week and does all the hard cleaning and washing," Ellie bragged often. "And she's got closets and closets of fine dresses and she and Grandfather go to the picture show every week!"

Her father's parents, were also the topic of many conversations with Pearl. "Gramma and Grampa Rosell didn't leave my father anything when they died." Ellie had told Pearl. They didn't have much. Meemaw says she doesn't know why Mother married Father. "

Most times Ellie and Pearl played well together. They strolled their baby dolls around the yard or, if they were at Ellie's house, they played dress up with Noreen Rosell's fine dresses and costume jewelry. In that way, Ellie was a good friend, she shared her things and even at school stood up for Pearl when other children chided her for being so poor. But other times she ridiculed Pearl for her family's outhouse or lack of a vehicle. Ellie boasted about how much prettier her hair was, told Pearl she was plain looking and was forever teasing her about never wearing shoes.

"She's the baby, left at home with her brother and sister all grown up and moved away. Ellie's parents have spoiled her rotten." Lottie would soothe Pearl when she'd find her daughter crying or distraught from Ellie's chiding. But Ellie was Pearl's friend and she took her "warts and all," she'd soon dismiss any cruelties Ellie threw her way and forgive quickly, as Ellie was simply the only friend Pearl had.

On occasion the Rosell and Scaggins families got together and drove to Wilmington to the picture show. It was the only time Pearl got to see the motion pictures. She liked them fine, especially Clark Gable.

And a few times a year Noreen Rosell would relent and join her husband for a day of picnicking at the banks. On these occasions Noreen always made certain that her hair was tied in a scarf, the color usually matched her clothing. Her pullover sweater would be stylish though modest and her polished nails matched the lipstick that she checked and reapplied often. In contrast, Lottie wore rolled at the ankle dungarees with one of her husband's shirts tied at the waist. Her curly dark hair blew loosely in the coastal breeze. The two women spoke politely to one another and were at ease with each other as they joked about their husband's peculiarities, but there was no doubt Lottie knew she did not fit into Noreen's world.

Pearl's parents were just the opposite of the Rosells. Lottie and Jess had married when they were both seventeen years old and by the time they were thirty they had become an old married couple. The bond between them was iron clad as a steel girder. Their trust in one another was palpable and their support for one another was fierce. They never spoke cruelly to one another nor threatened violence. Both longed for children in the beginning, but it seemed the dream of having them was not to be.

Lottie's first two pregnancies ended in miscarriage. The third time she gave birth to a boy child, he weighed barely four pounds. After four months Lottie and Jess believed everything was going well, until the child caught the flu and died. Lottie stayed in bed for one whole month, wrapped in sadness, and then as if an alarm had gone off she was out the door, never to mention it again.

It was an amazement, when in her mid-thirties, Lottie realized she was pregnant once again. She quit fishing with her husband, and had friends come to pick the vegetables from the garden. Jess helped with the canning, refusing to even allow her to pick up a pot or container weighing over a pound. Lottie sat in her most comfortable chair in the living room and listened to the radio, and as spring neared she relaxed in the rocker on the back porch watching Jess tend to her flower garden. Before she had the chance he was on his feet to get her a glass of water, sweep the floor, make the beds, or anything else that required her to exert any energy.

When the girl was born she was watched over and tended to like a fallen baby bird. It was in the fall of the year and so, as if preparing for winter, Jess caulked all the little cracks and crevices that might leak cool air into their home. Still having some warm days, he walked around the house opening some windows and closing others, and checking her clothing to make sure she never got too hot or too cold. Pearl was most definitely pampered.

As the little one grew stronger and taller, learning to walk and talk, Lottie and Jess fell deeper and deeper in love with her.

CHAPTER ONE
1940

Within minutes of casting his line, Jess caught three good
sized mullet; Leo Weldon landed two pompano and another
mullet. Lottie and Leo's wife Carla busied themselves
gathering pieces of drift wood for the fire, then cleaned the
fish while the two men walked to the sound to catch a few
blue crabs to boil in the iron pot they'd brought along. Pearl
laid out the contents of the picnic basket, nestling the
wooden bowls of boiled potatoes and deviled eggs into the
blanket covered sand. She dragged the big pieces of
driftwood logs kept behind one of the dunes to the fire for
everyone to sit on.

The crabs were boiled orangey red and the fish fried up
crispy on the outside. When broken apart to eat, the steam
rose along with the delicate seafood aroma. Pearl grabbed a
crab, broke off a claw and sucked the sweet meat out
loudly.

"Yum," she closed her eyes and puckered her lips, "Lordy, that's good," She said, "think I'll have another."

"No need to slurp, Sweetie," Lottie corrected her daughter. She winked to remind her that they were in the company of others and that what they did at home wasn't acceptable now.

"Yes, Ma'am," Pearl winked back.

"Tastes so darn good, makes my tongue wanna slap my brains out," said Jess as he stuffed another fingerful of mullet into his waiting mouth. He sucked his fingers loudly and looked over at Lottie. She rolled her eyes.

"Ain't nothing good as pompano tail." Leo joined in shaking his head from side to side as he crunched on a freshly fried fish tail. He threw the gnawed bones onto the sand for a nearby seagull. "Everybody eats today," he said.

"Men." Laughed Lottie and Carla simultaneously. Leo and Jess let out a loud belch and laughed.

"Looks like all's done here," Lottie reached to gather the empty bowls as Carla folded the blanket.
With everything eaten and the fish bones thrown in the ocean, the wooden bowls and the pots rinsed out too, the adults began their discussion of local politics and gossip. Pearl took her cue and wandered to the shore's edge to hunt for whelks, then made her way up the steep dunes to find her favorite, purple heather.

Across the sound from Sears Landing, the families loaded into Leo's old Model A, all except Pearl who had chosen to walk home rather than ride with the adults. She watched as the boat trailer swayed out of sight, thinking that perhaps she should have ridden with them, but the walk was only a few miles, and she loved strolling on the dirt and feeling the afternoon sun. The pockets of her dress bulged with the two whelks she'd found on the beach. Knowing that the sand dollars would get crushed if she'd put them in with the whelks, Pearl had settled them in the cleavage of her breasts. For fun she shook them from side to side, giggling as the sand dollars nestled even further against her softness. The muhly, she'd bundled in a checkered napkin and it lay bush-like in the crook of her arm.

She thought of Paul for a moment and how he would tease about wishing he was a sand dollar. She smiled - he was still chasing her up and down the sand dunes. Sometimes she let him catch her. Her mind wandered away as the trill of a red-wing blackbird echoed in the nearby woods. Her eyes made a quick scan of the oaks and junipers then rested on her bare feet as the dust from the road covered them. It was even creeping up to where her cotton dress swished against her knees. Pearl lifted her face to the sun and felt the slight breeze tousle her unkempt hair. Stretching her arms wide, she felt the breeze float through her dress, only the slightest bit of coolness gave the hint that winter was on its way.

Turning again to seek out the trill of the red-wing black bird she'd just heard, Pearl stepped to the side of the cart path, nearly in the weeds, and peered about. Again the bird trilled, closer this time, and she spotted it in the shortest of the water oaks, not fifteen feet away. She tried to imitate the sound, no luck. "Just wasn't blessed with a singing voice," she said aloud to herself as the bird flew away. She stood quietly, hoping to hear the trill again but instead heard the clop, clop of horse's hooves.

There were three of them - men in tan uniforms, astride tall dark horses. They looked stern and sat erect in their saddles as they trotted toward her. Nearing, she could see their faces - eyes focused straight ahead, shoulders squared and lips drawn tightly. The dust from the road clouded the horses' legs, as they came closer and Pearl squinted her eyes to shield them from the coarse dirt.

"Ma'am," one of the soldiers said as they slowed their horses to a walk. He tipped his hat and his lips turned up at the corners making a slight smile. The soldier's eyes looked directly into hers just for a second, then, as the riders passed, the men moved their horses back to a trot.

Pearl's heart beat so loudly that it startled her. "Hubba, Hubba," she tittered. "He was cute," Pearl was giddy as she felt her face flush. She watched as the men rode farther and farther away, the cloud of dense dust from the horses obscuring her view as she tried to recall the faces of the men. Of the three, *his* face was the only one she remembered.

27

"Those blue eyes, Lordy, they were *so* blue," Pearl said aloud. "And he looked at me. Yes, he looked straight into my eyes." Pearl felt the sand dollars, they were uncomfortable now. She touched her breasts to settle them back into comfort and felt her heart, thump, thumping loudly, once again.

Continuing her casual stroll along the dirt path, Pearl wondered what the men could possibly be doing. There wasn't anything between her home and the banks. *What could they want?* Then she remembered what her father had said – something about an Army camp in Holly Ridge. Something about lots of soldiers coming here. As she walked, slower now than before, she kicked the dirt with her feet.

"Geez, that stinks, dog gone Army." She thought of how the Intracoastal waterway had changed things when it finally came to be. No, they could not take the cattle across any longer. Her brow furrowed, *now an Army Camp, things are really going to change.* Then the image of the soldier she'd seen only minutes before came to her mind. "He had blue eyes, blue eyes," Nodding her head and smiling, Pearl repeated, "He had blue eyes... and his hair looked black.... That hat of his covered up most of it. Wonder how he wears it? *Oh, it has to be short if he's in the Army.* Pearl smiled again, swished the skirt of her dress and curtsied. "Nice to meet you," she imagined meeting the soldier.

She was nearly home now and still thinking of the young man's face. *"Blue eyes, dark hair ... he had a broad face and a straight nose... it was a nice nose ...."*

Pearl walked up the few steps to the screened-in porch of her home, lost in thought.

"Well, gal, what you smiling about?" Asked Jess as he rocked slowly in the straw backed chair, "Must be pretty good, 'cause I seen you coming down the road swishing that dress and laughin'."

Pearl lowered her eyes, trying to act as if nothing special had happened to her. "Oh, I was just wondering about some soldiers I saw riding down the road toward the banks. What are they doing here?"

"Well," Jess leaned back in his rocking chair, "I didn't want to mention anything that would spoil today, but looks like it won't be long before we can't go over to the banks anymore."

"What?" Stepping back in disbelief, Pearl gasped.

"I thought I told you about the Army camp coming to Holly Ridge."

"Yes Daddy, but you didn't say anything about the banks. What are they going to do at the banks?"

"When the Army builds the camp up there in Holly Ridge, they're going to take over the banks for some kind of artillery range."

"What do you mean?" Pearl nearly dropped the muhly she held cradled.

"It means just what I said, gal. They're going to be taking guns and shooting at targets - there's going to be all kinds of shooting going on over there and not with guns like what I got sitting behind the door. I'm talking 'bout big guns that have bullets this big." Jess stretched his hands wide to show the size. "Should have known something like this was going to happen with them putting in the Intracoastal waterway and doing all that dredging. Should of known a few years ago when we had to quit taking the cattle over, that something was up."

Pearl climbed the few steps to her father's side and put her arms around him. "I can't believe this, first we can't take the cattle to the banks anymore and now they don't even want us to go over to the banks. Gee Whiz, Daddy – what's going on?"

"War."

Pearl had heard talk of war for years also. She had hoped that the waterway was just talk - that the Army camp was just talk, but they had turned out to be facts of life. What was that her father had said, "Accepting change is part of growing up." But not being able to go to the banks at all – war? She did not like growing up at all.

She gave her father the perplexed look he recognized, though he had been seeing it less and less in the last year or so. His daughter was becoming a woman, Jess realized as he gazed at the lanky girl before him. It seemed like overnight she had began budding, changing. But the laugh was still there, the wonderment in her eyes was still there.

He held his hand out, "Gal, everything is going to be fine. We'll get through this. Don't we always find a way?"

"Yeah, Daddy," Pearl sighed, "It didn't hurt our cattle that much, we only have a few. But those other people, with big herds, now they're in a pickle." Pearl stood upright and furrowed her brow to frown at Jess, "But I still don't like those darn Army people taking our island. Where am I going to get . .."

"Your weeds?" Jess finished her sentence.

"Humph." Pearl pouted, "Daddy, what's going on. Are we really going to go to war with Germany like I keep hearing on the radio?"

"Maybe, gal. I hope not, but maybe. Our country's been helping out the Brits for a while now. And ,,,"

"My teacher said we're giving them tanks and other things,"

"That's right. We lend them our fire power and they lease us some land for military bases."

"We might as well be in the war, if we're doing that."

"No, gal. You don't want a war. That's why our country is giving the English and those other countries supplies; we're hoping they can win this thing before we have to enter it." Standing and reaching his arms in front of him, Jess interlaced his fingers; they crunched as he bent them back. "But it looks like we're going in it one way or another."

"Why?"

"One of Hitler's U-boats sunk one of our cargo ships."

Pearl was silent, her perplexed expression evidence of her naiveté, her furrowed brow belying a curiosity of more serious matters.

Jess reached to tousle his daughter's already mussed hair. "Those men you saw are scouting out where to put a bridge to the banks. Carl Burns says they been asking about a place to build a bridge. He told them right there at Sears Landing is the closest way to get there. So what you saw was some of those soldiers scouting out the best place to put one."

"A bridge would be nice. I could ride Topsy over there …" Pearl rolled her eyes and sighed, "Oh, that's right, won't be able to go over there anymore." She fumbled with the bouquet in her arms, "Humph."

Talking of impending war with his daughter was not something Jess enjoyed. He remembered being her age, but he did not remember being as naïve as she. But things were different, he thought, she was an only child - maybe he and Lottie had sheltered her too much, maybe he wanted only the best for his daughter.

He had been the only boy of five siblings. He was taught to be tough – had to be tough to help make ends meet in his family. Though he never kept things from Pearl - never tried to disillusion her about life, he struggled with the idea of his daughter growing up. He watched Pearl struggle with adulthood, her relationships with the opposite sex and the naivety about whom to trust. Probably the most demonstrative instance was her insistence on gathering the purple weeds. As some children held on to a blanket or baby doll, Pearl clung to her purple heather.

Jess's eyes rested on Pearl's messy hair and sandy feet, he chuckled to himself, " Now, I'll ask you again. What were you so happy about coming down that road?"

Pearl could feel the flush come back in her cheeks as she smiled broadly. "When I saw those three soldiers, one of them looked at me and smiled."

Jess laughed then reached out to tug lightly on Pearl's long pale locks. "What's Paul gonna say to that? You been seeing him, ain't you?"

"Paul, oh he's just a friend. I like him okay. And then...well, ... all I said was that one of the soldiers smiled at me."

Jess laughed again, "Okay, knew I had a heart breaker the moment you were born. Go on now and put them purple weeds in water before they get any more puny lookin'."

Pearl looked down at the muhly; it was starting to droop a bit. She nodded her head and ran quickly inside to put them in water.

CHAPTER TWO

Jay had noticed the girl long before she noticed him. From a distance he watched her as she peered into the marshy woods. And from that distance she had looked like a broad old woman. But as he, Sergeant Dailey and Sergeant Hansen neared it became clear that this old woman was nothing of the sort. This was a young girl.

Trotting his horse closer he could see the outline of her body through the thin cotton dress; her hips were not as broad as they appeared from afar, rather something in her pockets was making them look so. The top buttons of her dress were undone just enough to see the swell of her breasts. She stood barefoot, the dirt from the road covering her feet, and she was tanned by the sun.

The girl's hair was mussed and windblown and very near to the color of the stems of the weeds she held in her arms, but streaked by the sun with blond. As he slowed his horse to get a better view of her face, he noticed the line of

34

freckles across the bridge of her nose and the green of her eyes. He wanted to speak. But he knew Sergeants Dailey and Hansen would frown on it, they had been adamant about fraternizing with the locals, especially the women.

Jay tried to get his horse to walk even slower, but it was no use, it wanted to keep up with the other two and as he passed he tried for the longest time to keep her in his peripheral vision. *That's a pretty girl* he thought, as they slowly passed.

Moving the horses to a trot and getting out of ear shot, one of the Sergeants spoke, "they grow them pretty down here, Corporal Bishop. Don't you think?"

"Yes Sir, they sure do."

Nearing Sears Landing the soldiers dismounted from their horses and stood near the cattails and reeds where water sloshed against the shore. "Stinks," said Sergeant Hansen.

"Low tide," Corporal Bishop removed his cap and took a deep breath of the musky air. "My grandpa lives over by Padre Island in Texas, smells a lot like his place."

"I guess this is where they're going to put in the pontoon bridge," one of the Sergeants spoke. Soon as they do that, Bishop, you can bring the horses over."

"Yes sir. But I don't know why I can't bring them on over now and just let them graze on the island. Sir, there's plenty of wild grass over there for them."

The Sergeant grunted, "I'll look into that."

Nearly every day Pearl walked the dirt road to the banks hoping she would catch another glimpse of the young man she'd seen the week before. Twice she'd seen hoof prints in the dirt and was sure they must have been from the horse the blue eyed man had ridden.

She fantasized about meeting him again and what she would say. "Hello, my name is Pearl. My Daddy named me after an oyster." She shook her head in disgust.

"Hi, my name is Pearl, I ..."

"Hi, my name is Pearl, I'm a nice person."

"Hi, my name is Pearl. You look like a nice person."

"Hi, my name is Pearl. Are you in the Army?"

And so she rehearsed over and over in her head something that would sound smart yet welcoming. She wanted to look nice if she ever saw him again and made sure that her hair was brushed and pulled back from her face. She put Vaseline on her eyebrows to darken their light color. Pickled beets juice added a reddish blush to her lips and so Pearl took to eating beets, before her walk.

All this did not pass by Jess or Lottie and they gave each other a knowing look as they watched their daughter.

"Where you goin', gal?" Jess asked as Pearl made her way toward the door.

"Just going for a walk to the sound."

"Ya know I told you it won't be long before you'll have to stay off that road. After they put in the bridge they'll be bringing in them armored trucks and artillery from that camp in Holly Ridge." Jess knew that Pearl was longing to see the young fellow she'd met on that day, but he dare not embarrass her by mentioning it.

"She doesn't gussy up like that for Paul," Lottie spoke softly to her husband, "And she's even put on shoes. Now Jess, if she's putting on shoes, she's really smitten," Lottie raised an eyebrow and nudged her husband.

"If she doesn't see him pretty soon, she'll take them shoes off, if I know my little gal." Jess sniggered. "Maybe she won't see him again."

He watched as his daughter opened the screen door and hollered out to her, "Be back 'fore dark."

"I will Daddy."

Jay had ridden the dirt road to Sears Landing twice since seeing the girl and hoped to see her before the bridge was completed and all the movement toward the island began. *She'd be sure to stay off that road with all the artillery coming down. No daddy is going to let his daughter be around all that,* thought Jay. Both times he'd ridden the dirt road, it had been late in the day. Today he had left work earlier and would not take a horse. This time he'd be faster, he'd take the Jeep.

Leaving the camp and crossing the railroad tracks, Jay slid into third gear as he reached the dirt road. Dust clouded behind him as the Jeep sped ahead into fourth.

"Slow down, slow down," he spoke loudly to himself. She's probably married or already got a boyfriend…. She's probably dumb as a doornail, she's probably … well, this is stupid." He shook his head and slowed, downshifting to fifteen miles per hour. "I don't know anything about this girl, and *this* is stupid. I'm not looking for anyone, just taking a leisurely ride to the water. Just want to poke around, maybe do some fishing." He told himself as he glanced into the back of the Jeep. He hadn't even thought to bring a fishing pole. "I'll just catch a few crabs for me and the guys tonight. Yep. I'm just going crabbing."

Pearl kicked the dirt softly with her shoes as she slowly walked toward the landing. The color of her brown shoes was nearly hidden by the light colored dirt. She looked down at them, and then raised one foot to wipe on her calf, then the other. Doing so made the shoes looks shiny again. "That will do," she said to herself. "He's not coming anyway."

Nearly to the landing and still not having met up with the young man, Pearl resigned herself to forgetting all about him. After all, there had been no hoof prints in the dirt road today. *Probably never see him again* she thought. "He's probably married or already got a girlfriend, anyway," she pouted.

In the distance she heard the growling sound of a truck. It sounded sick, just like Mr. West's truck sounded. She figured that he was going to the landing to pick up his crab traps. He kept several there and checked them a few times a week. Often, if there was a good size catch, he and his wife Francis, would invite her family for a big pot of boiled crab. She shuffled along, gazing into the trees now and then to see if she could spy a red-wing blackbird, ignoring the truck as she heard it approaching. Pearl suspected that once it got near enough, Mr. West would stop and ask if she wanted a ride. "Good evening, young lady," he would question. "May I ask where you are going on such a fine day?" This is what Mr. West always said. And always with a distinguished tone in his voice — a made up tone, since he always liked to tease and play. Pearl liked Mr. West and his wife Miss Frances. They were fun to be around and when they came to visit it was always a good time.

As she heard the vehicle drop into a lower gear, she waited for the familiar, "Good evening, young lady," but there was none. Instead an unfamiliar voice spoke, "Hi."

As Pearl turned she met the eyes once again, the blue eyes that had mesmerized her so only a few days before. Neither she nor the young man spoke for what seemed the longest time. Then she heard a familiar voice say, "Hi, my name is Pearl . . . I'm named after..." She saw the puzzled look in the young man's eyes and caught herself. "My name is Pearl."

The young man gazed at her for a moment, and then smiled broadly, his white teeth showing. He cleared his throat and spoke, "Jay, I'm Jay." Pearl nodded her head and smiled back.

"I'm going crabbing down at the landing," the young man said.

"Me too."

"Want to ride with me?"

Pearl answered by opening the door to the Jeep and hopping onto the seat. Jay slid into first gear slowly and crept along until jerking the shift into second and then third gear. They were both quiet as they drove to the landing only a few hundred yards away.

"Did you bring your string?"

Jay looked at Pearl perplexingly.

"For crabbing."

Jay shrugged his shoulders, "guess I forgot. Thought it was already in the Jeep. Do you have any?"

Pearl shook her head no and shrugged. "But there's usually some around here somewhere. People leave string all the time." She moved her hand to open the door as the Jeep came to a jerky stop. Jay jumped quickly out of the Jeep and to the door to open it for her.

"Oh, golly, thank you." She said sheepishly. She thought of how Paul never opened the door for her, but then the only car he'd ever taken her riding in had no doors. Pearl stepped out of the Jeep, "You know, I just bet you that there is some crab string tied around here to some stick and I bet there's an old bucket or wash tub around here too."

Jay turned around to search the back of the Jeep for some kind of discarded food, "Looks like I got an orange peel and an old chicken bone here that ought to work."

Pearl made her way through the weeds and marsh grass searching for discarded string and if she was lucky, an old bucket left behind by one of the many fishermen that frequented the site. She found various lengths of string and tied them together until they were long enough for each to have a decent sized crab line.

"Wish we had a net." She called, still scouring the weeds.

"We'll use my hat," Jay offered.

"That piece of orange isn't going to work," Pearl spoke as she kicked off her shoes and waded into the water. Slowly lowering her hands she scooped up a small minnow. "I'll use this." Piercing the minnow through the gills with a small stick, she threaded her string through the body. Jay fastened his string around the chicken bone. They sat quietly on the driftwood stump fixing their lures, tying an oyster shell to them for weight. Each threw the string out just far enough to keep it in sight. Quietly they watched as the "bait" floated about under the water. They waited, turned to smile shyly at one another, and then looked back to the bait.

"One will come along any minute now, this place is full of blue crab . . . Shhh," she whispered as she poked Jay in the side and nodded toward her line. A crab was sidling slowly toward the minnow tied to her string. As it approached she slowly pulled in on it, bringing the crab closer.

Jay watched as Pearl maneuvered the crab closer and slowly gathered his hat. Using the broad brim for a handle he gently lowered it into the water and like a flash scooped up the crab.

"Into the tub you go old man."

"Jay. You got one, you got one." Pearl pointed to his line, still in the water. She had been holding his string while he netted her crab and she moved to give it back.

"No, you hold on. I'll net him up too."

"You better take off your boots, don't you think."

Jay looked at his already muddy boots."Too late for that," he said as he stepped into the shallow water to scoop the crab.

Pearl laughed and shook her head.

"Okay, okay." He unlaced the boots, sliding them off and rolled down the sopping khaki socks.

"There's another one on your line," Pearl reached for his hat. "What are you going to do about this?" She held up the dripping hat, before tossing the crab inside into the tub.

"I'll tell them I fell in," Laughing, Jay looked down at his wet slacks.

The couple relaxed into easy conversation as they watched for crabs, ignoring their lines as they became more engrossed in asking questions about each other.

"I'll be moving the horses over to the island before long, as soon as they get the stables built."

"Those are some big horses. I noticed when I saw y'all the other day, they're a lot bigger than the ones we have at home."

"Ain't all that big, I got a Clydesdale cross at home, stands over eighteen hands"

"Lordy that *is* a big horse."

"Yeah, Pop used to use him for plowing, but we got a tractor a few years back and so we mainly just use him for fun. Mom likes to ride him, says he goes nice and slow, just like she likes."

"I miss riding the horses over to the banks." Pearl said wistfully. "We used to drive our cattle over there."

"Yeah, I heard that's what the people around here used to do. Good place for it."

Pearl began telling Jay how she helped out on the family's small farm with canning vegetables and working with the animals, about the trips to Wilmington, its tree lined streets and about the school in Hampstead where she graduated the previous spring.

"And you don't like wearing shoes," Jay teased.

"Oh," she blushed and lowered her head. "I just took them off 'cause we're crabbing."

"No, you didn't have any on the other day when I saw you. You were barefoot."

"Well, if you must know, I hate shoes." Pearl rolled her eyes and teasingly said, "And I guess if that matters to you ..."

"I hate shoes too, if I wasn't in the Army I wouldn't wear any either. Only time I wore them back home was when I was working cattle."

"You got cattle?"

"Yeah, my family's got nearly six hundred head." Jay grinned proudly, "I'm from Texas."

"Golly, that's such a big place."

"We got twelve hundred acres of land," he said.

"That must be a job in itself, to move them around."

"Well, you know how it is if you got cows, they kind of take care of themselves. We just make sure they're dipped for ticks and try to keep them healthy. We also got a fruit orchard with grapefruit and oranges." Jay could tell he impressed the girl; her eyes were wide with excitement.

"You must be rich." Pearl blurted out, and then quickly lowered her head, "I'm sorry, that wasn't a very nice thing to say."

Jay laughed, "That's okay, lots of people think I'm rich when I tell them about the land and cattle, but no, we aren't rich. Out in Texas twelve hundred acres isn't much at all. Most ranchers got a couple thousand or more."

The afternoon had become more about talking than crabbing. Now and then they'd net up one of the crabs that came to nibble at the depleted bait. And what seemed like only a short time grew long as the sun began to lower itself in the sky as darkness crept up.

Pearl leaned back, tossing her hair, seeing the darkening of the sky, but not acknowledging it as she stayed rapt in the presence of Jay as he attempted to secure a crab. She laughed as she watched him jerk his hands away and stumble backward.

"Hey, did you see that? That critter just tried to take my finger off - pinched the heck out of me!" Leaning closer to Pearl to show her the red marks on his finger, he smiled, laughing.

Feeling his closeness, Pearl felt herself gasp. She was surprised at the way it made her feel – almost as if she could not breathe. Jay paused too as their eyes met and held. Pearl could feel the blood pulsing through her. Her whole body tingled and then Jay moved even closer, then rose and stepped back a few paces. Pearl rose too, noticing the change in the sky all at once.

"What's the matter?" Jay leaned in.

"Oh my goodness!" Daddy's going to kill me. I promised I'd be back before dark.

"Don't worry about that," Jay said as he pulled in both their strings and tossed them in the nearby weeds. He reached for the tub of crabs, "I'll have you home in five minutes, come on."

As Jay slid into fourth gear, the Jeep sped up. "I sure did have a lot of fun this afternoon." He looked over at Pearl.

She was holding on to the edge of the seat with one hand and to the door with the other.

"Going too fast for you?" He asked.

"Never gone this fast before," she smiled. "But I'm okay; I don't want to get home too late." Pearl paused for a moment, and then added, "Daddy's not going to like me riding with someone he doesn't know." She looked at Jay with questioning eyes. Their eyes holding for a second, they sat silent as Jay drove onto the rutted drive of the Scaggins home.

Pearl could see her father sitting in the rocking chair on the screened porch as they drove down the lane to her home. As the Jeep approached Jess stood and walked out the screen door and waited on the last step. Jay raised a hand to wave, Jess did not wave back.

"Hello, Mr. Scaggins," Jay called as he jumped from the jeep to open Pearl's door." " I'm sorry I got your girl home so late. I hope she doesn't get in trouble. I'm stationed at the new camp in Holly Ridge, Camp Davis and had the afternoon off and wanted to do a little crabbing and Pearl said she was going crabbing too, and it just seemed the good thing to do since we were both going crabbing and we got some crabs..." He realized he was talking too much as he watched Jess's brow furrow.

"Sorry sir," He said, stretching out his hand and hoping Pearl's father would reach to shake it."My name is Jay Bishop, Corporal Jay Bishop."

Jess took the young man's hand and firmly gave it a quick shake. "You know my girl's only seventeen."

"Well, no sir, I wasn't sure just how old she was. I'm nineteen."

"Look Daddy! We got a whole mess of crabs here in the tub."

Jess and Jay walked to the rear of the Jeep and grabbed the handles to lift it out. There were a good twenty or so there.

"Staying for dinner?" Asked Jess sternly. The request sounding more like an order.

Jay's face lit up for a moment. He ran his fingers through his hair to smooth the long bangs that weren't there. The Army had taken care of that.

"If it's no problem, sir, it would be nice and I'll help with the crabs."

"You bet you will," Chuckled Jess.

"Joined the Army when I was seventeen, sir. Mom and Pop weren't too keen on me going in, but I kept begging them and begging them. You know how it's been lately. With hardly anybody being able to get ahead and with two of our bulls being brought down by coyotes, well, sir, we lost quite a bit when that happened. I figured the Army would feed me and give me a place to live and I could send Mom and Pop a little money every month to help out."

"We know about losing bulls," nodded Lottie, her tone stern.

Jay smiled at her. She was older than his mother, but she had that same protective air.

"Yes, son, losing a bull can really hurt, "Jess propped both elbows on the table and cleared his throat, "We lost one a few years back and it took a long time to get back to normal. Seems we were robbing Peter to pay Paul the whole time – playing catch up."

"Yes sir, know what that's like. Couple years ago we had a freeze and lost most of our citrus. That really hurt. That was our cash crop." He gnawed a row of corn off the cob, and then continued. "So, with all that going on and us not having much money and me not knowing how to do much of anything except work cows and horses, I thought the best thing would be to join the Army."

"Not a bad thing to do, son." Jess leaned back in his chair to pat his slim belly. "Probably exactly what I would have done. Trying to help your folks out is not a bad thing."

"The Army's got me working with the horses, doing farrier work, right now. But I just got back from Mitchell Field in New York and they taught me all about that new thing called radar."

"Yeah," Jess leaned in to listen. "I've heard about that, seems you can see things from miles away."

"Yes, sir. You sure can."

"What's this radar look like? How's it work?"

Jay leaned in too, using his hands to demonstrate the location and description of the new innovation. "Well sir, it's set up on a platform, or it can even be set up on a flatbed. Then there's a couple of motors that rotate the antenna...."

"Must be big."

"Yes, sir, about fifty-five feet tall." Jay's eyes grew wide with enthusiasm. "It's got thirty-six half wave dipoles backed with huge reflectors and it's operated at one hundred and six megahertz."

"Whoa now, all that's over my head, I don't think I could understand any of this, son, but just how far off can you see things?"

"Near to one hundred and fifty miles, sir." Jay's head bobbed enthusiastically, "One hundred and fifty miles."

"I'll be. They're coming up with new fangled gadgets all the time."

"Yes, sir. They sure are. But right now they've got me working with the horses until they decide where they want me to go. Some men were sent down to the Philippines a few months back and then some were sent to the Panama Canal. Got no idea where they'll send me."

"Maybe you won't have to go anywhere," Lottie finally spoke up as she gathered crab soaked newspaper from the table.

"Hope not, I've only got about a year and a half before I get out and I'd really like to have a place of my own."

"You planning on farming?"

"Yes ma'am."

"And you said your parent's have a cattle ranch down in Texas?"

"Yes, Daddy." Eager to join in on the conversation, Pearl answered the question directed at Jay, "He's got six hundred head of cattle." She beamed toward her father whose eyes disapprovingly fell on her. Pearl knew that look. It meant that she should be quiet and not interrupt. Pressing her lips together tightly she looked away then back to watch the two men speaking.

She realized her daddy was sizing up the young man. All the banter between the two was designed to feel Jay out – see what kind of man he was. Pearl had seen her daddy do this sort of thing in town or around business people and had never really acknowledged what it was all about. Now, she sat back a little in her chair and watched her father's reactions, listened to his follow-up questions and how *he* watched the young man's movements and responses. Smiling to herself, Pearl continued eating her meal.

The conversation between Jay and Jess continued between bites of food. "Yes, sir. Nearly six hundred head - got eight bulls - a couple of Hereford, a couple Brahman, and Pop just got four Angus. He says everyone down home is getting them. They're supposed to be real hearty."

"I heard the cows threw puny calves."

"Haven't seen that, Mr. Scaggins. No, I'd say by the time they go to market they're up near seven hundred pounds."

Jess nodded his head as he listened to the boy. He sure was knowledgeable – about all sorts of things. He liked him. But just what was he doing with his little girl? She'd come home, her face flushed, not daring to meet his eyes. This was so unlike the evenings when she came back from riding with Paul. But this young man hadn't backed down when invited to stay for dinner. He hadn't turned away when he looked in his eyes.

He doesn't agree with everything I say, that's good. Never could stand a brownnoser – and he's polite. Jess thought, watching Jay as he talked. *Seems honest. Keeps his napkin folded in his lap, so his momma must have taught him something.* Jess noticed how he smiled when he spoke to Lottie and how he looked at Pearl when she spoke. It was as if he lingered on her every word, searching her face. He noticed too, how Pearl turned her eyes downward when she caught the boy looking at her.

"In a couple weeks we're moving our little herd on over to another pasture. You're welcome to come help us if you like."

Both Lottie and Pearl looked at Jess when he said this.

"Well, if he's gonna be seeing our little girl we may as well get to know him a little better." Jess said, justifying his invitation.

"Daddy!" Pearl blushed. She couldn't believe her father had said it right out loud.

"Sir, I'd like to get to know y'all better too. And you're doing the right thing. Pop would have said just like you did, if some fella came driving up in his yard with my sister Marsha."

"Got any brothers?" Lottie asked.

"No Ma'am. Just me and Marsha. We're tight as ticks, too. Pearl reminds me a little bit of her - loves walking in the woods …. and doesn't like wearing shoes."

"She must be a wise girl," Pearl rested her chin on her hand, and raised an eyebrow, "How old is your sister?"

"She's sixteen. You'd like her, Pearl. She likes fishing and can ride a horse almost as good as me."

CHAPTER THREE

Jay visited the Scaggins home several more times before he came to help move the cattle. On Tuesday after his work day at Camp Davis he drove to their home for dinner, pork roast with gravy and mashed potatoes. Thursday it was meat loaf with red potatoes and green beans, Sunday it was fried chicken, cole slaw and biscuits. He came the following week too, upon Jess's invitation and came to be expected at least every other day. He helped clean the table and put away the dishes. Then sat on the porch with the family to listen to the radio or talk about the day's events. Never alone with each other, Pearl and Jay touched their feet together under the table, brushed sleeves as they cleared the table - Pearl letting a giggle escape now and then.

A couple of times they all went out in the skiff to fish in the sound for trout until dark. Jay and Jess cleaned the fish and Lottie and Pearl fried them up.

A few evenings before the cattle drive Jay offered to wash the dishes, Pearl quickly rose with him from the table, "I'm drying." Lottie glanced at Jess, shrugged and they rose to cross through the breezeway into the living room where they listened to the radio. Finally alone, Pearl and Jay stood side by side, touching – filling the sink with sudsy water, leaning in to one another as he washed a plate and then a glass - she dried them, her fingers touching his as he held out the item to be dried. Quietly they passed the glassware, touching fingertips.

"What y'all talking about in here?" Lottie walked briskly into the kitchen, "Your Daddy and I would like a glass of milk while we listen to Amos and Andy and could you please keep it down we can hear y'all talking all the way across the breezeway." The couple heard her boisterous laugh as she existed the kitchen.

"Your momma is something else."

"Just like they don't trust us to be alone," Pearl added as they quickly finished the dishes and joined Lottie and Jess to listen to the radio.

Two days later Jay took everyone for a ride in the Jeep, but rather than drive the road from Holly Ridge to the banks, they drove the lanes to the pastures of the Scaggins' land. Jess showed off his Hereford bulls and stand of hickory trees he kept for smoking hogs and colder winter nights.

Jess was proud of his land and the condition in which he kept it. The posts of the fences were all uniform in height, not an easy task since he was known to pull out his tape measure to make sure each post was level to the other. Fencing in between might have been rough, but his corner posts and all others were uniform. He liked them that way and he'd even hewn them to a smooth roundness.

Lottie accused him of whittling them down to toothpicks, and chided him about the peculiarity of trimming something that to her point of view made no matter. Jess retorted that if she could have her gater tail, he could have his fence posts – end of discussion. But he liked things just so and he liked feeling roughness graded into smoothness. He also took great pride in his land, never allowing old tires or rusted equipment to be left on any pasture land – that sort of thing went to the quarter acre designated for trash. He didn't like leaving stumps in his pastures either and had pulled them up when clearing his land, thus his pastures looked nearly mowed rather than gnawed by cattle.

Lottie could tease Jess all she wanted about the finicky way in which he hewed his posts, but she couldn't have been more pleased with the trellises he made for her in the backyard of their home. They were tall, and rather than made square and frame like, Jess had made them rounded and scrolled at the edges. They were fancy for a simple farm and Lottie dressed them up even more with climbing roses. Nearby she planted an assortment of flowers that, despite the time of the year, seemed to be always in bloom.

"Mrs. Scaggins, you sure do have a pretty flower patch," Jay commented. "My mom likes Peonies."

"They don't grow that good here in this sandy soil," Lottie answered. "I wish they did, I think they are such a pretty flower."

After the ride Jay sat on the porch and helped with the making of ice-cream. Jess and Lottie watched as he churned the cream, ice and salt with Pearl sitting by his side.

"You know churning is usually my job," said Pearl teasingly. "But I like the way you churn much better than me. Yes, you do that *so* much better than I can."

Jay grinned devilishly, "I know I do."

"What?"

"I probably do everything better than you," Jay sniggered.

"Well… just who caught more crabs the other day?"

Jay's tone changed to one of endearment, "I wasn't thinking too much about crabbing the other day."

Pearl blushed as she fell silent. She looked over to her mother and father who were on the far side of the porch. A slight grin moved across Jess's lips and Lottie, trying to cover the broad smile on her face, turned her back and began talking to Jess about the weather.

As evening came, Jay said good-bye to Jess and Lottie. They watched as Pearl walked with him to the Jeep and as Jay reached for Pearl's hand.

"We ought not be sitting out here watching those two. We've been like hawks the last couple weeks, maybe we ought to back off a little," said Jess as he stood and motioned for his wife to follow him inside the house."I know Pearl sure does like him a lot... and it looks like he likes her a lot too."

"He's in the Army Jess, and you know how those Army boys can be. I still want to have a little talk with Pearl... and maybe you need to have a little talk with that young man."

"Already did."

"Yeah, what did you tell him?"

"Told him that if he hurt my little girl in any way, that one day he'd just disappear. Told him that between the gators and the sharks, they'd never find him."

"No, you didn't."

"No, I didn't put it that way, but I let him know how good a girl Pearl is and that he better take care with how he treated her."

"What did he say?"

"The right words."

"Huh? And just what were those right words?"

"Doesn't really matter now, does it Sweetie, you and me's been watching that boy like a hawk and we've made up our minds about him. Wouldn't you agree?"

Lottie nodded, stroking her husband's muscular shirt covered arm.

"He didn't say nothing you and I haven't already decided about him – that he was raised the right way. That he is an honorable person... I like that boy. He's hard working, polite and down to earth. I think he's a good man. My only worry is all this talk about war. And if we get into war with Europe, no telling what will happen."

Lottie liked Jay also. There was something about him, something that made her feel that Pearl would always be safe with him. "He's respectful to us, and he's a feelin' man," she told Jess that night as they lay snuggled in bed close together. "He *feels* obligated to help out his parents. I like that about him."

"Naw, he's a thinking man. He *thinks* about how his parents are faring and he *thinks* about what you and I *think* about him."

Lottie rolled her eyes, "same thing. He's a *feeling* man."

"I'm a *feeling* man." He cooed as he laid his large hand on the small of her back and pulled her close. Kissing her neck, Jess whispered, "I *think* I *feel* like a man."

The morning was cool and crisp, but by noon it had warmed to over seventy-five degrees - not unusual for fall. All the riders were tired and sweaty and even the horses had worked up a lather after chasing the calves that ran off to frolic and butt heads with one another. Jess and Lottie brought up the rear as Pearl and her friend Ellie rode to the side. Jay rode the opposite side of the herd, keeping a keen eye out for drifting cattle or calves.

Pearl wished that Ellie hadn't invited herself along, but once she told her about Jay, Ellie jumped at the chance. "I've got to see this Jay of yours. He sounds like he's really good looking. I'll just bring that little Bay of mine and ride along with you – I have to take a look at him."

"Why'd you invite Ellie?" Lottie sneered as she stepped into a stirrup.

"Shhh, Momma." Pearl took the reins and moved her horse close to her mother's. "She might hear you, and I didn't invite her, she just wanted to come."

"Wanted to get a peak at Jay. Huh?"

Pearl nodded. "That's all. Just wanted to see what he looked like."

"Watch out for her, sweetie. She's sneaky."

"I know."

As she rode along, half listening to Ellie chattering about one thing and the other, Pearl found herself hoping that Ellie wouldn't like Jay very much. She knew that if she did, her flirting would be unbearable. And that was one thing she was not going to put up with.

Looking at Ellie mouth words she wasn't listening to, Pearl fashioned a scenario: *'Oh Jay', would you help me get on my horse?' Jay lifts her by the waist as she grasps the saddle horn. Unbeknownst to her Pearl has cut the girth and as Ellie throws her leg across the saddle she slips and falls on the other side of the horse into a mud puddle.*

A smile crosses her lips as Pearl begins another scenario: *'Oh Jay, would you bait my hook....'*

Pearl! Did you hear what I said! An annoyed Ellie screeched.

Waking from the daydream, Pearl focused on her friend's face. "What?"

"I said you were right."

"Right about what?"

"You're right, he sure is dreamy," Ellie chortled. "I bet he kisses real good, huh?"

"He hasn't kissed me yet."

"No? What's wrong, doesn't he like you?"

"Every time I see him we're around Momma and Daddy."

"Well, you need to do something about that. If I were you I'd be dragging him out behind the barn or something."

"Momma says that it will happen when it's the right time."

"Yeah? The right time for you or for her," Ellie flipped her hair to the side then fell silent for a moment as she reflected on the relationship she had with her own mother. There was no way she could ever talk to her about boys. In fact, the thought of talking to *Miss Noreen Paris Portman,* (as her father so often referred to her), about them turned her stomach.

She was quite aware of the closeness between Pearl and her parents and long ago she'd learned never to ask her to do anything without their permission. Still it irked her to know they were so involved with Pearl's life. "You're not going to get anywhere if you tell your parents everything, and Jay's never going to kiss you as long as you hang around them."

"Ellie, Momma and Daddy like Jay. Why don't you just mind your own business, smelly Ellie?"

"Yes ma'am, Miss Pearly White, goody two shoes – oh, that's right, you don't wear any shoes," A sneer crossed Ellie's lips as she crossed her eyes and flipped her hair.

Pearl stuck her tongue out at her friend, and secured the straw hat she wore. Oh, how she wished she had never mentioned Jay to Ellie. Why would she think it would be any different this time – telling Ellie anything exciting was like spitting in the wind – She always degraded her happiness - always rained on her parade – as her mother often stated.

"We're going to Wilmington next week got to get a new pair of shoes."

"'Bout time."

Pearl rolled her eyes again and shook her head in disgust.

"All right, all right, I'll behave....I saw some really cute ones with straps across the top in the Sears catalog. I think they called them Mary Janes."

"Oh yes, I know what you're talking about. I like them too, maybe I'll get them."

Jay had slowed his horse to allow the girls to move ahead of him. He knew they'd been talking about him, He'd seen the dark haired girl, the one named Ellie, point at him. She was pretty. A little more up town than Pearl. He'd noticed the rouge on her cheeks and bright colored pins in her hair. She wasn't shy like Pearl, and when they had been introduced she looked boldly at him as she tossed her hair to the side. He wondered why Pearl had invited her to come along on the cattle drive. He'd been hoping to be alone with her this time, or at least alone enough to talk more and maybe even get to kiss her. That was all he seemed to think about, kissing Pearl. Her lips looked so soft and the way they fell across her teeth when she smiled made him envy them. He had never felt this way before. And it felt so good to know that Pearl wanted to be with him too. He felt it in the way she gazed into his eyes and in the way she talked to him. Smiling to himself he watched her as she rode along, secure that the day would be a good one. Any day with Pearl was a good one.

There weren't that many cattle to move and he knew it wouldn't take but a few hours. Back home on his ranch in Texas, moving cattle took several days. But with just fifty head and only a few pastures he'd figured they would be finished by noon. Then he would have the rest of the day to spend with Pearl. Maybe he'd ask her to ride out and check on the cattle again. Or he'd suggest they go for a ride to the sound – anything, he just wanted to be alone with her.

"I'm going to ride back and ask Momma what we're having for lunch." Pearl noticed that Jay was no longer in sight and she briefly glanced back to see where he was. Waving to him, she turned her horse in the middle of her conversation with Ellie.

"Hey! I'm going too."

"No, you have to watch these cows! Don't let those calves run off. We're just about to the south pasture."

Pearl rode to her parents, slowing her horse as she neared. Pretending not to look in Jay's direction, she asked her mother the first thing that popped in her head, "What are we having for lunch, Momma".

Jess let out a huge laugh."Lordy, gal, I swear. Your momma and me's been sitting back here watching you girls and watching that young man of yours - all sneaking peaks at one another. I suspect you're wishing you'd never asked Ellie to come along. Now, you ain't fooling nobody." He laughed again.

"We're having roast pork sandwiches, leftovers from last night's dinner," joined in Lottie, pausing for a moment to think of some way to help her daughter. "I'll tell you what we're going to do – you're going to ride on over to Jay and I'm going to ride on up to where Ellie's at and keep her company and your daddy's going to stay right back here where he's at. Now, go on."

Grinning broadly, Jess took his hat off and shooed it at Pearl, "Go on gal."

As Pearl trotted next to Jay, he turned and smiled. "I was wondering when I was going to get to talk with you." It seemed that all his shyness had disappeared as he reached his hand out to hold hers just for a moment. Nodding in the other direction he said, "So your friend, Ellie. Is she a *good* friend of yours?"

Pearl thought for a moment, recalling the previous conversation between herself and Ellie and thinking of the scenarios she had devised. She felt guilty for thinking such things. "I guess she is. She's the closest friend I have around here. There's never been anyone else to play with, except at school. Ellie's okay. Kind of lonely, I guess. At least that's what Momma says."

He couldn't keep his eyes off Pearl as her hair flowed in the breeze. It seemed even more freckles had popped out across her nose and the greenness of her eyes seemed to rival the towering pine trees that surrounded them.

Pearl felt his gaze on her and she blushed, "We're having sandwiches for lunch when we get in."

"Good, I'm starving."

"I was thinking that if you'd like to we could wrap a couple of them up and ride down to the sound."

"There's nothing I'd like better," Jay responded and nudged his horse closer to Pearl's.

After the horses were put away, everyone gathered around the kitchen table where Lottie had set the roast pork from the night before. She'd already sliced the bread and set out the mustard from the refrigerator. "Help yourselves," she called out as she walked to Ellie's side, "You let them two alone, now. You hear me. They been dying all day to be together and for the life of me I don't know why Pearl invited you over."

"Mrs. Scaggins, I don't know what you mean. I was invited because Pearl was bragging so about this new boyfriend she's got. She said she wanted me to see him."

"More than likely you invited yourself. You're not fooling me, Ellie Rosell. And I don't mean to be unkind to you, but I've known you since you were a child and I've seen it with my own eyes, and heard it with my own ears. If you don't have it, it's not any good and if you do have it, it's the best in the world. I just don't know how good a friend you can be to anybody. Always got to lick the red off of somebody else's candy, just can't stand to see someone else happy."

Ellie tightened her lips and balled her hands into fists."I'll have you know that I never said a bad word about him. I think he's nice."

"Well, all that's fine and good, but just the same, you just quietly slide out the door and get on that little bay of yours and go on home. I thank you for helping with the cattle today, and you say hello to your mom and dad for me. You can visit on another day."

"I'd like to have my own restaurant some day."

"You mean you don't plan on getting married and having a bunch of babies?" Jay's voice teased but his eyes searched Pearl's earnestly.

She nodded her head as she took a small bite of her sandwich. "Well, yes, someday. But wouldn't it be great to have a little restaurant by the sound and sell roasted oysters and fried flounder. Daddy says he's been saving up a little bit every year and taking some of the money from his oystering and shrimping so that he and Momma and I could have a little oyster roast restaurant. He said I could keep the books. Said it was really important for me to learn about business. Says it's more secure than farming."

"Your daddy is smart. That's the best way to find out about a thing, from the inside out."

The couple sat on the log where they had gone crabbing a few weeks before, speaking easily with one another. But as he gently brushed her arm, the mood changed. Moving his hand slowly down to hers, he clasped it in his own. Pearl laid her head on his shoulder trying to ease her own breathing. She could feel her heart beating so loudly that it drowned the thoughts in her head.

To Jay, Pearl's smell was intoxicating, sweet and fresh, like the smell of fresh flowers. He whispered her name as he nuzzled his face in her long hair. She turned and lifted her face to his, his lips brushed ever so slightly against hers. Pearl kissed him back, pressing harder, Jay responded by drawing her closer to him. He felt her breasts soft against his chest as his hand reached to the small of her back. He pulled her even closer, feeling her belly against his own.

"Whew!" Jay shook his head, and gently pushed the girl away from his hungry body.

She gazed at him, her eyes rapt in his. She felt the pulsing of her lips and then the aching of her cheeks as she realized the broad smile she had suddenly made."That was nice."

"I've been wanting to do that since the day I met you," Pulling her close once again he looked intently into her green eyes, then at the freckles across her nose, the wisps of hair across her forehead, and smiled back. Slowly taking her shoulders in his hands he bent to kiss her once more. This time her mouth was waiting, her lips slightly parted.

The taste of raw cherries filled his mouth and he held Pearl against him tightly once again, but this time he resisted pulling her in as closely, though he knew she would have let him.

CHAPTER FOUR

By midsummer of 1941 anti-aircraft training was already taking place at the banks. Nonmilitary were not allowed to go there. Barracks, warehouses, fire stations, stables and recreation buildings had been built on the island. Where the cart path ruts that led from the banks to Holly Ridge had once been, a dirt road had been constructed. It seemed always busy with a procession of Army trucks and wagons carrying supplies and artillery, or was crowded with troops of soldiers marching along, raising dust from the dry sandy soil. Things had changed quickly at the banks, as they had in Holly Ridge, where before 1941 the tiny community had been the home to a train depot and a gas station. There had been less than fifty families. Now, all kinds of businesses were springing up. Now, with Camp Davis as part of Holly Ridge, the population was over one hundred thousand.

The construction of Camp Davis was nearly complete with close to a thousand buildings being erected. Rows of barracks could be seen from Highway 17, the crossroads to the banks. Some of the largest buildings Pearl had ever seen, even larger than those in Wilmington, stood where once had been acres and acres of forest.

Enid Abbott, a young local boy who drove many of the top brass around Camp Davis in the camp station wagon offered to take his new friend Jay and the Scaggins family on a tour. It was fascinating and even Jess spent most of the time with his jaw dropped in amazement at the complexity of Camp Davis's endless paved streets that led to warehouses, a commissary, fire stations, a post office, a laundromat, the largest hospital any of them had ever seen, movie theatres, and a post exchange where the enlisted could purchase just about anything they wanted. Then there were the rows and rows of barracks that went on and on. There seemed to be so many people where once there had been nothing. It was overwhelming; Pearl was impressed and proud that the young man she was dating, and yes, they were dating – the thought made her tingle inside – yes, he was part of all this.

Holly Ridge itself had grown in the short time since Camp Davis had become part of the landscape. There was a new general store, a couple of barber shops and beauty salons, several new restaurants and plenty of bars where the servicemen could relax off base. Things had certainly changed. There were even street lights.

The five miles that lay between the banks and Holly Ridge was still pretty much the same though, wooded, with small farms here and there. A few families bought land or rented cabins and moved in for the jobs at Camp Davis. Some of the women from the Pike and Burns families were working at the Laundromat. Will Pike was working at one of the fire stations and Rawl West was working construction. He had even helped with the construction of the new pontoon bridge that led from Sears Landing to the banks.

The pontoon bridge, operated by pulley and winch, was a novelty to the area and many locals came to simply gawk at its wonder. Everyone commented how much easier the bridge would have made getting over to the banks as they stood watching the military men and machines board the pontoon platform and move across the dredged waters to the banks where they used to fish, graze cattle and picnic.

Things were moving fast. Changes were occurring daily, it seemed. Many welcomed it, others stood clear, wary of what all the newness would bring.

CHAPTER FIVE

"You got this in Mexico?"

"Sure did, bought it in Reynosa, Mexico. Sam's store has the finest leather goods around . . . and I bought this – just for you." Jay laid the finely tooled saddle across the sawhorse and reached to hang the bridle on the post nearest the tack room in the barn.

"Oh Jay!" Pearl wrapped her arms around Jay's neck then kissed him hard on the lips; the kiss grew softer as he pulled her into him.

"Merry Christmas," he whispered. "Wish you could have come with me. But the Army doesn't pay for anyone but family.

She pulled back, her eyes questioning his.

"I told my mom and pop about you."

"What did they say? Do you think your parents will like me?"

"Marsha really wants to meet you. Says you must be a gal after her own heart if you hate shoes and can ride a horse."

"But what did your parents say?"

Jay thought of the disapproving look in his mother's eyes when he mentioned the girl. His father on the other hand smiled.

"You think she's the one?" John Bishop had asked as they walked among the grapefruit trees of their orchard.

"I know she is, Pop. I've never felt like this before. She's wonderful! She can ride and she's not afraid of work and she loves fishing."

"Sounds like she's your sister," John chuckled.

"She listens to me, Pop. She takes time with me. We can sit for hours and talk or go for a ride and just say nothing at all."

"Must be the perfect girl for you, Jay. But be sure, it's the rest of your life you're talking about. You've only known her a few months. Give it another seven or eight and if you still feel that way – make her yours."

As much as he wanted to ask Pearl to marry him, Jay heeded his father's words. He looked Pearl fully in the eyes, "They said that you sound like the perfect girl for me."

For the next few months Jay visited as before and the couple took trips to Wilmington to see movies. They went fishing, sometimes with Lottie and Jess, sometimes without. They went to pig pickings and fish fries held by the local families - each evening before parting, falling into each other's arms, kissing and wrestling, falling into a passion that both wanted so badly to consummate but would not.

"There will be a time when it's right," Lottie warned.

"It feels so right now, Momma."

"I know it does, sweetie, but that's one thing you have to try not to do. Has he asked you to marry him?"

Shifting her eyes from her mother's, Pearl sighed, "No."

Jay brought Pearl to the banks often. They visited the Officer's Club where they dined at tables with white linen table cloths. Smartly dressed waiters brought glasses of wine and Pearl ordered dishes she'd never heard of before, like filet mignon, or veal parmesan. It was all very new and exciting for her. But when it came to the seafood, she always complained about the overcooking. There was no one who could boil up a pot of shrimp or fry flounder and hush puppies like her momma.

"Do you mind if I ask Ellie and Paul to come over some time?" Pearl cooed one evening as they dined at the club.

"Are you sure that is such a good idea?

"Oh Jay, Ellie's promised to be good. For the life of me I can't believe she hasn't started throwing herself at you. She's always been such a flirt." She shrugged her shoulders, "And Paul, well, you know he used to be sweet on me. We grew up together, he's like a brother and sometimes, well, I feel sorry for him."

"Sorry for him?"

Pearl nodded her head, cutting another piece of filet mignon. "Jay, he's so poor. And ..."

"Okay," Jay took the napkin from his lap to wipe his mouth. "Look, I'm never going to tell you who to pick for your friends, so you bring them along next Sunday and we'll all go swimming, but I can't bring all of you here to the club. I can't afford that. Okay?"

"Maybe we can come in and have a Coca-Cola?"

"We'll come in and have a Coca-Cola." Jay nodded as he squeezed her hand gently.

"I can't wait for them to see just all that has been done here at the banks. They're going to be so surprised at everything."

Ellie sat next to Pearl as they watched Jay and Paul throw the football back and forth along the shore. Ellie's tanned skin glistened against her white two piece bathing suit. "Tie my straps back up for me Pearl," she purred, as she lifted her long dark hair above her neck.

"Aren't you afraid your top will fall off when you undo the straps, Ellie?"

Grinning sheepishly Ellie took her hand away from the bra of her suit, nearly letting it fall. "Oh, don't look so surprised, I'm not going to show everyone what I've got.

Besides, for some odd reason, that boyfriend of yours has eyes only for you."

Wrapping the straps into a bow, and settling back on her heels, Pearl smiled widely, "I know. I love him Ellie, and I just know he loves me too!"

"Y'all getting married?"

"I don't know. I'd like to. He's so much fun and he's so smart."

"Smart?"

"He knows all about working cattle and he helps Daddy to make the seine. He knows how to do just about everything." Pearl could hardly contain her excitement. "And he says I'm the prettiest girl he's ever known."

"Why don't you grow up, they all say that."

Pearl slid a glance toward her friend and responded sarcastically, "No Ellie... Smellie Ellie, no they don't."

Ellie closed her eyes and pursed her lips, "they *do* say that... to get in your britches. Then once they do, the next girl is the prettiest."

"Well, I'm not going to do that. I'm saving myself for my wedding night."

Ellie rolled her eyes, "What's it been, nearly a year? And you're telling me that you haven't done anything?"

"It's only been about eight months." Pearl ignored the question, "But I wish we could get married. There's just nobody like him. Nobody."

"There's soldiers all over the place, Pearly White. Just look at them." She motioned toward the dozens of young men in swimming trunks scattered along the beach either swimming or ogling the few invited women bathers. "It would be so easy to get one." She paused for a moment and eyed Pearl questioningly. "Ah, that's it. Jay's got money and he's always spending it on you. That's pretty smart, girl." She relaxed back on her elbows and laughed loudly. "You're the one that I'd say is smart. And if you can get him to marry you, well, you'd be out of this God forsaken backwoods place."

"You're coo coo." Pearl looked at Ellie as if she were a stranger. *What in the world is she thinking? What in the world is wrong with her?* She thought.

"All these guys will spend money on you. It's just a matter of picking out the right one to take you home to meet momma. Just last Saturday, one of them – uh – Shep – I think that was his name, took me to the Paradise Club in Holly Ridge. It was sooo fancy, lanterns everywhere and palm trees everywhere – inside – they were growing inside."

"Jay says it's not as good as the Officer's Club's food."

"And the night before that, another one – oh what's his name – Carl, yeah – he's from Massachusetts. He took me to the movie theatre at the camp."

"Jay takes me to the movies in Wilmington, says he doesn't want all those soldiers ogling me."

"So what, I like them *ogling* me. Pearl, they could get us away from here. Don't you want to get out of this rinky dinky, nowhere town?"

"No." Pearl held her knees to her chest and scrunched her toes in the sand. "No. I don't want to leave here. I love it here."

"You've got no ambition, Pearl. No ambition. What in the hell is there to do here?"

"There may be nothing for *you* to do here, Ellie. But there is plenty for me to do. And I hope Jay wants to do those things too."

"You're boring." Ellie stretched her neck back letting her long dark hair brush against the beach blanket.

Momma was right. She is spoiled. Pearl thought as she watched her friend, propped on her elbows, stretch her long legs, close her eyes and bask in the rays of the sun. *Oh how I'd love to wipe that smirk right off your face.*

"Hey girls, come on in the water," Jay called from the shore as he tossed the football toward them.

"You go on, Miss Goody Two Shoes. I'm going to get my tan, and I don't want to get my hair wet."

"I'll sit with you, Ellie," Paul spoke, as he strode from the shore. Shaking the water from his hair and leaning to grab a towel, he bumped against Pearl. "He's a nice fella. I like him. And he's crazy about you."

Though he was smiling, Pearl recognized the sorrow his eyes held. She knew she had hurt him. But her feelings for Paul were nothing like those for Jay. She wanted to tell him she was sorry, but instead reached out her hand to his and pressed softly. "Thanks, I'm crazy about him too."

"He's waiting for you out there," Paul nodded toward the water where Jay stood knee deep, hands on hips.

Pearl grabbed the ball, tossing it as she ran toward him.

"That Paul's not a bad guy," Jay caught the low thrown ball.

"We've been friends forever. And he is too nice to have Ellie for a cousin." Pearl jumped on Jay's back and they waded farther into the water. "I hope he can find a nice girl and get away from his father. But it just seems he's so unlucky."

"Mmm, I'm the lucky guy."He stroked her legs hanging about his waist." If I hadn't joined the Army I would have never found you. Maybe he should join the Army."

"Find the girl of his dreams and bring her back. Huh."

"Sounds like a plan,"

"You know, I don't ever want to leave here."

"What makes you say that?"

"Ellie."

"Smellie, Ellie? She doesn't know anything. We'll have two homes, one in Texas and one here."

Pearl giggled as she jumped from Jay's back and pulled him beneath the oncoming wave.

"Hey!" Jay swooped her up in his arms only to dunk her beneath the next swelling wave.

On shore, Paul and Ellie watched as the couple played, taking turns dunking each other, then wrapping their arms around each other to embrace in a kiss. "She loves him," Paul spoke sadly.

"She loves his money."

"His money?"

"Yeah, his family has a big ranch in Texas and they've got a thousand head of cattle and six citrus groves."

"I didn't know that."

"He's filthy rich. She's just trying to get him so she can move away from this place."

Paul's eyes searched Ellie's. In their darkness there must be truth, but he could never figure her out. He wasn't even sure he liked her, his own cousin. He thought of what his daddy often said, "You can pick your nose, but you can't pick your family." Paul sniggered, recalling the euphemism. "You're so full of it, Ellie."

Ellie's dark eyes slid a sly glance toward him. She tossed her hair, gathering it into a ponytail before stuffing it into the flowered bathing cap. "Do you know differently?" Rising from the blanket, she kicked her sandy toes toward Paul and ran to the shore to dive into the next oncoming wave.

Paul wrapped the towel around his shoulders as he sat down on the blanket. He watched Pearl and Jay laughing and flirting with one another and wondered if there was anything to what his cousin had said; she so often embellished stories. But if what she said was true, maybe he still had a chance with Pearl.

CHAPTER SIX

Pearl pulled off her hip boots one at a time as she watched Jay pile the oysters against the log. "This is going to be sooo good. Of course, they'll be better next month when it gets a little cooler."

"Where's the crackers? Jay questioned as he lit the kindling near the log.

"Oh shoot, I knew I'd forget something." Pearl drew her knees close to her body. "But I really don't even like them with crackers."

"Me either, I like them with you." Jay plopped next to her in the sand, rolling Pearl away from its warmth to nuzzle against her soft hair.

"You know, it's been almost a whole year since we met."

"Time flies when you're in love."

Pearl looked intently into Jay's steel blue eyes. "Gosh, I just can't believe all that has happened since then."

"Your little island has come alive."

"I don't know if I like that or not, Jay." She moved closer to him as she sat up. "I like the bridge. It makes it a lot easier to get over. But we can't even go fishing over there anymore."

"I've taken you fishing there and I even took your daddy a couple times. We've done lots of stuff over there."

"No, you know what I mean. It used to be that all the families would get together and we'd picnic and seine fish. And you remember me telling you about how we all used to graze our cattle there. So much has changed."

"What about me?"

Pearl kissed his cheek softly. "You're the best thing that ever happened to me."

"And you don't have to go all the way to Wilmington to see a movie anymore. And there's a bowling alley at the camp too and Mr. Poke's big new store in Holly Ridge- well, he's got everything you could want. And all those fancy restaurants..."

"I know, there are a lot more things to do now that the Army is here." Pearl rested her chin against her up pulled knees. "But I still wish I could go to the banks whenever I wanted."

Jay slid his knife into the crevice of an oyster, popped it open and scooped out the meat, "Open wide."

"Ummm. Where's my butter and hot sauce?" Reaching into the embers with a cloth covered hand, Pearl grasped the small jar, swirling the butter as she added hot sauce to it.

"If you like hot food, I need to take you down to Texas. We'll go to Reynosa, to Sam's where I got your saddle. He sells food too." Jay reached his hand to wipe a wisp of hair from Pearl's face. "Sam's is like Poke's — he has everything, only cheaper... and he's got the best Mexican food around."

"I'd love to go to Mexico. What's it like?"

"Ever seen any Tom Mix movies?"

"Yep."

"That's what it looks like, miles of nothing and mesquite trees." Jay dipped an oyster in the sauce, and then slurped it down. "That was a big one."

"Hmm...." Pearl slid a disapproving eye toward him, "Pretty barren down there, huh?"

"We can always go down to Monterey — there's the saddle back mountains there and the sunsets — you'd think the whole world was on fire, they are so brilliant . . . it's beautiful." Stretching to touch her, Jay caressed her arm softly.

"It sounds nice, Jay. I hope we can go sometime. I know you miss your home, but — well, I miss the way it used to be here." Pearl reached for another oyster and began maneuvering the knife along the edges to open it, "When I say that things have changed so much, Jay, I don't dislike all the new things that have come here. I like not having to wait until Ellie invites me to go to Wilmington to see a movie, and I like going bowling and eating out — especially at the Officer's Club. But..." she slurped another butter dipped oyster.

"I know what you're saying. I didn't like it much when the government puts in a check-in station at the border. I used to just walk in or ride my horse on over. It's changed."

"Just wish we had the banks back."

Jay pulled Pearl close to him, "I tell you what, why don't I take you on over to the banks and we'll get a couple horses and go riding next Sunday. How 'bout that? You can pick some of those weeds you like so much."

"There should be plenty of heather there now."

"We'll go take a look. Let's not think of what used to be, but what is going to be."

Pearl nuzzled her head into Jay's chest. She could hear his heart beating and feel the warmth emanating from his body. "It would be nice, even if there's no heather," she reached her hand to caress his face and pull him in for a long kiss.

The couple rode bareback along the beach, northward from where they had gone swimming in the summer and northward still, past the Officer's Club. It was a nice, crisp day for the month of September and the couple rode their horses far into the water, splashing water on each other.

"Should have worn my swimsuit."

"Yeah," Jay arched his eyebrows up and down and let out a wolf whistle.

"Ellie's right, you're all alike," Teased Pearl as she headed toward the beach.

"What is Ol' Smellie Ellie up to these days?

"I think she's seeing some soldier by the name of Chuck."

"We got lots of Chucks. I can think of three Chucks at the camp right now that have been out with her. She gets around." Jay kicked his horse to move faster.

"She just hasn't found the right man."

"That's a laugh! She ain't nothing but trouble waiting to happen."

"That's what my momma says." Pearl dismounted from her horse. "This looks like a good place. Come on!" She waved her arm beckoning for Jay to join her as she ran up the dunes. Reaching for his hand she led him to the top. "It's all over the place" She said excitedly, looking across the dune valleys. "The purple heather, lordy, it's so thick." She raced toward the clumps of wild beach grasses, "Watch out for stickers," Pearl called as she motioned for Jay to follow her.

"Ouch! Too late. I found them already!" Jay sat down in a sandy area to pluck sandspurs from his bare feet.

Pearl laughed aloud, "They hurt don't they?"

"Should have worn my shoes," Wincing as he tugged on a sandspur, Jay pulled his foot closer and leaned in to eye the spiny sandspur.

Pearl knelt beside him and helped pull them out, watching him grit his teeth as she pulled one from between his toes. "Just look where you're going and you'll be all right." She stood to make her way among the blue stem, yuccas and hairawn muhly. Gathering a small bunch in her fist, she jerked her hand sideways to break them off, and then touched her nose to the blooms as if to smell. "I'm always hoping they will have a nice smell, but they never do." With the fistful of muhly in her hands, she walked back to where Jay was still sitting in the sand rubbing his sore toes, and sat next to him. "See." Tousling the purple blooms, hair-like fuzz floated in the air.

"I bet your mom likes dusting your room." Jay sniggered, still rubbing his toes.

"Nothing or nobody's perfect, says my daddy. Gotta take a little hell with your heaven."

Jay put his arm around Pearl, flicked his hand at the blooms and watched the fuzz float in the air. "Okay, they're pretty, but different" He laughed as he reached for her, pulled her close and kissed her nose, then her soft lips. She responded by leaning into the curve of his body. She felt his hands move along the small of her back and to her shoulder blades, pulling her in even tighter. Her skin tingled, growing warmer and warmer.

"Anything you like I'll get you. Anything you want me to do, I'll do it for you." Jay pushed Pearl to arm's length to look at her face. "I really do love you. Marry me."

Pearl's breath escaped her lips in a gasp. She felt her throat flush. "I love you so much too, Jay." Dropping the muhly to the sand she wrapped her arms once again around his neck. "You make me so happy. Oh yes, I'll marry you."

She could feel the warmth of his body against hers as the coolness of the late September day swept against her bare arms.

"Ummm…." Jay felt her warmth too; he could feel his passion rising then reluctantly held her to arms length once again, "We better find something else to do," he sniggered. "Come on; let's ride to the big hill. It's not far."

The hill was so high that nearly the entire island could be seen from it. The view was breath taking. Dunes seemed to roll one after another toward the ocean. Water oaks shaped by the wind grew everywhere. The terrain of the island curved in and out with marshes as lace along its edges. It was the home of the hermit crab, the otter, mink, gator and a various assortment of ducks. Then there was the redwing blackbird. Its trill so enraptured Pearl that she often spent hours on the back porch of her home listening as the birds sang in the trees of the marshes.

Small islands that dotted the waterway could be seen from the top of the hill. There were many between the mainland and the banks. Some were small and during a good nor'easter would be swallowed up by the rising waters. Others were larger and habitable for the livestock that local farming families kept there. Some farmed the fertile isles, planting corn and other vegetables, while others had small fishing shacks where dories and skiffs were kept.

The north inlet, where the ocean came tumbling in, could be seen from the hill plainly. These were dangerous waters and as Pearl gazed she recalled her father's words, "NEVER go in the water there, the ocean will drag you down and out to sea. Sharks will chomp on your legs and crabs will eat your eyes out." The first time her father had said these words to her, she cried, and running to her mother for consolation, screamed the horrible things Jess had said. Her fears were fortified when her mother repeated her father's warning, "Never go into the water there. The swirly water will pull you down and the sharks will eat you and crabs will eat out your eyes. We'll never find you; you'll never be able to see us again." Their words were meant to scare Pearl. Her parents had seen the horror before, when the Allen's young son had vanished, only to be washed ashore a few days later with chunks of meat missing from his legs and black holes where eyes had once been.

"Pearl winced as she recalled the words of her parents.

"What's the matter?" Jay noticed the sullen look on Pearl's face as he nudged his horse closer to hers.

"Just thinking of the inlet and how dangerous it is. Some people just don't know."

"Yeah, one of the fellows almost drowned out there this summer. That's no place to go swimming, that's for sure."

The pair stood atop the hill taking in all that could be seen, sea oats standing like flags on the sand dunes, some were already starting to lose their buds. A few brown tinged bells dangled from the tall Yuccas that still stood staunchly in the dune valleys. But her purple heather blazed against the dullness, it was its time of the year – from late summer till winter it would bloom its most brilliant purple.

By January the white bells of the yucca would have turned brown and fallen to the ground. The stalks would turn brown as well. The blue stem and muhly would become the weeds that her daddy and Jay always joked about. The sea and the sky were the only things to add color to the gray winters of the banks.

Jay helped a few more times moving the cattle at the Scaggins home and went fishing and oystering with them often. He was a regular at the dinner table and became more and more like one of the family. Jess and Lottie came to feel as if he were already part of it and wagered chores as to when the couple would announce an engagement.

"Your daddy and I are going turkey hunting tomorrow. I think I'll have a talk with him about us then." Jay spoke confidently, protectively, as if Pearl were now his.

"I hope he says yes, Jay. I just don't know what I'd do if he wouldn't let me marry you."

"Pearl, this is 1941, you don't need your parent's permission to get married. And anyway, you know he's going to say yes. Now, you know that. Don't you?"

She smiled at him and leaned to kiss his lips softly, "Yes, yes. I know - he likes you, Momma likes you and even the other day they were asking me if we had talked about getting married, but I didn't say a word."

"I can't wait Pearl. It's going to be so grand. I've got about six months and I'll be out of the Army. I'll take you down to Texas and show you to Mom and Pop – I've written to them and they can't wait to meet you. They're going to love you."

"I can't wait either, Jay. It's all so exciting." Pearl wrapped her arms around his neck and Jay lifted her in the air, twirling her, and then lowered her to face him. Their kiss was deep, long and slow. She could feel his chest against her breasts and his belly against hers. She felt a desire in the pit of her stomach and she knew she wanted him even closer. "I can't wait until we're married, Jay."

"I can't wait either, but we're going to," he said sternly.

There had been several times when he'd reached for her, wanting to truly love her. And they'd talked about how they wanted to be together in that way. But it had to be different this time – not like the girl in New York - Ellie kind of reminded him of her – dark haired , brazen, but loud – obnoxiously loud, even as they walked to her hotel room. He couldn't even remember her name –it was quick, definitely pleasurable, but when he looked around the cockroach filled room, he felt immense dissatisfaction with himself.

"I know we have to wait until we're married." Pearl persisted with Jay nodding his head in agreement.

Pearl was the one he wanted to share the rest of his life with. She'd become his best friend, his most cherished confidant. He felt at ease with her almost from the start and her family had welcomed him into their home as if he was one of their own.

Jay envisioned a life not unlike the one he had in Texas with his own parents; a life of living off the land. He daydreamed about living near the Scaggins, having a little place that was close to Pearl's family. He'd share his acreage with theirs. They had been so kind and welcoming to him he wanted to share his life with not only their daughter, but the whole family. He wanted to have cattle, maybe even add to their herd. It wouldn't be as big as his place in Texas, but then there was so much more here to do. There was fishing and oystering. Maybe he'd buy a place for Pearl and her parents. He'd heard them talk so often about how they wanted to open an oyster shack where they could sell oysters and other seafood. A restaurant, that's what they wanted.

That's what I'll do, I'll buy some land and we'll build a building with nice tables and have a dance floor...." he dreamed on, wanting for it all to happen the next day, not to wait till April, when they planned to marry. Oh, how he wished he could get out of the Army now. Dreams of success and children filled his head. Yes, tomorrow when he went turkey hunting with Mr. Scaggins, he would tell him of his plans and how he wanted more than anything to marry his lovely daughter.

Pearl seemed excited and giddy the whole morning, and to Lottie this could only mean one thing. She'd won the bet and now Jess would be mucking out the barn next go round. She smiled to herself as she watched her daughter peeling potatoes in preparation for the Thanksgiving feast that night; she elbowed her lightly in the ribs.

"What's up?"

It spilled out of her mouth barely before Lottie finished the question, "Momma, Jay's going to ask Daddy if he can marry me," tears spilled down her checks. "Oh, Momma, I love him so much. I want to marry him so much"

Lottie held her daughter as she smiled and stroked her hair. "I think that it's wonderful, Sweetie. I know your daddy is going to like the idea very much. I like the idea very much. Now, dry your eyes. Everything is going to be beautiful for you." Lottie dabbed her own eyes with the corner of her apron. "Jay is a very good man and I know he loves you very much. He'll make a good husband. You'll be the prettiest bride ever. We'll even go to Wilmington and pick you out one of those store bought dresses to be married in. How about that? "

Pearl's face beamed, "We could have the wedding down by the landing and Daddy could kill one of the hogs and everybody could come over – oh, it will be the best....we're going to announce it at the dinner table tonight," Pearl said, borrowing the edge of her mother's apron to wipe her own tears away.

CHAPTER SEVEN

"And your daddy says he's gonna get that big hog even fatter for your wedding party. Miss Bella Abbott is making a three tiered cake and Sarah Burns and Francis West are doing the whole place up in flowers from their gardens. By April they should have some really pretty spring blooms out." Lottie's eyes were lit with joy and tears hung at their edges as she displayed pictures of various wedding dresses Noreen had brought back from Wilmington. "She's going to take us to Wilmington right after Christmas so you can pick out your wedding dress." Leaning in to kiss her daughter's cheek, Lottie smiled widely and raised her eyebrows high with gleeful anticipation.

"Just three more weeks until Christmas, Momma. Just three more weeks and I can pick out my own wedding dress." Excitement filled Pearl's bedroom as she and Lottie planned the wedding. "All of this is going to cost you and Daddy so much, Momma. How are you going to do it?"

"It's not that much. You're our only little girl, and besides, your daddy says he's going to oyster extra and he's going with Leo to South Carolina to do work on one of the shrimp boats. He'll make a good amount of money off that."

"You're getting a new dress for my wedding, aren't you Momma?"

"I'm making my dress, dear. Always wanted a green, dotted Swiss dress. And if your daddy makes enough money, I'm going to buy the material for it."

"Jay says that he'll probably be able to get leave for a few extra days and we can take the train down to Texas and see his parents. I can't wait to meet them."

As Pearl held her mother's hands she looked deep into her face, though excitement washed over it, it seemed somehow different. She watched her dab at tear soaked eyes. Why had she not noticed before the deep furrows above her brow or the tiny wrinkles on her cheeks. Sitting down next to Lottie, Pearl squeezed her hands gently, "Momma ….." She didn't know where to begin as her heart welled with love for the woman who had always been there for her. She had always seemed like part of her, an extension, someone who knew her thoughts and always calmed her fears. "Momma . . ."

Lottie looked into her daughter's eyes, searching them for the woman she knew Pearl was becoming. "Baby, everything is going to be fine. Everything is going to be beautiful."

93

Jess Scaggins decided he wanted to give his daughter an engagement party. He'd read about such things in the newspaper, on the society pages where big families in Wilmington announced the engagements of their daughters and how lavish parties were given. His daughter would be no different. She would have the best. This hog he had been fatting up just for such an occasion. He never doubted that Jay would propose to Pearl, not once. It was for this day he planned, walking to the hog pen each day with extra corn and slop. It was going to be some fine party for his only daughter. He smiled to himself as he ran the knife against the whetstone.

Lottie watched her husband from the kitchen window, a long thick apron wrapped around his waist, covering his overalls. Her face drew up in a grimace as she watched him slice open the belly of the hog, the intestines spilling out into the tub beneath it. Though she could not smell them from the distance, she instinctively covered her nose with her apron. "Those things stink," she said aloud to herself as she walked to the screened in porch. "Hey Jess! Come here for a minute."

"Whatcha want? Can't you see me and Carl's out here readyin' this hog so we can stick it on the fire! Gotta have it ready by this evening. Now, whatcha want?"

"Just want you to cut me off the tiniest piece of liver. You know how I love it fried up."

Reluctantly Jess slipped the knife across the innards, holding a small portion between his fingers, he called out.

"This big enough?" He didn't wait for her answer, just began making his way toward the house.

"Just how many people did you invite over for this shindig, Jess?" The warm mixed smells of collard greens permeated the air and swept through his nostrils as he entered the kitchen. "

"Everybody!" Slapping the dark red meat on the kitchen counter he reached out to sample the apple cobbler. Lottie slapped his hand sharply with the wooden spoon she held. "Just wait," she grimaced.

"Humph," Scowling intently at her, he turned and strode onto the back porch, the screen door clacking loudly behind him.

"Jess! Come back here and close this kitchen door...you're letting in a draft and I'm baking bread." She teased him, wanting to see his face once again, knowing he was lost in preparation of the hog; *he's doing his man thing.* "It's got to be warm in my kitchen."

Jess strode back, his long strides taking him within arm's reach of the door, "Seems it would have been easier for you to just close it yourself."

"Thank you darling," Lottie fluttered her eyelashes and blew a loud kiss to him.

"Doggone women...."

The rest was unintelligible mutterings that Lottie ignored. Besides, she loved pulling his chain. And she knew that whenever her husband was excited he got bossy. He'd get over it and later would apologize. She looked forward to his apologies, *he acts like a bad little puppy dog, Lottie* smiled in anticipation of the hugs and offers to fetch things that would most certainly come about in the near future.

One week had not been much time to prepare for a big party, but Lottie was up to the task; she liked the idea too, though never letting on to her husband that she was as enthused as he. As soon as Jay made the announcement at Thanksgiving about the marriage, Jess had begun devising something special for his daughter, a party. Of course Lottie knew she would be doing most of the work. *All he's got to do is kill that pig and brush it with sauce now and then,* She laughed to herself, as she watched from the kitchen window, *you'd think the governor was coming by for a visit.* She giggled at the stern concentrated look on Jess's face. Lottie was proud of her husband. He had always been a doting father, though honest and never one to hide the truth. It seems his love overcame all obstacles.

After church that morning Pearl had come home and changed into her overalls. She and Jay were going to get oysters for the party that night. It didn't take too long to gather a couple bushels and she'd promised they'd be back soon. Sarah and Francis promised they'd bring a covered dish to the party and Bella Abbott was bringing a smaller version of the cake she planned to bake for the wedding. Lottie envisioned layers of white coconut cake, sprinkled always with powdered sugar.

It was nearly two o'clock, which left her only three more hours to finish up with the cooking, bake the bread and get her kitchen in presentable order. Lottie looked forward to the cook - outs and parties, there were always good friends, food and music. Will Pike was the best fiddle player around and she loved hearing him play Orange Blossom Special and Tennessee Waltz. She especially liked hearing Nobody's Darlin' but Mine and believed that Jay and Pearl considered that to be their song. She had watched several times before at oyster roasts and pig picking parties when Will played the tune, how they gazed into one another's eyes and sang the words to one another as they danced.

Lottie hummed the tune and moved her feet to the beat as she kneaded the dough she was making for rolls. Leaning across the kitchen counter, with floured hands she turned the knob of the radio and heard the click as it sprang to life with crackling sounds. Adjusting the dial to get a clearer tone, she tapped her foot to a lively tune. Singing along and lost in the moment she lifted the kneaded dough into a bowl, then covered it with a dishcloth to wait for it to rise.

"Oh, darn....." Lottie turned to check the collard greens and speared a forkful to taste. The radio station crackled again; the noise began fading in and out. "Poop," she muttered, walking to the back porch to see just how far along Jess and Carl had gotten with the preparing of the hog. She was glad the bleeding was over with, she hated that part. There was always so much blood, not like a gator that seemed to have barely any at all. But the hog tasted so good once cooked up. "Let's see what else is on." Lottie moved the dial and it lit up along the line of numbers.

"Of America was suddenly attacked by naval and air forces of the Empire of Jap…." The crackling resumed as she frantically searched for another static-less station. But it was all over the radio, every station blared the news of an attack by the Japanese.

"Oh, my God, Oh dear God! Jess! Jess!" One of Lottie's house slippers slipped from her foot as she scrambled down the porch stairs and toward the shed.

"Jess! It's on the radio! What's it mean?"

"Hold on there, sweetheart. What you talking about?" He set the pint jar of clear liquid he'd been holding behind one of the big kettles and motioned for Carl to do the same.

But it didn't matter much to Lottie about the moonshine she knew he sipped on occasion when friends came over. "Jess! Something about us being attacked by Japan. I guess it was Japan. I didn't hear it all." She spoke frantically, taking turns twisting her apron in knots and dusting the flour from it.

"Us?" Jess looked around the circumference of his property. Then he thought of Camp Davis and the artillery at the banks. "They hit the banks? I didn't hear anything."

"No… maybe… I don't think they were talking about the banks…. It was Hawaii…I'm not sure, Jess. Come and find it on the radio. It started crackling like it usually does until it warms up good… that damn radio"

Carl followed the couple into the house and stood near the counter as Jess fumbled with the dial.

"This morning at 7:53 Japanese naval and air forces attacked Pearl Harbor, Hawaii. The attack lasted until 9:45. Hundreds, no, thousands are presumed dead as three battleships were struck and sunk at Pearl Harbor."

Carl, in his soft low voice, moaned as loudly as Jess or Lottie had ever heard. "I better get on home to Sarah," he scrambled to his old Ford truck to get home as soon as possible, leaving the hog still cooking on the pit grill. "Be back in an hour or so," He called out as he drove away.

Lottie and Jess wrapped their arms around one another. Sobbing against Jess's broad shoulders she muttered, "This is no time, dear God, no time for this." As so many unknown things in his life had taken place, things he had struggled through, Jess calmed his wife, "This ain't God's doing, wife – you know that."

"They made him leave, Daddy - just when we had both bushels and were putting them in his jeep. These men drove up and told Jay he had to go to Camp Davis." Jess reached to help Pearl out of the military truck. "I don't know if he's coming tonight or not. Oh, I wish we had a telephone."

Jess looked questioningly at the drivers. "Don't know, sir. I was just told to make sure he got back to Camp Davis as soon as possible."

"Thank you, son."

"The oysters are in the back. We'll help you get them."

"No need." Jess opened the tailgate to the truck, grabbed the bushel baskets of oysters and set them on the ground one at a time.

"Thank you, sir."

Jess nodded his head in response, "Sorry, gal. Important stuff, I guess. Important things are happening now and he's needed."

"What? What's going on?"

"The Japs bombed Hawaii. Pearl Harbor – where all our Navy is. They sunk our ships and a lot of people got killed."

"But Jay's in the Army."

"Come on in the house. Let's get you a nice glass of iced tea – talk with me a bit."

The two climbed the steps to the back porch and opened the door to the kitchen. "Sit down, gal."

Pearl sat in the nearest chair at the small kitchen dinette; her legs pressed closely together, her hands in her lap. She gazed up at her father, eyes questioning and damp with tears.

"I know you know about the war in Europe between England and Germany."

"Yeah Daddy! Of course I know." She took a deep breath as her face reddened. "Please don't talk to me like I'm a little girl." Pearl noticed the forlorn look of her father's face, and calmed herself. "That darn Hitler is trying to take over the world."

The perplexed expression on his face did not leave as he struggled to talk to his daughter. "It's more complicated than that, but that's mainly it. He invaded Poland and killed lots of innocent people."

Pearl nodded her head, "I know that, Daddy. I'm not a child," she snapped. "I do know about things going on in Europe. I know about that, but Japan?"

This was the first time Jess had heard his daughter talk to him in such an angry tone of voice. But rather than admonish her for speaking to him so disrespectfully, he stayed calm, understanding that she must feel lost and terrified at the same time. "Yes, Japan." Now his tone was admonishing. Pearl lowered her eyes. Jess paused for a moment trying to gather his thoughts and think of how to present them to his daughter. "You *understand* about the war in Europe."

Pearl nodded, took a deep breath and stretched her neck backward. Her father's patience and desire to explain things to her as if she were a child annoyed her for the first time. "Tell me, tell me," she said impatiently while motioning with her hands.

"Germany and Japan are allies."

"So if we go to war with Japan we will go to war with Germany….Daddy I understand this. All I want to know is why Jay had to leave *now*."

Again the perplexed look crossed his face. "And Italy," Jess continued, ignoring his daughter's aggravated demeanor. "I was hoping things would calm down in the world or at least that we wouldn't get involved, but it looks like it's going to happen."

"Jay has barely five months left until he's out of the Army. It's not fair that he should have to be in this."

Pulling his chair closer to his daughter's, Jess reached for her clasped hands. "Maybe they won't send him anywhere since he's got so little time left in the Army. And he works with the horses mostly. So what's he gonna do? The Army doesn't use horses in the military like they used to." Jess stroked Pearl's hair, as he thought of the new innovation of radar Jay had been trained to use.

"I hope you're right, Daddy... I'm sorry for getting angry with you," Pearl paused, "I know you want to protect me - to explain things to me. But I know *things*. I just want you to ..." Searching for the right words, she realized there were none and that her father was merely trying to explain as he always had. She looked at him in a new light, and smiled to herself, nodding to her father – "Thank you, Daddy."

"Besides, you got a big engagement party tonight."

"I just hope Jay can come."

"You let me take care of that."

CHAPTER EIGHT

If anyone could reach Jay it would be Enid Abbott. He was always at Camp Davis and was always driving the big wigs around, so Bud Rosell and Jess drove to Enid's home and left word with his young wife Bella that it was of the utmost importance for him to reach Jess. Sure enough, it wasn't three hours later that Enid came driving down the rutted path with a message from Jay.

"Mr. Jess, sir," Enid hopped from the jeep, "that soldier that's been seeing your girl... Jay, he wanted me to drive down here and tell you that he wasn't sure he could make it to the party tonight."

"Nothing he can do?" Jess leaned against the Jeep, rubbing his brow; he shook his head in dismay. "That's too bad, tonight was his and Pearl's engagement party."

"I know, Mr. Jess. That's what he told me. And I told him about my friend the Captain."

"Who?"

Enid threw back his head in laughter. "My friend the Captain, he loves the stuff, you know, Clarence's brew. I tell you what. You come on with me and you bring some of that stuff you keep hid from your wife. Let's go have a talk with him."

Enid Abbott may have been young but his friendliness, sharp wit and intellect earned him respect and opened many a door for him. He was a go-between for officers and locals, and was able to procure anything from moonshine to a date with the prettiest local girl. Not much got past him and even at such a young age he knew how to take care of himself in just about any situation. He used tact and diplomacy when working deals and smoothed over many a would be fight.

"Yes, sir. This Captain told me just the other day how he'd sell his momma for some good stuff. Says he used to buy it from a guy down in Florida. Says it's better than anything bought legal."

A broad grin crossed Jess's face, "You don't say."

Jess and Enid walked to the shed where Carl stood mopping the roasting pig with sauce, "Hey, Carl, how's the family doin'?"

Carl nodded and smiled, "fair to middlin'"

Jess grabbed the jug set on the dirt floor of the lean-to shed.

"I don't think one jug will do, Mr. Jess." Enid winked at him,

"You get it from Paul's daddy, Clarence, right?"

"Yep." Searching for the well known moonshiner, Jess finally spied him standing by his truck with several other men.

"Hey Clarence," Jess waved his arm to get his attention then made his way toward the truck. "Clarence, you got some more of this stuff with you, don't you?"

"Sure do," a broad smile showing crooked yellowed teeth spread across the man's face. "Whatcha need?"

Jess looked to Enid questioningly.

"Three more?"

"Got that Clarence?"

"No problem." Reaching beneath a tarp Clarence pulled out three more jugs of homemade whiskey.

Turning to the man, Jess nodded his head, "Catch you tomorrow with the cash." He handed the jugs to Enid.

By six o'clock neighboring friends were arriving at the engagement party, not sure of what was going to take place but ready to share their knowledge of what had occurred on that day. Carl's wife Sarah was helping Lottie spread the tablecloth over the long makeshift table made by laying long boards across two sawhorses. Rawl and Francis West were there with their young son, David, only a few months old. The smell of roasting pork wafted through the cool evening air and the men gathered around the cooking pork to poke and prod at its meat, loosening it. It had cooked to perfection and the meat simply fell from the bones.

"That looks mighty darn good, Rawl said as he quickly stuffed a fingerful of pork in his mouth. Jess, got any of that moonshine hid around here? Sure could use a snort."

Clarence Rosell chuckled as he reached behind a thick beam for his mason jar. "I need to do my drinkin' in peace," he snorted sarcastically as he lit a hand rolled cigarette and walked toward the thick brush just beyond the lean-to. A few of the men followed, most lighting cigarettes along the way, and carrying their mason jars of shine. "

"That's right, leave me here to tend the pig," called Carl as he continued his prodding of the meat. "It's always me, left to do the cookin' while they tell all the good jokes."

"His wife'd have a hissy fit if she caught him out here drinkin,'" Clarence chuckled deeply.

It wasn't long before all the fixings were set out on the makeshift table. Lottie's baked beans and collards sat covered with dish cloths; their aroma wafting through the evening air. Her rolls turned out soft and shiny on top. Sarah Burns brought baked squash, Carla Weldon brought candied yams, Francis West brought rutabagas and Bella Abbott brought her famous coconut cake.

The oysters, as appetizers, were already being dug into by most and nearly a whole bushel had been consumed before the honking of a jeep could be heard as it rumbled down the little road to the Scaggins home.

"Here comes the groom!" Several of the men shouted, turning to watch the dust trail clouds of Jay's jeep.

"Glad you could make it," Jess reached out his hand to grasp Jay's.

"Sorry, sir."

The men exchanged a knowing look. "Damn Japs," Jay shook his head, scuffed his feet in the dry soil and balled his hands into fists.

"There's worse words for 'em son, but we're in mixed company now." He winked, "Damn this having to come right now. But don't you worry about it tonight. Tonight's your and Pearl's night."

Jay's eyes searched the huge yard for his bride to be. He found her leaning against the light pole by the dock. In its glow she looked like an angel, with her flaxen hair lying in soft curls about her face and shoulders. The bodice of her dress was tight against her body with the skirt flaring out just a bit. He laughed as he looked at the pumps she wore on her feet.

"Tonight must be special," Jay walked toward Pearl, her face glowed with rouge touched cheeks and the slightest smear of color on her lips.

She curtsied low, "Why yes, Mister Bishop, I curled my hair especially for you." Pearl wrapped her arms around Jay's neck, tilting her face up toward his for a kiss.

Jay placed his hands on her shoulders to push her to arms length.

"Whenever you have something important to say to me you do this," She moved back, closer to Jay, as she had been before. "I know about Pearl Harbor. I know that we might go to war, Daddy said so. He said he knew it was coming, sooner or later." Her eyes begged his for the word "no", for any response other than the one she knew would come.

"Pearl, all I can do is what they tell me. But we most likely are going to war, and it looks like they'll be sending me off."

"Where?" Her eyes filling with tears, Pearl's shoulders slumped as she pressed herself into Jay's chest.

Jay pulled her in even closer, nuzzling her soft curls. "I don't know."

From the grill, Jess had been watching his daughter and her new fiancé. Recalling his youth, he remembered how it felt as if your heart would burst and what it meant to hold the one you loved. He was overjoyed for the happiness he knew his daughter felt. But then another part of him ached for the confusion she must also feel. The day's news brought uncertainty to their plans. The thought brought him back to the time of the Great War. Of the time when he had tried to join the Army and Lottie's reaction; *their* reaction to what might be.

"Thank God," Lottie had sobbed when he was turned down. The only son among five children and belief that his father had greased someone's palm had kept him out of the war. He was embarrassed about that part of it, but relieved deep down in his heart when he saw friends come back in boxes. Others who came back alive never seemed quite the same. Maybe in years to come they settled into the old ways, but there was always that look of agony in their eyes when asked about the war.

"Gal!" Jess hollered out to the couple. "Y'all come on up here and get some of this pig."

"I can smell it all the way down here, Mr. Scaggins." Jay kissed Pearl's forehead. "Things will be fine. Now, we need to get on up there to the rest of the people, they came here for us, you know."

"And it's "Jess" from now on, son. No more of that Mr. Scaggins stuff." Jess handed a plate to Pearl and nodded toward the end of the table for Jay to get his own.

"And no more Mrs. Scaggins either." Lottie reached up to tousle the young man's hair.

"Yes, Miss Lottie, no more Mrs. Scaggins." Jay smiled widely, as he gazed into the eyes of a woman that felt so much like his own mother.

The evening progressed into a lively montage of laughter, food and music. The pig, laid open on the grill, soon was reduced to bone; even the crisp brown skin had been devoured. An occasional guest took to the platform to tell a "clean" joke, while the men ambled off around corners of buildings to sip shine, and tell "real" jokes.

With the food disappearing, the musicians for the night walked to the makeshift platform. Will Pike pulled out his fiddle, and began to rosin his bow as young Enid adjusted the strings of his guitar. The banjo and mandolin players plucked at their instruments, tuning them and the crowd of local farmers and fisherman began to gather, waiting for the men to begin their music.

Will scraped the bow across the strings, grinning at the crowd, relishing their anticipation of the tune he had honed to perfection. The Orange Blossom Special rang out as the guitar, banjo, base and mandolin joined in. Toes were tapping, ladies swayed their hips to the rapid tempo and the mood of the engagement party swept into high gear. Pearl started the dancing as she slipped her hand into Jay's and pulled him to the dirt dance floor. Others joined in- who couldn't smile from ear to ear with the magical tune of Orange Blossom Special. Will, Enid and the others played on and on as the party took on a liveliness and glee of its own. It seemed to Pearl that even the sad news of the world had stopped for her that night.

"And now, the special song of the evening... I'm dedicating it to newly engaged couple; Pearl and Jay, who will be getting married, come this spring. May your love be as sweet and last as long as the sun shines." Enid adjusted his guitar strap and began strumming the lead in to Nobody's Darlin' but Mine.

As the couple took to the dance floor, the crowd backed away to watch as Jay led Pearl in the slow country waltz. His arm cupped around her waist, Jay gazed into her eyes. "You *are* nobody's darlin' but mine – and never forget it."

Jess and Lottie entered the dancing area as well as Rawl and Francis West. Carl and Sarah Burns followed suit and by the end of the waltz nearly every couple had joined in.

"Why don't you want to dance with me, Ellie?" Paul asked as the two watched from one of the nearby picnic tables.

Ellie shook her head no, "you're my cousin…"

"When did that ever stop ya? We've been dancing together since we were kids."

"I'm a grown lady now."

Paul guffawed, "Seems like since the Army came to town, you're too good to dance with *your cousin.*"

"I like upbeat music. This is too slow and all the parents are out there – even mine." Scrunching her nose in disgust, she fidgeted about, swishing her skirt, "I wish Mr. Pike would call a square dance, then I'd probably dance with you."

Paul glanced again toward Pearl and Jay, "I hope she's happy."

"No you don't. You're hoping right now that there's a war and that Jay gets sent overseas and never comes back."

"Good God, Ellie." Paul rolled his eyes as he moved a few steps, distancing himself from her. "I don't want us to go to war!"

"But you wish that was you there, holding her, kissing her – and you know what else."

"Stop it. All girls aren't like you."

"Well, you do wish it." A slight grin crept upon her lips as she turned her glance away from Paul.

"Maybe you're right. Maybe I do wish that it was me dancing with her and getting ready to marry her. But that doesn't make me wish anything bad for her."

"Bad for her?"

"Bad for her," Paul retorted. "If and when we have a war and Jay has to go off and fight in it, just how do you think she's going to feel?"

Tossing her hair to the side, Ellie fumbled with the ribbon in it. "She'll get over it. And besides, while the cat's away the mice will play."

"Not Pearl, she'll be faithful to Jay for as long as it takes him to come back."

"Humph."

"That's the kind of girl *she* is." Paul's eyes looked sternly at Ellie. "And I hope he comes back, because I want Pearl to be happy."

"Liar. And if he doesn't come back, you'll be there for her to pick up the pieces."

Paul turned away from Ellie and strode to the grill to pick a strand of pork from the nearly bare bones. He glared at Ellie who was still watching him as he chewed on the succulent meat. Swishing her skirt about, she motioned for him to come back as the fiddle player announced that a square dance would be coming up next. Paul ran his fingers though his hair, then reached for the jug hidden behind a wooden beam, walked off into the night, flipping his palm out quickly, as if to say, get lost.

CHAPTER NINE

December 8, 1941 war was declared on Japan. On December 11, Germany and Italy declared war on the United States.

"What a Christmas! What an awful Christmas this is going to be! Lottie fumbled with the wrapping paper. "I can't even make a damn bow!"

"Momma! I haven't ever heard you cuss before."

"Well, there's no time like the present." Pushing the gifts aside, Lottie sat on the edge of the bed. "Sweetie, I just hate all of this for you. And this *damn* war, this *damn* war." Tears streamed down her cheeks as she continued to fumble with the bow.

"It'll be over soon," Pearl pushed another gift aside as she sat next to her mother. "Jay says it won't last six months, maybe even less, and then he'll be back home. Maybe even in time to keep our wedding date in April." She smoothed her mother's graying hair away from her face. "You're more upset than I am, Momma."

Lottie wiped her eyes and smiled, the lines about her eyes folding deeply at the crease. "I've always wanted the best for you, though your daddy and I could never give you much, we always wanted you to have the happiest life possible."

"But I am happy, Momma."

She can't possibly know the worry, the fear that is going to wash over her when Jay leaves. There is no possible way... but she will know. Lottie's eyes teared again as she thought of the inevitable pain her daughter would feel once Jay left for war.

"He says his unit will be leaving in a couple weeks, right after Christmas. But he's not sure where they are going to send him"

She's lost in love, Lottie smiled to herself as her daughter, seemingly without a care, snipped Christmas wrapping paper. *I'm not going to ruin this for her. Let her have her peace.* "So, what did you get that man of yours for Christmas?"

Leaping from the bed, Pearl rushed toward the bedroom door, "You gotta see it, Momma. I made it!"

Now what has that child made? What could she possibly make, Thought Lottie as she gathered the wrapping paper into a neat stack on the bed.

"I made it from an old blanket, one of Jay's, so that it would be Army regulation." Pearl handed the vest to her mother. "Buttons can break off, so I made them out of material, but they still fit through the buttonholes."

Lottie ran her fingers along the seams of the garment. It was all hand stitched, yet smooth as if done by a machine. The buttons were as her daughter had said, made of the same material, yet large enough and dense enough to resemble a button. There was no way they were coming off.

"It's really cold in Europe. This will help keep him warm." Pearl shuffled through the bright papers on the bed and chose a green sheet with red holly berries, "I need a bow too."

Lottie reached for the spool of red ribbon, cutting off a good yard or so. "This will look pretty."

As Pearl wrapped the vest, and tied the ribbon, curling its ends with scissors, her voice softened to a nearly inaudible sound," Momma, I am scared. I know Jay could ..."

Lottie sat closely, next to her daughter.

"I know Jay could... get hurt...I know... I know you think I'm still your little girl. But Momma, I understand a lot more than you think I do. And Jay and I have talked about this."

"Well, Sweetie, you just have to learn to be strong."

Pearl shifted her body toward her mother's, "You sound like Jay ... be strong. But I guess there is no other alternative, is there Momma?" Pearl straightened her back as she continued wrapping the gift.

The ring was simple, a yellow gold band with one small diamond chip. Jay slipped it on her finger Christmas Day while Pearl's parents watched, then cheered. "And this is my special gift to you, I made it also," Jay handed a neatly wrapped present to Pearl and nodded toward the opened gift box where his vest lay.

Pearl scratched at the paper, trying to figure out just where the tape was.

"I used glue."

"No wonder I'm having such a hard time doing this." She laughed nervously, finally pulling the edges of the paper apart; she dug into the white box that seemed so heavy. "Oh my gosh. Jay, how in the world did you do this?"

"Is it a paper weight?" Jess asked from across the living room.

"It can be." Jay reached for the glass globe Pearl held in her hands. "It's sort of like a snow globe, but it has sand instead of white flakes. See." He held the globe closer to where Jess and Lottie sat, turning it upside down and back right side to watch the sand drift slowly down.

"I see you got Pearl's weeds inside it."

Lottie laughed, "Jess, shame on you." She gave him a gentle sock to the arm, and took the orb from Jay's hand. "But it is pretty. It's different."

"A guy at camp made it for me."

"I thought you said *you* made it?" Pearl reached to take the globe from her mother.

"Sorta, I made it ...sorta. I designed it and I'm the one who got the sand and weeds... I mean flowers."

Pearl shrugged, "I've come to terms with y'all calling them weeds. Dandelions are weeds and they're pretty. So weeds they are, pretty weeds."

"I gathered the *purple flowers*. Then there's this guy at the camp that makes all sorts of things with glass, so I had him make this. I hope you like it."

Quietly she sat holding the globe, pondering not what was in the globe itself, but the new feeling that rushed through her. For a fleeting moment Pearl felt the child that had once relished picking scores of purple heather; that lived to pick them and decorate her room to overflowing. Now, the plant inside the globe meant something else.

"You do like it, don't you?" Jay's voice broke her concentration. She raised her head a slight bit and looked at the man she loved with new light.

Pearl was quiet the rest of the day. During dinner she ate little, watching instead the interaction between her parents and Jay. It was if she had never noticed the way he moved - reaching out to accept a dish of desert from her mother or the way he cocked his head, smiling, eyes twinkling as he thanked her - or how he leaned back in his chair when talking to her father, a relaxed look about him as they spoke. Why hadn't she noticed before the flecks of brown in his black hair or the small lines near his eyes or the way he leaned in to speak, the way his shoulders rounded when he sat intensely listening.

"Pearl? Are you off in lala land today, or what?" Jess looked at his daughter's barely eaten plate of food. "You feeling okay?"

"Yes, Daddy. I feel just fine. I'm just not real hungry."

Lottie and Jess shot a quick knowing glance to one another, thinking that this might be the last time the couple saw one another for a long time. Excusing herself from the table, Lottie motioned for Jess to help her gather the dishes as Jay and Pearl rose from their chairs. "We'll just take these to the sink, y'all go on in the living room, we'll be in there shortly."

Pearl looked to her father as he nodded his head in compliance with Lottie. "Go on now. We can take care of this."

Arm in arm, Jay and Pearl left the kitchen and walked through the breezeway into the living room.

"I think it finally hit her," Jess whispered as they gathered dishes and placed them on the kitchen counter.

"I think it finally hit them both, did you see how they were looking at one another during dinner?" Lottie scraped the bits of food from the dishes into the trash can.

"Yeah, this was all so quick. With the war, and Jay having to leave, I guess it threw her for a loop." Jess turned the knob to the faucet, plugged the drain and added the dish soap. Neither he nor Lottie heard the living room door close.

A crisp coolness filled the night air and Pearl moved closer to Jay. She could feel his hips move against her side as he pulled her close. She gazed up to the starlit sky, then nuzzled her head into his chest.

"Pearl, my dear sweet Pearl."

They walked on toward the dock and stood silently listening to the slap of the water against the boats, watching as they swayed to and fro with the tide.

"I'll be back."

"I know."

"As soon as I get back we'll get married."

"I know." Pearl didn't bother to fight back the tears that flowed down her cheeks. She didn't try to wipe them away either as a trembling sigh escaped her lips.

Walking slowly across the yard, leaves crunching beneath their feet, they stopped at the barn. "Let me say good bye to old Topsy," Jay's words quivered as he released Pearl's hand to open the barn door.

"I sure am going to miss this place." Jay patted the horse on the hind quarter, and tried to lighten the mood. "Your family's been really nice to me – reminds me of my folks back home...I love the vest. All the guys are going to be jealous when they see it."

Pearl stood gazing at him. Understanding what he was trying to do as she touched the ring he'd slipped on her finger. "This is so pretty," she held it up close to her face; Jay reached for her arm and pulled her close to him.

This night, when he held her close, pangs of loneliness consumed Pearl. It was as if she had already lost him, and at the same time, as if she had never really kissed him before. She ached to hold him closer, kiss him deeper; searching for answers to all the confusion. She felt his tears as she pressed her cheek against his. Then as always he pushed her to arms length. "Whoa, gal," Jay said weakly."

Pearl said nothing in response, only slid her hand across his cheek and then to his hair; her fingers grasped the short strands, pulling his face close to her own. She felt his lips on her skin, against her neck. Heat shot through her as Jay drew his hands to the slip beneath her dress, caressing her thighs. She bent to the curvature of his body and felt him against her as she reached her hand beneath his shirt. Together they slowly knelt into the mounds of hay, lying together as one.

CHAPTER TEN

"Well, that's done." Lottie untied her apron and smoothed her dress as Jess placed the dish towel on the oven handle. "Guess those two are on the sofa smooching." She giggled, putting her arms around Jess's neck to give him a quick peck."We can keep her busy planning that wedding of hers while he's gone."

"Hope there is a wedding."

"Look on the sunny side, always on the sunny side," Lottie sang the words to one of her favorite songs and nudged Jess to smile. "Gotta believe he will, dear."

"Better prepare for if he don't." Jess held the door for his wife as they left the kitchen and entered the breezeway.

"You prepare for if he don't, I'll prepare for the wedding. That boy loves that girl, he'll *be* back." Lottie leaned against the breezeway frame and looked out into the cool starlit sky.

"I know he loves her, what I'm saying is, what if he can't come back."

"Jess, you have to know I've thought of that. I prefer to believe he will." Lottie pushed open the partially closed door to the living room. "Where'd they go?"

"They better not be…." Jess walked to Pearl's bedroom and flipped the light switch to find her bed neatly made.

"They're out there," Lottie smiled sadly as she held the curtain aside. Jess heaved a sigh of relief and then peeked through the partially open curtain to see his daughter and Jay leaning against the Jeep. Pearl's head was nestled against his chest while Jay's hand caressed her hair. A kiss was exchanged, tears flowed, and they watched as Jay gently pushed their daughter to arms length. He wiped her tears. They spoke in muted sounds then turned toward the house, Lottie and Jess quickly closed the curtain.

"I guess it's that time," Jay's steps sounded heavy as he entered the room. His cheeks were tear stained, as were Pearl's. "I'm not sure when I'm going to be leaving. Could be a couple days, could be tomorrow. You know how those things are in the Army."

"If you don't leave tomorrow, are you coming back over?" Lottie asked hopefully.

"I'll try. They're sending me up to New York first before shipping me overseas." Jay breathed a clumsy guffaw, "don't ask me why. You know it's…."

"The Army," Jess finished Jay's sentence.

"If I can, you know I will come before I leave out." His words seemed to beg for the possibility of return.

Jess reached to shake Jay's hand. "Son, you hurry on back now."

Lottie reached out her hand to Jay, and pulled him close for a tight hug. "Boy, we're here waiting for you. We'll be planning that wedding. Okay?" She forced a smile, aching both for her daughter and the young man she loved. Lottie had come to think of him as the young boy child she had lost so long ago. He had become a son.

Bending to kiss Pearl, Jay gazed into her eyes, smiled slightly and whispered gently against her lips, "I love you. Be strong for me."

Their kiss was soft, gentle, a mere brush against the lips. "I love you so much Jay." Pearl took a deep breath then stepped back from him, lifted her chin, and squared her shoulders. "I'm nobody's darlin' but yours."

Jay did not come the following day, but Enid Abbott drove to the Scaggins home to deliver a letter from him. His words were tender with expressions of love filling nearly half the page. Then his tone turned to optimism about their future and the wedding that was planned for April. He reminded Pearl to thank her mother for the wonderful meals she had fed him, 'beats the heck out of the mess hall,' and asked Pearl to remind Jess that he would be back soon to help with the cattle.

New Year's Day, the Scaggins prepared their annual pig pickin' and the regular local families showed up to enjoy the good food and the music that was once again provided by Will and Enid.

Pearl's spirits were in fine form as she carried a letter from Jay in her dress pocket. It had arrived only that morning. "He's still in New York." She answered Ellie's question gleefully.

"Well, I will tell you one thing, Miss Pearly White, tonight you look really pretty. And I hope that beau of yours comes back soon."

It wasn't often that Ellie retracted her claws when it came to men. But tonight she seemed almost giddy herself. Chuck asked me to marry him," she whispered in Pearl's ear."

"Oh, Ellie, I'm so happy for you." Pearl flung her arms around her friend. When? When are y'all getting married?"

"Fifteenth of this month. Me and him are going down to Florida. He wants me to meet his parents." Lottie held out her hand to show the ring on her finger. The stone was several times larger than the chip in Pearl's ring.

"Wow, that's some rock."

"Yeah, Chuck's family has two thousand acres of orange groves down there. He says we could live there when he gets out of the Army."

"Is that what you want to do?"

"You know that's what I want to do." Ellie searched her friend's eyes, "Get the heck out of this place." Sighing deeply, she reached for Pearl's hand, "come on, goody two shoes, let's go in your room, I want to talk with you."

Pearl flipped the light on as she entered her room, and sat on the edge of her bed. "Okay, Ellie, what's up?"

"I've got a bun in the oven," She gently patted her stomach."

Pearl searched Ellie's face, and lowered her head, thinking of the night Jay had left. She hadn't even considered that their love making would result in her own pregnancy.

"Is that why you're getting married?"

Heaving a sigh, Ellie looked again at the engagement ring on her hand. "He'd ask me anyway. He thinks I'm the best thing since sliced bread." Ellie tucked her legs beneath her dress, settling herself more comfortably on the bed. "He's always buying me things. And he always takes me out to the nicest places. And," she signed once more, "He's always telling me he loves me."

"But do you love him?"

"Of course I do." She answered quickly. Smoothing her dress, Ellie giggled, "I'm going to live in Florida."

"I've been told it's pretty there and warm all year round."

"Yeah, hardly any winter at all."

Pearl paused for a moment before asking, "How far along are you?"

"Little over a month."

"What did Chuck say when you told him?"

"He asked me to marry him, dummy. He said it was the right thing to do."

Pearl contemplated telling Ellie about her and Jay the night before he left. "Just one time?" She added shyly.

Ellie's eyes grew large, "are you kidding, we've been *doing that* just about since I met him."

"But…"

"He was always careful, you know what I mean. *Careful*"

"Pearl's puzzled look annoyed Ellie, "Oh, that's right. You wouldn't know. Well, just for future reference, always remember to ask your beau to use *protection*. He'll know what you mean."

"If you and Chuck used *protection*" why are you pregnant? Pearl thought of the mistake she would be making if she confided anything to Ellie. Her lips tightened as she listened to Ellie continue.

"One night we just got lost in the moment. Hasn't that ever happened to you? I mean, how long have you been dating that cowboy?"

"Little over a year."

"And you never did it?"

"That's none of your business." Walking to the window she watched Will drag his bow across the strings as he played the first notes of the Orange Blossom Special. "Come on, let's go outside."

"Don't change the subject. Did you or didn't you? Pearl walked to the side of the bed where Ellie sat; she looked childlike with her dress spread out across the bedspread.

"Tell me now." Ellie purred, trying to coax an answer.

"No."

"I don't believe you. You had to have done something after a year. I *know* you did."

"We got close." Pearl shrugged, figuring that she would give her enough to stop the questioning, a few intimate details, but that would be as far as she would go. She knew Ellie, and knew that at some point in time she would use whatever information she could to taunt or ridicule her. That was just Ellie's way.

"How close?"

Shrugging her shoulders, Pearl's lips turned up at the corners.

Tap, tap, tap. Paul had been watching the two girls talk for nearly a minute, though he hadn't heard a word of their whispered conversation. He tapped again on the glass.

Pearl and Ellie raised their heads to peer at the window where Paul stood motioning for them to come outside. "You're missing the party, girls," He hollered through the glass. "Come on!"

Ellie turned to Pearl, grabbing her arm, "Not until you tell me. Now did you or didn't you?"

"Oh, come on Ellie, let's go outside. And I promise what me and Jay did wasn't much – second base, that's all." She sighed, "Well, now you know and you know me, ol goody two shoes." Pearl flipped her hair and headed for the door, I'm going dancing."

Ellie followed reluctantly, still curious about the intimate details of Jay and Pearl's love life. She arched an eyebrow, and then she saw Pearl wrap her arms around Paul. "Ahh, little mouse," she said to herself as she watched Pearl prop up her drunken cousin.

"I see you've already found your date for the night." Ellie nodded toward the jar of whiskey Paul held.

"I'm free, white, and twenty-one."

"Twenty-two," Scolded Ellie. "And I don't care what color you are, you're starting to get on my nerves, cousin or no cousin. In fact, if you don't stop all this drinking, I'm not even going to claim you."

"Oops, sorry ma'am." Paul swallowed the last of the whiskey and leaned down to set the jar against a tree.

"I'm worried about you too, Paul." Pearl moved close to him, taking his hand, pausing as she remembered how Jay had warned about her friendliness to Paul, that he might misinterpret it. She let go of his hand. "I'll always be your friend, Paul, no matter what you do." Then taking a scolding tone, "But *you* need to quit drinking so much."

"Why? I don't bother nobody."

Ellie threw back her head in laughter, "That's the truth. What girl in her right mind would want to be *bothered* by you. You're drunk all the time?"

"You didn't always drink." In Paul's defense, Pearl glared at Ellie. "You never drank when you were around me, did you, Paul."

Paul smirked, as he kicked the dirt.

"He ain't around you now, that's the problem."

"Shut up, Ellie!" Paul shoved her more than gently. "Why don't you just shut your mouth once in awhile?"

Grabbing his shirt as he turned to leave, Pearl shot a venomous glance toward Ellie. "Come dance with me, Paul." Taking his hand she led him to the dance floor, settling one hand on his shoulder, the other in his palm.   "She's mean. I don't know why I'm friends with her."

"She knows how to get people to trust her... and then…. Well, you know what I mean, Pearl. She's a snake in the grass."

"Yes, I've come to realize that, but we've had a lot of fun together, all of us. Remember all those times on the banks and playing pirates and tag?" Pearl winced as Paul stepped on her foot. "But she has a point about your drinking so much."

"You ain't telling me anything I don't know already. I don't even like the stuff."

"Then why…"

His eyes said it all. Pearl held her breath, a tinge of guilt swept through her as she recalled the dates she had gone on with Paul before she met Jay.

"I've always liked you Paul. We've always been friends. All the times we've been to the banks and going fishing, you know, we grew up together."

"I always liked *you* too". Paul moved to hold Pearl closer, but felt the resistance in her body.

"I know." As the music ended, Pearl released her hand from Paul's. "Let's go sit down by the dock."

Paul looked for his cousin as he and Pearl walked to the dock. He certainly did not want her along.

"I like Jay, Pearl. He's a good man."

Pearl touched the ring on her finger, and smiled as she turned to Paul. "Yes, he is."

"But I always thought it would be me and you, ever since we were kids. And then you started seeing Jay, well, I sort of figured it would be like Ellie, you know, date him for a while and then he'd move on. "

"I'm sorry."

"There's nothing to be sorry for. I should have known. You're not like Ellie. A man just couldn't help falling in love with *you*."

"I do love him, Paul. And I miss him so much."

"He'll be back soon. This war isn't going to last too long. He ought to be back by spring, summer at the latest."

Smoothing her hair and curling it around her hand, Pearl nodded. "That's what he says. That's what Daddy and Momma say. And I hope everybody's right."

Paul reached his arm around Pearl's shoulders, nudging her, "You just plan for that wedding, and remember that if you need me, I'll always be around."

"And you're going to stop drinking so much."

Paul scrunched his face, "How in the Hell does my dad drink that swaller?"

She's been the same since she was twelve years old. Like clockwork. Lottie sorted through the bathroom waste basket. *She usually soils the sheets a little at night too. Oh Lord. What has that girl gone and done now.* Lottie bobby pinned a few stray hairs from her forehead as she considered, through her own calculations, that her daughter might be pregnant.

From the breezeway Lottie caught sight of her at the dock. She was scaling a fish Jess had caught that morning.

"Pearl!" She called out.

"Yes ma'am!"

"When you get done with that fish, come on over here for a minute, if you please!"

"Yes ma'am!" Pearl threw the head and guts into the water, then leaned back and watched as little minnows picked at them. How normal, no mundane, life seemed without Jay. Rinsing her hands in the water, she wiped them on her dungarees and walked toward the house.

"Yes ma'am?" She questioned her mother as she walked into the kitchen and sat at the table.

Lottie slid a chair from beneath it and sat to face her daughter. "Sweetie...I was cleaning out the bathroom." She drew a deep sigh. "I know it's about your time of the month. Last week should have been your time, but every once in a while everybody gets a little late."

Pearl drew her thumbnail to her mouth and began nipping at the edges. "I was afraid to say anything."

"Afraid?"

Pearl nodded, "I just keep hoping that I'll start. But I'm well over a week late now... and I haven't heard from Jay in over a week either."

The distraught look on Pearl's face dissuaded Lottie from raising her voice in anger and she watched as her daughter wiped a tear from her cheek.

"I get a letter at least every other day, and now, I haven't gotten anything from him."

Lottie scooted her chair next to Pearl's. "Why don't I talk to your daddy? Maybe he knows some way we can find out where Jay is. We'd just have to move the wedding up a little, that's all."

"Tell Daddy? Oh my God. He will hate me!"

"There, there, your daddy will never hate you. Lottie stroked her daughter's hair as she laid her head on the table, sobbing. "Let me tell you a secret."

Pearl quieted for a moment as her mother began. "You remember your Aunt Dinah?"

Pearl nodded her head.

"Well, during The Great War, she was in love with some boy she met up in Wilmington. He'd ride all the way out here to see her, at least once a week. Well, your Aunt Dinah was just gaga over him and told Grandpa that they wanted to get married."

Pearl sat up as she listened to her mother speak softly and with compassion about an aunt she barely knew.

"But your grandpa didn't like the boy very much, didn't like the way his own daughter had talked about getting married rather than the boy coming and asking for her hand."

"Was that all?"

"Back then it would have been enough for your grandpa, but there was something else."

"What?"

"The boy hadn't done anything, but his daddy had been in prison. And you know how Grandpa is, he believes the apple don't fall far from the tree."

"That's so silly, Momma."

"Be that as it may, he told Dinah he forbade the marriage. Well, lo and behold, this makes her even more determined, 'cause you know your Aunt Dinah's got that stubborn streak in her just like your daddy."

Pearl, sniggered at the remark, and straightened in her chair. "What happened then?"

"She went off with that boy and ended up..."

Inadvertently Lottie glanced toward her daughter's belly.

Gently touching her stomach, Pearl's eyes teared. "What did she do? Did they get married?"

"No, seems Grandpa wasn't too wrong about that young man, after all."

"What do you mean?'

"Well, sweetie – Leonard, that was his name, Leonard, took his daddy's Model T and decided he and Aunt Dinah would go to South Carolina to get married. Except along the way, they decided to steal some laundry."

"Steal laundry?"

"You bet, they were stealing laundry. All the way down to South Carolina, every time they'd come upon someone's wash in the backyard drying, he and your Aunt Dinah would stop and sneak up and take the laundry right off the line. The back seat of that Model T was full to nearly overflowing."

"What'd they do that for?"

"Beats the stuffing out of me, but sure enough, that's what they did. And finally, they stopped at the wrong house. The Sheriff's house and he was just getting up from his noon day nap and saw them out the kitchen widow while he was getting himself a glass of water."

Pearl's laughter was uncontrollable as she held herself around the waist. "This can't be true."

"It sure enough is true. But don't you dare ask your daddy about it. He swore me to secrecy long ago."

"What happened then?" Pearl asked, stifling her laughter.

"Of course, they both got arrested. And knowing your Aunt Dinah, I wouldn't put it past her that she put poor Leonard up to all the stealing, she was always a clothes horse."

"They both went to jail?"

"Leonard did for a few days, Dinah didn't. Grandpa paid more than a few dollars to get her out of that mess. Then, since the war was going on at that time, Leonard got off scot free when he joined the Army."

"I guess Aunt Dinah didn't know she was carrying his baby. Did she?"

"No, Sweetie, but it wasn't long before she did and Grandpa went down to the courthouse and had her named changed to Mullins and sent her out to Arkansas to live with his sister Mollie. And, except for the one time she visited us, she's been out there ever since."

"What ever happened to Leonard?"

"He got killed in the war."

CHAPTER ELEVEN

"You still haven't heard from him?"

Pearl shook her head no as she stepped into the flats boat.

Searching for the right words, words that would not hurt, Paul reached to rub her back. "Have you asked Enid if he can find out anything?"

"He can't, says nobody out there knows anything once someone leaves the camp."

"Well, you're going to have to do something pretty soon, Pearl. You're going to start showing." Paul untied the line from the piling and shoved the boat away from the dock.

It had been over a month since Jay left and Pearl had heard nothing from him in the last three weeks. "It wouldn't be so bad if I wasn't...you know. I know that sometimes girls don't hear from their men for weeks at a time when they are shipped out. But..."

"Have you thought of writing to his parents?"

"What would I say? Hello Mr. and Mrs. Bishop, I'm going to have your son's baby so I need to find out if you know how I can reach him?" She shot a sarcastic look toward Paul. "Momma was talking to me about changing my last name and moving away... I'd change it to Bishop."

"Do you want to move away?"

"No, I don't want to leave here." Shaking her head demonstratively, Pearl breathed a heavy sigh. "What if he comes back and I'm gone. What then?"

"If he does come back then everything will be fine. And you'll already have his last name."

But the thought of leaving her family and friends was unbearable. And the thought of having to live like Aunt Dinah, shamed, away from her family forever, made her nauseous. This could not be – and why was it happening to her?

Paul jerked the motor cord, "I'll marry you." His voice was loud over the sound of the outboard, but his eyes were gentle and pleading as he took the tiller and motored into the sound.

"He's coming back, Paul," Pearl lifted her chin and wiped a tear from her cheek.

"I'm just saying that if he doesn't, I will." He leaned to yank one of the braids she had plaited her hair into, "Hey gal, he's coming back. He'd be a fool not to."

Pearl pulled her hat down to guard her ears from the wind and buttoned the top button of her coat. "Lordy, I hate this time of year. It's always so cold." She fidgeted with the oyster rake in the bottom of the boat. "Course, oysters are better the colder it gets."

Paul nodded in agreement. He watched her gaze out into the marsh, settling her elbows on her knees. The wind whipped her braids behind her neck. "You sure this ain't going to hurt the baby none?"

"Momma says as long as I don't strain or pick up anything too heavy, I'll be alright."

"Okay." Paul gently guided the boat toward a small island, "You haven't said anything to Ellie, have you? You better not have."

"There is no way in the world I would tell Ellie. Do you know what she'd do if she knew?"

Pearl recalled the conversation of only a few weeks before and how Ellie had bragged about her own sexual activity. How glad she was that she had not told her that night of Jay and she making love in the barn. "Humph.... So, have you heard anything from her since she's been in Florida?"

"Mom got a postcard from her. It had girls lying on the beach with palm trees and the ocean. Looks nice down there. And she said it is really warm."

"Paul....promise me you won't let on to Momma that you know anything about me ... promise you won't let her know that I told you."

"You told me? Hell, I guessed it. You were pukin' all over my boots, Jeez." Paul laughed. "That ain't the first time I saw anybody with morning sickness... But I knew it before then."

Furrowing her brow in doubt, Pearl smirked as she pulled her hat down again over her ears. "How?"

"That far away look in your eyes, your refusing to eat any of Mom's chicken and pastry. I knew it, I knew it. If you didn't want any of my mother's chicken and pastry, I knew something was wrong with you." Pausing as he turned the skiff southward, Paul spoke, "And I'll ask you again. Marry me Pearl. It's going to look real bad if you don't marry somebody, or go away. And you need to think of your parents."

It had not occurred to her before how the shame of her unwed pregnancy would affect her parents. They would be humiliated and ostracized by the community. She knew how the people gossiped about other folks. Her parents might feel unwelcome, even at church. "If I don't hear anything by the end of this week, I'll do something."

"Something? What? You don't have a lot of choices.

"I know." Pearl touched Paul's arm, "It wouldn't be fair to you, Paul." Her eyes searched his for understanding.

"To marry me?"

Nodding her head, Pearl smiled weakly and touched his arm again. "I just don't ….."

"Love me?"

'Gee Whiz, Paul. You know what I mean. Yes, I love you…but…"

He saw the pain in her eyes, and could not fault her for not feeling as he did, "I know, I know…I'm like your brother."

Pearl shrugged, "Yeah, sorta. But I do love you Paul, you're my best friend."

They gathered the oysters, Paul doing most of the raking, while Pearl sorted through and chose the ones she considered the best. They talked about Ellie and what a rascal she was, about how she was faring in Florida.

"I can see her now, the belle of the ball getting all the attention she can muster. I bet she's got that family wrapped around her fingers." They both laughed about Ellie and how, despite her arrogance and snobbiness, she could sometimes be loving and considerate. "But not often," Paul added, laughing. They talked about the upcoming gathering that evening. Both commented on how they really didn't want to be part of it; Paul stressed his dislike of how loud and obnoxious his father became when he drank. "And you know he's going to drink tonight. He's always got to boast about his moonshine and how he sells it to the big shots, which of course, makes him a big shot. "Yep, both Dad and Ellie got something to sell...shinola," Paul teased. "Sure can tell they're related.

"We got three bushels of oysters, Momma." Pearl called as she sat on the porch and pulled the tall rubber boots from her feet.

Paul echoed her words as he placed the last bushel near the steps. Flipping open his knife, he edged the blade along a crevice, opened an oyster and gulped it down. "They're good too, nice and salty."

"Let me have one of those," Pearl leaned out of the screened door and grabbed an opened shell, cupped her lips to the edges and swallowed the raw oyster. "Would be better with some hot sauce, but its good. Want one Momma?"

Lottie stood at the door to the kitchen, her hands holding several unfolded sheets of paper. Pearl's eyes brightened as her first thought was that of a letter from Jay. Then as she noticed the look of pain on her mother's face, nausea welled in her throat. She flew to grab the pages from her mother's hand.

"Sweetie, I'm sorry." Trying to comfort her daughter, Lottie knelt beside her. "It's from his momma, Mrs. Bishop. She wanted us to know. .. she says he wrote about you all the time. Said he couldn't wait till you and he were married....I think it was so kind of her... it had to be hard to write such a letter."

Pearl's eyes raced over the words, *Missing in Action,* a small guttural sound raised from her throat.

"Mrs. Bishop says she felt it. One night she just woke up and knew. Oh my God... that is the worst thing.... to *know.*"

"Pearl, you have to make a decision," Jess's voice was stern. He had lost patience with Pearl's indecisiveness. "He's not coming back!" Walking to the fireplace he threw in a split log too harshly, sparks popped about the kitchen. "Three quarters of those boys that go over there and get listed as missing in action, don't ever come back!"

Pearl knew his words made sense. She had heard how bodies were torn in so many pieces that they were unidentifiable. And how soldiers were put into camps where they were beaten and starved. The thought was unbearable. Believing that those things could happen to Jay, made even the hope of his life seem cruel. It would be a sin to wish him alive if only to be tortured."Oh, Daddy!" Rushing into her father's arms she sobbed against his shoulder.

"It's time to let go, gal." Stroking her hair, Jess spoke the words as kindly as he could. He gathered her in his arms and sat her on his lap, as if she were still his little girl.

CHAPTER TWELVE

Their wedding was a simple ceremony preformed at the Justice of the Peace in Wilmington. Afterward, the couple drove to Wrightsville Beach and rented a small cottage. That evening they dined at the Lumina Pavilion. Pearl even danced a few times with Paul on the sparkling dance floor that overlooked the ocean. Jay had taken her there once before. They had danced well into the night and strolled on the beach afterward. She recalled his kisses, their laughter, but she dare not tell Paul; she didn't want to "lick the red off his candy," as her mother would say.

She had felt so numb since learning about Jay. It was as if the world around her was a foreign place; she moved through it like words on a page. Now, nothing mattered. Not anymore. And when Paul had asked once again to marry her, the only answer she could conceive of was to tell him yes. What did it matter anyway? She could not leave a place where she saw Jay in fleeting images – as he rode helping drive the cattle, as he held his hat, scooping crabs, or as in the barn where he helped her saddle the horses and had made such sweet love to her.

At first when Paul had reached for her on their wedding night, she thought she could close her eyes and feel Jay and that with enough effort it would be Jay. Though Paul was gentle with her that night, the smell was wrong, the movements were wrong and for Pearl it felt strange to hold someone other than Jay - to kiss someone other than Jay. But it did not matter.

"I guess we'll have to live at my parent's house until we can get our own place. Hope you don't mind." Paul drove with one hand on the steering wheel and the other around Pearl's shoulder trying to make small talk, looking for some sort of affection. He recalled the night before too and how unresponsive Pearl had been, she seemed that way now too. "You know last night we didn't have to..."

She smiled at him and shrugged. "It's okay."

"Did I hurt you?"

"No." She looked down at the band on her finger, moving it around with her thumb, thinking of Jay's ring that lay quietly in a hidden compartment of her jewelry box.

"All you would have had to say is no. I wouldn't have done anything if you had said no."

"You're my husband now."

"I've always been your friend," Paul's voice was sarcastic and cutting as he removed his arm from around her shoulder.

As they rode in silence, Pearl's thoughts turned to Jay once again. She wanted so desperately to feel his touch, to hear his voice soothe her but instead she heard Paul whispering as he leaned against her.

"I am your friend. Maybe last night is not what a friend does, but to me it was love. I have always wanted to be part of you. Don't you understand that you have always been part of *me*. That it was you who saved me. Don't you remember how I used to run to your house and we'd go fishing or go riding old Topsy. I was running to you to get away from my mom and dad. He beat the shit out me and she'd stand there and watch. You were always kind to me, always trying to make me laugh and you always included me in things. Ellie, my own cousin wouldn't do that. But you helped make me want to keep on living…. I will never hurt you, never make you feel ashamed, never make you feel like you are anything less than the wonderful girl that always makes my heart fill with love.

Pearl turned to face him. She had known that Paul's family was what was called *rough.* She'd heard of Clarence getting into fights and how mean he could get when he was drinking, seen his wife's scarred face but she'd never imagined that things were that bad at home for Paul or what it all meant. Caressing his hand she looked deeply into his eyes, "I'm so sorry." She looked at him as they drove along. She had known him her entire life and Jay only a little over a year. It should be Paul she would know the best, but as she had lain with him the night before, she realized she did not know him at all. His body felt strange; she felt awkward, as if it was wrong —as if she were being unfaithful.

Turning her face again to watch him as he drove the truck she noticed the pox mark high on his right cheek and the coarse stubble on his chin. It was light colored, like his hair. He was so different than Jay. Then she remembered her mother's words, *Jay is not here. Don't blame Paul for not being Jay and don't blame him for what you did.* It made sense; she had to let Jay go. *In time you will love Paul more than you ever thought of loving Jay.* Pearl knew that could never be.

When she had touched his hand Paul felt her sympathy. He did not want her pity. As he stared at the road ahead he began thinking of what type of future lay in store for him and Pearl. She had said nothing but "I'm sorry," but what was she sorry for? This morning, after a strange and confusing night, it seemed they could not speak easily to one another. Words had never been a problem in their friendship. He tried again to open communication.

"Did you enjoy the Lumina last night?"

"It was nice." She tried to think of something else to say, but her mind, still held Jay's image.

"Are you sure I didn't I hurt you last night?"

Pearl looked meekly into his eyes, "No, of course not."

"I was just thinking that with the baby and everything that…"

146

"No," Pearl pressed against her still flat belly and smiled. "It's probably the size of a turtle egg now. I don't think that's going to hurt."

"I was just thinking that maybe we shouldn't... you know."

Pearl shrugged "I'm your wife, now."

The statement seemed matter of fact, like one of compliance; he tightened his grip on the wheel, trying to find a subject that might brighten up the drive home. "Sure do like this truck. It was nice of your daddy to let us borrow it. Do you know what your daddy paid for it?"

Conversation seemed strained and awkward but Pearl tried to sound enthusiastic about the new truck. Other than the old Model T that sat rusting in the woods, this was the only automobile her family had ever owned. "He bought it from Mr. Grayson in Verona. I think he paid a hundred dollars."

Paul let out a loud whistle, "That's a lot of money."

"Yeah, he's been oystering more and went down to South Carolina a couple times to seine fish, so he could save up some money."

That was the money he was saving up for Pearl and Jay's wedding. Paul's jaw tightened and he felt his face redden. *God, I'm so stupid. Me and my big mouth.* "Well, uh...we'll stop at my house and you can come on in, Mom says she's got the room fixed up really nice for us."

Pearl glanced quickly at him and smiled. "We're getting a telephone too and Daddy's going to put in indoor plumbing.

They won't have to go to the outhouse anymore." Touching his arm again, she giggled softly.

Paul's mood lightened a bit as he put his arm around Pearl again. "You'll be able to talk with your mom and dad whenever you want then."

"Yes." Nodding her head in agreement Pearl thought again of the conversation they had when she agreed to marry him: "Paul, I can never thank you enough for….but I still love him…what if he comes back some day?"

He had answered with as much consideration for her as he could, "I don't want to hear about it. We've done what we've done and the rest is up to us." Paul hesitated for a moment, "You can decide to dream about Jay or you can be my wife. I hope you'll be my wife, Pearl. You know, and I won't say it no more, I've always loved you and I ain't never going to stop. But everything is up to you."

Josie and Clarence Rosell stood at the doorway of their small house and watched as the couple walked to the front porch. Josie held a small handkerchief to her eyes, letting it drape down to cover her smile; she held out her other hand to Pearl. "Oh, Sweetie." She hugged her tightly – Pearl could feel her small frame against her own; she could see the patches of missing hair that appeared to be teased over.

"I'm so happy for you and Paul. I just always knowed it, always knowed you and my boy would one day get married. I know it's not much, but we fixed up Paul's room for you, let me show you y'all's room." Josie tugged at Pearl's arm, taking small steps as she made her way down the narrow hall to where Paul had always stayed.

The room had been fixed up nicely, a new star burst quilt lay across a newly built bed, the windows of the room had trellised curtains of yellow and pink roses, and the tall chest of drawers smelled of new paint.

"I just knowed, my whole life – ever since you two was kids, that one day you'd get married." She repeated as she wiped her eyes again, then pulling Pearl in close, she hugged her tightly. "I always said it, Paul was always crazy 'bout you. And you, honey, you are just the sweetest thing."

"Thank you, Miss Josie." Pearl returned the hug. "The room sure does look pretty."

"Later this year we'll sneak on over to the banks and get some of them purple flowers Paul says you like so much."

Pearl cast her gaze toward Paul, who winked back at her.

"Well, young lady," Clarence nodded to his new daughter-in-law, "looks like you're going to be living with us for a while. Least 'til your husband can build a place of his own." His condescending tone sing songed and he glared at the couple, "yep, that bed looks real comfortable."

Clarence Rosell, unlike his brother Bud, was not a pleasant man. He resembled his brother physically; both had blond hair and blue eyes, both were thin, but that was where the resemblance ended. Where Bud's voice was thin and twangy, Clarence's was deep and gravely. His eyes held a much harder gaze than any Pearl had ever seen from Ellie's father. A large wad of tobacco usually bulged from his lower lip, leaving brown tobacco residue at the corners of his mouth and down the front of his overalls.

Clarence and Josie Rosell's home was small and bare. Decorations on the walls could have been used to hide the many holes there - evidence, no doubt, of Clarence's violent temper. The doorways seemed slightly askew and there were long scratches carved in the wooden floors. Where they had come from was a source of curiosity as Pearl recalled Paul's revelation of how his father beat him.

A few hundred feet from the home stood an old barn with one remaining door dangling at an angle. Several rusting automobiles lay to the side of the decaying barn. From the look of things it was obvious that Clarence lacked the knack for farming. Most assumed he simply didn't have the desire to work very hard at all. Other than the small patch of garden, that Paul and Josie worked, the rest of his fields lay barren and strewn with discarded furniture or rusting machinery.

Over the years Clarence could always be counted on to help with the fishing in the fall. He was a strong fisherman, and he kept a small oyster bed in the nearby sound. These things he was good at. But he rarely did more than was required, leaving his family dependent on his whimsical work ethic. To his credit, Clarence did have one asset – his main source of income - a still hidden far in the woods. It was his pride and joy. If he was not there, he could be found at his house napping off a drunk. His sister-in-law, Noreen, always referred to him as the *lazy* brother. Clarence Rosell referred to his brother's wife as *that naggin' bitch*.

"Hope at least that *you're* a good cook," Clarence sniggered sarcastically as he slid a glance toward Josie.

His wife ignored the slight, "I hope you like the room. It's small, but I think it will be just fine," Josie's eyes widened in delight. "It will be nice to have some company while Clarence is off working during the day."

Pearl listened intently to Josie; it was hard to resist the woman's gentle demeanor and sparkling eyes and she found herself smiling as she listened to the gentle lilting voice.

"We was planning to make the room bigger... you know... since we had the two boys in there... then, since Phil went away... but I guess that time just got away over the years, and..."

"That's enough, Josie." Clarence growled at his wife, "This little girl ain't interested in all that." He turned his attention to Pearl, "If your new husband will get off his ass and get a job, you won't have to be so cramped up." A guttural snigger rolled from his throat, as he turned to spit chaw toward the opened door.

Watching Josie ignore the glob of tobacco that lay spattered on the living room floor, Pearl reached for her new mother-in-law's hand, "It will be just fine. I like the way the windows are set, we'll have morning and evening sun.

Each morning Pearl rose early to make the bed and straighten the bedroom. She helped Josie prepare breakfast for the men and helped her mother-in-law clean the small cluttered house. Usually she wore an apron to try and conceal her growing belly, but it was not many weeks later when Josie revealed her knowledge of the pregnancy.

Leaning in to Pearl as she stood washing the dishes, Josie whispered, "It's going to be a boy."

Quickly Pearl turned to her, "What?"

"Dearie, you never were that skinny to begin with, and you can only wear that apron so loose."

Pearl blushed, "I was going to tell you in a few days." She nodded toward Clarence, "Does he know?"

"That man wouldn't notice if I grew warts on my nose. And besides, when you and Paul got married right out of the blue, I figured there was a bun in the oven." Josie laughed softly as she stroked Pearl's hair, "I'm so happy... and it's going to be a boy."

"How do you know?"

Josie smiled widely, exposing her chipped and missing teeth, "you're carryin' him really low, that's how I know it's a boy. Now if it was a girl, that baby'd be all up in your bosom."

Pearl lowed her head as she wiped another dish, and blushed deeply.

"When are you due?"

"Sometime time around the end of October," Pearl lied, adding another month to the original date. *First babies are usually a little late,* she remembered her mother saying. She hoped she was right.

"What's your momma say?"

"She's happy too. She's been crocheting socks and other things for it."

"I remember what a hard time your ma had with her babies, and I'm gonna make sure you keep yourself healthy."

"Yes ma'am, she's talked with me about that too and she's warned me against doing too much or picking up heavy things."

"And missy, standing up on your feet for too long ain't good for you, neither. I want you to start taking it easy around here. Okay?"

Pearl nodded, "I promise, I don't want anything to go wrong." She thought of how the baby was the only part of Jay she had and how desperately she wanted to hold on to that. This was *their* baby.

She still felt Jay's warmth, desired his warmth. How could she even consider forgetting Jay? But the guilt was overwhelming. Paul was so kind and eager to please her and she liked it when they laughed together – but how could that be, she loved Jay so deeply.

Ellie thought of making the turn into the Scaggins lane, but instead slowed her vehicle to a crawl as she neared the mailbox. She'd spied the mail carrier earlier and watched him as he lowered the red flag.

Ellie gathered the few pieces of mail and thumbed through them, stopping to read the bold print of one thicker than the others. It was addressed to Pearl Scaggins, *must not have known she got married,* thought Ellie. The return address was Donna, Texas.

"Ah, wonder what this is all about?" Ellie tore open the side of the envelope and read the words hurriedly.

Dear Pearl,

Jay wrote often about you and how special a girl he thought you were. We were looking forward to your wedding and meeting you, but I guess God has a different a plan for us all.

The last time I wrote to you was a very sad time. I had learned that my only son was missing in action. Only by the grace of God and with faith in Him have I been able to carry on.

I have gotten word from the government that Jay is alive in a prisoner of war camp in Germany. I have sent him a package and I hope he has received it by now. I know during war sometimes people do not receive things.

I wanted to let you know that our beloved Jay is alive. Whenever this horrible war is over I pray that the Lord will bring him home safely to us.

I know that you have not heard from me in a long while, but it was hard for me to write about my son. I hope you will forgive me.

My daughter Marsha is a Navy Nurse and she is overseas too and with both of my children gone from me it was hard for my husband and me to carry on. He had a stroke a month ago, right after he heard of Jay being missing in action. Marsha came home for a short visit to help me take care of him, but he passed away within two weeks.

I hope that you can understand why I have not written you sooner. I know Jay would want me to keep you posted on what is current. But with the loss of my husband of thirty years, I found myself in a sea of loneliness and despair. Without my good neighbors who came to help me and bring me food, I do not know what would have become of me.

I thank the Lord for answering my prayers about Jay and am only sad that my beloved husband could not have heard the news before he passed.

This war has been a curse to us all. The one good thing about this is that Jay met you. He wrote the first time he visited your family that he believed he had met the girl he wanted to marry.

I know you are just as happy to find out that Jay is alive. But we must pray for him every day that he will survive the conditions of the prisoner of war camp he is in. I hope you will write to me and let me know how you are doing. I will send you all information I get. Maybe you can write him a

letter. I know he would love to hear from you. He loves you
so much.
God Bless you,
Mrs. Madge Bishop.

"Well, I'll be damned."

The Rosell family drove the two miles to the Scaggins
home for the celebration. Clarence had thrown three
croaker sacks of oysters into the bed of his truck. Josie sat in
the front seat holding the cracklin' cornbread in her lap.
When they arrived at the Scaggins home the merkle bushes
were glowing a soft pink and they smoked perfectly as the
burlap bags of oysters were laid out.

It was a small gathering, just the two families celebrating
Pearl's pregnancy. Ellie had come for an unexpected visit
and sat with the other women while the men stood by the
fire, stoking the embers and taking a swig or two from the
jug of moonshine Clarence had brought with him.

Unusually quiet, Ellie helped set the side dishes on the
table and listened as the others talked about what the
future would bring and how careful Pearl needed to be
during this special time.

"Sweetie, I just want you and the baby to be as safe and
happy as can be. Now, you sit on down and let me set out

this food." Lottie turned to Ellie who was straightening a bow on her blouse, "And how are things coming along for you? You seem so quiet tonight." Lottie pursed her lips, "That's so unlike you."

"Momma?" Pearl admonished her mother for the sarcasm in her voice.

"That's okay; I know she doesn't like me."

"I don't dislike you, Ellie. I just never know what you're up to. Now, take tonight. You're awfully quiet. What's going on in that head of yours?"

"And why are you up here instead of down in Florida- and you're expecting a baby – I'd think the Bridges would want to keep you down there and take care of you." Josie interrupted, "You're momma and daddy never said nothing to me about you coming home for a visit."

Ellie fidgeted in her chair, lowering her eyes as she once again fumbled with the bow on her blouse. "Mother and Dad didn't know I was coming and I got in an argument with the Bridges and said I was coming home - if you need to know."

"And what was the argument about, young lady?" Lottie leaned forward, sarcasm filling her voice.
"What to name the baby."

"Well, I never heard of such a thing," Josie shook her head, "Miss Ellie, those people are puttin' you up in their home, now don't you think you ought to be a little more patient with them?" Meekly speaking the words, Josie lowered her

157

head and added almost in a whisper, "Shame on you now, shame on you."

"Good grief, why doesn't everybody just jump on me all at once!" Ellie turned to Josie and wagged her finger in ridicule, "and you, what business is it of yours Aunt Josie, who I argue with."

Pulling in her shoulders, Josie turned her face toward the house.

"Why don't you stop being so sassy? It's an ugly trait." Lottie looked sternly at Ellie, who shrugged and rolled her eyes.

"You being so quiet is out of character – makes us wonder, that's all. And you need to apologize to your aunt. That's no way to talk to her."

Ellie released a long held sigh, "Sorry, Aunt Josie."

"That's okay, child. Everybody's a little bit on edge with babies coming and a war going on. It's just a mess."

Pearl patted Josie's hand and nodded toward Ellie, "You know, usually you're the one with all the snide remarks and smart answers to everything. And tonight you *are* quiet. It's not like you. What's going on? Tell us."

"I don't know."

"Are you unhappy in Florida?"

"No, I really like Florida – love the weather," Ellie slid her dress off her shoulder to reveal the tan marks from her swim suit.

"Then why are you up here and why are you acting this way?"

"Isn't anybody glad to see me?"

"I am," Pearl reached her hand to touch Ellie's, as the other women looked at one another, rolling their eyes.

"I haven't done a darn thing but come up here to see my family... and friends," Squeezing Pearl's hand in return, Ellie lowered her head and dabbed at her eyes with a lacy handkerchief.

"We're sorry, Ellie. Like Josie said, it's just this war and everything that's going on."

"And my husband is one of those men over there fighting. You know, he could die! He could leave me all alone with a baby!" Ellie wiped a tear from her cheek and paused for a moment before blurting out, "They want me to name the baby Monroe. Who names a baby Monroe? That's why I drove up here; I just couldn't take them telling me what I've got to do with *my* baby."

"Monroe?" A puzzled looked crossed Lottie's face.

"Yeah, Monroe," Shaking her head and rolling her eyes, Ellie sneered.

"Where in the world did they come up with that name?" Josie tapped her foot and edged closer to her niece.

"Some uncle that Mrs. Bridge had - her favorite uncle."

"But that's a boy's name," Lottie leaned in to agree.

"I know. That's what I said. But they are adamant about it. That old biddy wrote Chuck about it and he wrote back to me that he likes the name too, says it's different."

"It's fine for a boy. But what if it's a girl?"

Ellie shrugged her shoulders, "They said it would work for a boy or a girl."

All the women grew silent, and gazed at one another. All thinking the same thing - Ellie was getting her just desserts.

"That whole family is against me. It's not fair."

Josie and Lottie gave each other the same puzzled look as before. *This is most certainly a different person. She needs to get pregnant more often if this is the result - a true feeling human being,* Thought Lottie.

"Having a child effects *every* woman in a different way," Josie echoed Lottie's thoughts.

"That is so true," Pearl released her arms from around Ellie. "Take me for example; I'm becoming the Queen of Sheba. Nobody lets me lift a finger to do anything."

"With your momma's history in child birthin' I think you ought to listen to her and not do too much, dearie." Josie whistled a *sh* from between chipped front teeth.

"Hey, why don't you old bags shut your squawking over there?" Clarence slurred loudly from the barn.

Josie leaned in to whisper, "Oh, Boy. There he goes. We better be quiet or he'll come over here and start something."

"He better not!" Ellie yelled loudly. "You old bag of worms! I'll talk as loud as I want and say what I want! Now you just get yourself back in that jug and shut up.!"

Lottie doubled over in silent laughter, "Now that's the Ellie we all know."

"Naw, she ain't changed none." The *sh* whistling through Josie's teeth again.

"And you, Miss Pearly White goody two shoes, you do what you're told and take it easy.

"Okay," Pearl rubbed the small bulge and smiled. "I promise I won't lift anything more than a milk bottle and I'll stay off my feet as much as I can."

"And if Mr. Clarence has anything to say about it, we'll just get Ellie up here to give him *what for.*"

"Wonder what them hens are cacklin' about over there?" Clarence slurred. "Damn women, always laughin', cryin', or yellin' about something. Ain't got no idea what hard work men gotta do." He jabbed Paul's arm, "See what you got to look forward to, boy."

"They're just having some fun, Pa."

"And by the way, when you gonna build you your own house, you got a kid comin' and we ain't hardly got no room for you now."

"When you going to pay me for delivering that moonshine to Mr. Walker?"

"What you talkin' about? I done paid you. Got a roof over your head and food in your belly. What else do you want?"

Jess and Paul gave each other a knowing glance.

"Have another swig, Pa," Paul nodded at the glass jar in his father's hand. "You're right about everything."

"You're damn right, I am." His face reddened as he bobbed his head, "And I tell you, when I was your age I done

built me a house and was out there fishin' everyday -
earnin' money."

"I always wanted to bring the farm back, Pa."

"That farm ain't worth a damn. Ain't got no good soil.
Ain't never gonna be nothin'."

"If I planted some tobacco..."

"I ain't got no money to buy no tobacco, boy!"

The women turned as they heard Clarence raise his voice.
"Here we go again," Josie shook her head in despair. That
boy better watch what he says to his Pa, he'll pop the living
mud outta him."

"Tobacco's always been a good crop for us and I don't
think your soil's much different than ours," Hands on her
hips, Lottie swayed back and forth.

"He ain't never let that boy do anything. Never let him try
his hand at farming. Wants him to work that still. You
watch, if he don't do what his pa says he'll run him off just
like his brother Phil." Josie sniffled and brought her
handkerchief to her eyes.

"I'm sorry," Lottie shrugged, "Josie, you rest knowing that
will never happen with Paul and Pearl. There will always be
a home for them at my house."

"Thank you, maybe I'm just running my mouth like
Clarence is always saying, maybe I don't know nothing. All's
I'm glad for is he never took up the drinking like Clarence,
you know, helping his pa run that still. But..." she squared
her shoulders and reached to pull back a stray lock of Pearl's

hair," Since he and Pearl's been married, I don't think I seen him touch a drop."

"Why's he so hard on him, Miss Josie?" Pearl leaned forward on the table, resting her head in her hands.

"Been that way since he was born. You'd think he was jealous of him or something. Every time Paul did something good and got a little praise from somebody, Clarence would knock him right back down again. Telling him how it weren't no good and how he'd never amount to anything." Josie's haggard face lowered, "Same with my boy Phil...he just had enough one day and was gone the next. Ain't never heard from him either."

The women grew silent as they recalled young Phil. A much more demonstrative youth than Paul, he lashed back at his father when struck and defended his mother always encouraging her to leave her husband. No one understood why she stayed for the beating of her children and herself, and finally Phil quit trying too and left.

The stillness was roused when Ellie chimed in, smirking – then blowing a heavy sigh. "I remember the time Uncle Clarence asked Daddy for some money to raise some tobacco. Said he was going to out do him and be a better business man than my daddy ever thought of being."

Josie tapped her foot rapidly and looked squarely at Ellie, "He took that money and put it all into that still."

"Daddy didn't ever let him have anything again. Mother made sure of that."

"So now, the mention of the word tobacco sets him off. He ain't never gonna give poor Paul a chance to do nothin'."

"He's always talked about raising tobacco and corn, ever since we were kids. He'd go on and on about putting up a tobacco barn and how much money there was in it."

"Yeah, it's a good idea too, but his pa ain't ever goin' to let him do it. And then he talks about how you two's bummin' off us." Josie nodded toward Pearl. "Don't get me wrong, sweetie, it wouldn't matter if you laid gold eggs. They'd be the wrong size and the wrong shape, according to him."

"He never says anything like that around me." Pearl spoke defensively.

"He talks one way around some folks and another way around others."

"I know he gets Paul really upset sometimes. I hear them arguing about things and I really feel sorry for him. If there was some way Paul could get ahead and we could get a place of our own."

"As long as he stays workin' with his pa, that ain't goin' to happen."

"Couldn't he work for someone else?" Lottie questioned, knowing full well the answer.

"Humph," Josie smirked. "People around here know they better not hire Paul behind his pa's back.

"After I have this baby I'm going to help Paul out more and we *are* going to get a place for ourselves. You just wait and see."

Raising her chin high, Ellie patted Pearl on the back, "You're good for my cousin, Miss Goody two shoes."

In the following weeks and months Pearl did as she was instructed, relaxing and keeping her feet up. She took up crocheting as she sat by the radio listening to her favorite game show, Truth or Consequences and her favorite day time drama, Against the Storm. On occasion Josie and she would drive to see Lottie and Jess. They in turn would visit too, but only after a telephone call to see if Clarence was home or not.

Not many days would pass without Clarence storming into the house accusing either Josie or Paul of stealing one of his tools. He kicked the furniture and if in the kitchen, at least one piece of crockery would be broken. He allowed no denials, no words of defense. Pearl learned to keep her mouth shut, as Paul and Josie did, and to keep out of Clarence's way.

CHAPTER THIRTEEN

"I'm going to be drafted anyway, Pearl."

"In a little over four months I'm having this baby and I know you won't be back before then. Why do you want to leave me now?"

"You can move back in with your momma and daddy. Then you won't have to put up with no more of my parents."

"Your momma is fine, she's nice."

"But my pa is never going to stop. He's never going to give me a chance and we'll be here forever and never have anything."

"You can't wait till after the baby is born?"

"No."

"Why?"

Paul sat down on the bed and motioned for Pearl to join him. "Pearly, you have to understand. I can send money home to you. If I stay here I won't ever have a damn thing and neither will you and *he'll* start in on that child. I'm *not* going to let that happen. He did it to my brother Phil."

Balling his hand into a fist he hit the bed, "Never a day, there was never a day that that son of a bitch didn't hit him or tell him how worthless he was."

Pearl reached for his hand; Paul pulled away.

"No, he was even worse to Phil than he was to me, but now that he's gone, Pa's taking everything out on me." Paul's eyes blazed icy blue as he looked into Pearl's. "

"That baby's got to be born at your home where there's no yelling or telling people they ain't no good."

"But Paul, you won't even be able to see our...I mean . . ." Pearl stopped and gazed at the embroidered pillow sham on the bed.

"It ain't got nothing to do with that, Pearl." He reached to gently rub her belly. "That baby is mine now. I'm doing this for all of us."

There were nights when Pearl thought of Jay, times when she thought she could feel his touch. But there had been no word. Since he had left, there had been no letters from him other than the few she had received in the first weeks after his departure. There had been no more letters from his parents in Texas. After the last letter from Jay's mother saying that he was missing in action, there had been no letter saying he had died or that he was alive. *He must have died*, she thought.

As Pearl pulled herself closer to Paul and put her arms around his neck she thought of the possibility of losing him also. "I'll miss you." She felt an ache not unlike the one she

167

had felt when Jay left. And then she felt Paul's arms around her and she laughed, "Can't get all the way around. Huh?" She wished he could hold her closer.

"Pearl, I've lived near the water my whole life and been out on that ocean more times than stars in the sky. That's where I'll be, out in the ocean.

"I've seen the newsreels and the Navy has lost ships and young men too.

"I could swim before I could crawl," Paul joked, as he raised Pearl's hand to his lips.

Pearl rolled her eyes, "There's just no talking to you I guess. You've made up your mind, haven't you?"

"Like I said, all the money will be coming to you and the baby." Taking her by the hand and helping her from the bed, Paul smoothed the hair away from Pearl's face. "So, what are we going to name the bundle of joy?"

Pearl thought for a moment. "What is your middle name Paul? You've never told me that."

"Aaron. You want to name the baby Aaron if it's a boy?"

Biting her bottom lip as she nodded, Pearl smoothed her dress across her swollen belly. "I'd like the middle name to be Aaron and the first name to be Frank. I have an Uncle Frank that I always liked a lot."

"Frank Aaron Rosell. Sounds good to me. And what if it's a girl?"

"Well, your momma seems to think it's going to be a boy and that's all I've thought of... boy's names. I haven't thought much of girl's."

"I've always liked the name Ginger."

"That sounds nice. And what about a middle name."

"Josie."

"Ginger Josie," Pearl crinkled her nose, "Really, Ginger Josie?"

"Well, Josephine. That's ma's real name - Josephine, but everybody calls her Josie."

"I like the name Josie...Josephine. And your ma is such a sweet person. It would be nice to name the baby after her."

"Okay, Josephine it is, and we'll think of another middle name. Okay?"

"Okay."

As they lay in bed that night, she tossed about, angry with herself for suggesting the name Frank. *Why did I do that?* She thought, twisting the pillow sham. *And Uncle Frank? God, that was stupid.* Pearl rose from the bed and walked to the window to sit in the small chair there. The moon lit the yard to almost daylight. She could see remnants of a flower garden; she supposed that Josie had tried at one time to pretty the place up. She could only imagine how her efforts would have been thwarted by Clarence.

Paul was right. It would be best if she moved in with her parents. And as much as she hated to admit it, it seemed right also that Paul join the Navy. Leaving here was the only way out. But what if he didn't come back? It would be like losing Jay all over again.

"Maybe, that's why I did it – why I told Paul we'd name the baby Frank," she whispered softly. Looking out into the ramshackle yard again with the discarded machinery and old boards she recalled the day she had been riding with her new beau. It was as clear as day in her mind as she recalled Jay and she riding along through the woods.

'Pearl, that's a pretty name, just where did you get it?'

Bumping her horse next to his, and laughing as it startled, she saw herself speak the words: my daddy says that he and momma are oysters and I'm their Pearl.' She could see Jay laugh - how his eyes crinkled in the corners and how his broad shoulders sat squared as he held the reins.

'And your middle name?'

'Lorraine.'

'Pearl Lorraine Scaggins'

'Yep. Pearl Lorraine Scaggins.'

'It's a pretty name, except for that Scaggins part.'

"What! There's not anything wrong with Scaggins.'

'It's going to sound better as Pearl Lorraine Bishop.'

Settling herself into a more comfortable position, Pearl wiped a tear from her cheek. It all seemed so long ago. As she felt the movement in her belly she drifted back to the conversation.

'And your middle name? Jay... Jay what?'

'Actually it's not Jay at all. That's just what everybody calls me.'

'Then what is it?'

'John.'
'John...good name. John what?'
'John Frank.'

"Are you okay?" Paul called to her, "Come back to bed.

"I'm fine, just thinking about the baby." Crawling back into bed she snuggled closely against Paul.

He could smell the richness of her skin and her hair seemed silkier than ever as he brushed it away from the nape of her neck. "I love you, Pearl," Paul whispered.

Pearl pushed her hands against the bed to move herself more comfortably and so she could look in Paul's eyes. "You know, if you don't like the name Frank, we don't have to name the baby that."

"No, I like that name. It's a strong name."

"We've got a few more months till the baby's here, we might change our minds."

"Maybe," Paul caressed the outline of Pearl's face and leaned to kiss her lips. "I love you."

"I love you too, Paul. You are so good to me."

He wished for once she would not add the "you are so good to me." It made it sound as if the love was an obligation. Though in the past several months he knew she had become closer to him. He did know that Pearl loved him, but not like the kind of love she once had for Jay. He wondered how often she still thought about him.

"When I come back we'll have enough money saved to get our own place, or at least to put a down payment on one."

"And you can build a tobacco barn and grow tobacco."

Paul nodded in agreement, "Mr. Lee in Sloop Point makes a killing every year from selling tobacco. It's North Carolina's biggest cash crop, you know."

"I know," Pearl searched his eyes. They were a cool blue color. She pressed her fingers against his lips. "You have such soft lips, Paul."

"The better to kiss you with, my dear." He pressed his mouth against Pearl's, he could taste the tears. "I won't be leaving for a while."

She felt the ache of loss again, as she pulled him tightly to her chest. "I'm so scared, Paul. You're going to leave me and I do, I do love you Paul. You are so good to me."

Jay tapped at the loose leather of his boot. The sole had worn thin and hung loosely from the body of his shoe. As he leaned against a wall, he slowly scoped the swaying room, eyeing the others in the box car. Most seemed to stare at the dirty walls around them, a few returned a blank look of hopelessness. They had become accustomed to the stench of feces, urine and rotting flesh, and clung silently to life as if it were the last leaf in a swirling eddy.

This would be the second dulag he had departed from. Now, he was to be sent to a new camp - a place fortified with guard towers and rows and rows of barbed wire. He had been told that it would be a place where all enemy soldiers could live out the rest of the war in comfort. But there were rules that must be obeyed. Wasn't there always? He knew what happened when you broke the rules... and got caught. At least he thought he did. It seemed that some paid a price just for existing.

He'd seen enough death in the dulags where those who wore yellow stars, pink triangles or purple triangles were treated with such vehemence that he had been tempted in the beginning to defend their weakness. That did not last much longer than the second time he saw the brains blow out of a fellow prisoner's head.

This new camp, a stalag, would have no prisoners who wore colored arm patches. It had been specifically built to contain non commissioned officers only. How many? He did not know. Where was it located? Some God forsaken mud hole. *Where in the hell do they get all the damn mud? How long would he be at this place?*

Jay reached his hand inside the heavy woolen coat; his thumb edging along the tattered armholes of the vest Pearl had made. The image of her face was clear in his mind and he half smiled as he recalled her hair blowing as they walked along the beach. He nearly laughed as he thought of her shoeless feet and how they had first met. Then with a quick jerk and jolt from the train the reality of what was about him wiped all of it away. His eyes glazed with determination and he thought – *insubordination would result in death, escape would result in death and illness would result in death – I won't get sick.*

CHAPTER FOURTEEN

Pearl sat in the rocking chair. The front and back doors to the house were open and with the breezeway allowing air to come in, coolness circulated throughout her parent's home. She was glad to be living here once again – glad to be safe with her parents. She was getting bigger and had gained nearly twenty pounds.

"Oh Momma, I'm getting so fat." Pearl rubbed her ever expanding belly.

"I lost my baby fat really quick, maybe you'll do the same."

"Hope so," Leaning back in the rocker, Pearl pushed her belly out farther. She closed her eyes and let her mind wander. She saw the smiling face of Jay and sat upright again.

"What's the matter, sweetie?"

Shaking her head, Pearl turned to her mother with a look both recognized.

"You have to let him go."

"I know."

"It's the best thing for everybody."

"But I feel so bad for his mother. It seems she would want to know that her son had a baby … that there was a part of her son still alive."

"Gal, I know how you feel. To lose a child is a terrible thing, a part of you dies - a part that never grows back."

"I'd like to tell her."

"You think about that for a minute. You've never met the woman and you don't know how she would react…think," Lottie tapped the side of her head. "Now, what do you *think* she's going to *think* of *you?* And why should she believe you? Why should she believe that's Jay's baby."

Pearl shrugged her shoulders. "I just thought…"

Lottie cocked her head sideways, "Thought? I want you to consider what would happen if you told the Bishops. They might want a piece of their son back, but dear, whether you tell them or not the child will be a bastard."

Gasping, and covering her mouth with her hand, Pearl shook her head, "No! No it won't.!"

"Then don't make it one. Never tell anyone who the real father is. And the best thing you can do for the baby is to let it know the one and only father it truly has… the one you're married to."

July 10, 1942

My dearest Pearl,

Today the ocean was really calm, almost like glass and a few of the guys fished off the aft. They caught a lot of tuna. They were really big; never saw tuna quite that big before. The cook cooked them up for us and it was really good.

Most of the fellows on the ship are easy enough to get along with, but there are a few city slickers who think they know everything. Boy, are they in for a surprise!

I think of you all the time and I have your picture hanging by my berth. (that's what they call beds in the Navy) Some of the guys don't believe you're my wife. They say you are too pretty for me. I think so too.

There are a lot of things I can't tell you. Like where I am and where I'm going. It all has to do with the war, we are all trying to be cautious and surprise the Japs.

I want you to know that I love you very much. And now that I am away from you I have lots of time to think. I understand more how sometimes you felt distant from me. I know with things the way they are and with all that happened that it must be hard for you. But I want you to know I will always be there for you.

There are only a few more months to go and little Frank or Josephine will be here. I was thinking of Loretta for the middle name if it is a girl. Isn't Loretta your Momma's long name? What do you think? Josephine Loretta. And if it's a boy, Frank Aaron, like we talked about.

Sometimes it takes letters a long time to get to where they are going. So even if you don't hear from me, keep writing. Keep safe and tell your momma and daddy I give them my love too. Write as soon as you can.
All my love forever,
Paul.

July 30, 1942

Dear Paul,

I was so glad to get your letter today and so glad to hear you are okay. From the date on your letter, you are right; it does take a long time for your mail to get here.

It is really hot here and since no one will let me even lift a finger, I sit on the porch all day and crochet or read. That is getting to be really boring. I am getting so big now and sometimes it is really hard to sleep. I think I've gained ten more pounds since I moved back home with Momma and Daddy. It's not all baby either.

It is lonely here without you, but Momma and Daddy keep me company. Yesterday we all drove to Wilmington to see a movie. It was Back in the Saddle with Gene Autry starring. It was good. We went to a restaurant later and ate. It sure is nice to have a car and go places.

I've had a lot of time to think too. I want to try to be the best wife I can for you. I remember how when we were kids you would pick on me, but you were always there to defend

me, especially with Ellie. Ha Ha. I guess I took you for granted, but now I understand things better. I hope you stay safe and catch lots of fish.
Love,
Pearl

August 4, 1942

My Dearest Pearl,

I miss you more and more every day and I can't wait to get back home to you. Are you getting the checks okay? Did you get my last letter? I think about what it will be like when I come home and we can start our life together.

Sometimes I think I made the wrong decision by leaving you alone, especially knowing that I won't be there when the baby is born. It will be so nice to have a real family.

My mom wrote me about how they came and visited you the other day and how Pa made a fool of himself again. He has always drunk too much and when he drinks he gets plum mad at everybody. She told me how he said you looked fat and that he thought our baby would turn out to be lazy too. She said he cussed at your daddy and even took a swing at him. Pa's always been jealous of anybody who doesn't drink. He says people who don't tie one on now and then aren't real men.

It is still pretty calm out here. I sort of wish we'd see some action. I look at your picture all the time. It will be nice to feel your pretty hair and walk on the beach with you again. Your skin always felt so soft to touch.

Wish I was there with you. When I get home we'll go at least once a week to the movies. We'll go to a drive-in, and then we can take the baby with us too.

I love you and I hope that you love me too. I don't want you to feel like you owe me your love. I just want you to love me the real way. Do you know what I mean?

Write as soon as you can. You don't have to wait until you hear from me to write a letter. It is so nice to hear from you. All my love forever,

Paul

August 20, 1942

My Dearest Paul,

I'm so glad to hear that you are safe. I think about you a lot too. I think that you going into the Navy was the right thing for you to do. I can see now how hard it was to live with your dad. I'm so sorry that he was so mean to you and your brother. Your mom has told me how he shot at Phil one night when he got drunk. That is why he left. That is so horrible and I don't blame him for leaving.

My momma and daddy are glad that I came back home. They said they didn't want to say anything, but they had a suspicion that things were bad at your home. I know your mom doesn't talk much about what goes on in your house.

I'm glad to be back home too. I have only gotten one check but I put it right in the bank. Daddy says the government is slow and that I will start getting them regularly soon. I just know that when you come home we will have a good amount of money saved so we can get land of our own and start that tobacco farm you wanted. I've talked with Daddy about it and he says he'll keep his ears open for a good deal.

I've been thinking about the name of the baby just in case it's a boy. I'm not sure about the name Frank. What about having his first name Aaron and his middle name Frank? Or we can come up with a new middle name. You think about it and let me know.

I remember how you used to drink sometimes and how sick it would make you. I guess you just drank when you got upset. I guess your daddy liked to get you upset. And he was always making you work that still for him. But those days are over. You don't ever have to go back to that house and live.

I miss going fishing with you. I wish I had been better on our honeymoon at the Lumina. It was a beautiful night and you were so sweet to me. When you come home I want to go back there and have a real honeymoon. I do love you and about the other (you know what I mean) that is gone. I want you to come home safe.

All my love,
Pearl

August 21, 1942

My Dearest Paul,

You'll never believe what I did. I got my hair cut and got a permanent put in it. I'll send you a picture as soon as I get the film developed. Momma loves it, Daddy hates it. But Daddy never did like short hair. I hope you like it. If not, I'll let it grow out.

Rawl and Francis West came by last night and Will Pike brought his fiddle. Enid brought his guitar; he sure can play that thing. He says he's going to be joining the Navy too, here pretty soon. Maybe you and he will run into one another sometime. Anyway, the music was great. Daddy killed a hog and we all ate bar-b-que and listened to music. It was fun. I sure wish you would have been here to dance with me. I guess I couldn't have danced anyway, I look like a pumpkin. The hog was delicious and Mr. West made the best sauce to go with it; it tasted really good. Momma says around this time everything is going to taste good to me. Ha Ha.

I hope that by the time you come home, I will have lost my extra weight. I want to look pretty for you.

Your daddy is so different from Ellie's Daddy. It doesn't even seem like they are brothers. Mr. Bud is so hard working and I don't think he ever drinks. I think Miss Noreen would let him have it if she ever caught him drinking. I wish your daddy could see what a wonderful man you are. When you come home we'll show him just what hard work and good people can create. I can't wait!

182

I heard from Ellie. She's still in Florida. She says that she likes it fine down there and that she been eating lots of oranges. She just goes outside and picks them right off the tree. Her baby is due any day now and I'll write to tell you about it when it happens.

I miss you so much.

All my love,

Pearl

August 31, 1942

My Dearest Pearl,

I have to start my letter off by telling you how dearly I love you. I have always loved you. We were in port for a few days and all I can say is that it sure is different. In your letter you said that Ellie picks oranges off the trees herself. I could pick bananas and coconuts off these. I never understood Ellie, it seemed to me that she was always using people, but then other times she would be just as sweet as she could be. Like my Uncle Bud always says: you can pick your nose, but you can't pick your family. Ha Ha.

I think Ellie and my dad are more alike than Uncle Bud and he. Uncle Bud never has a bad word to say about anybody. He just goes along and minds Aunt Noreen. Ha Ha. Dad says that Aunt Noreen married beneath herself. I think my mom married beneath herself. You know, sometimes I think you are too good for me too. You always try to share things with other people and you're so honest. I don't think you'd ever mean to hurt anyone. I just know I'm proud that you are my wife. As for me, sometimes I get so angry that I just want to push everybody away. Sometimes I feel like everybody looks at me like I'm not any good - that I'm just like my father. I feel like I've got to prove them wrong. I'm going to make a fine tobacco farmer and we're going to have a nice house, without all that junk like my dad has lying around his place. I'll never be a worthless drunk like him. God did me a favor my making me get sick whenever I drink.

I kind of like the names we settled on for the baby. Frank is a good strong name. And I remember you said your favorite uncle was named Frank. I think naming a child after someone you love is very important. I'm sure glad my mom didn't name me after my dad.

I hope I haven't said too much. It's just that you have always been my best friend, Pearl. I could always trust you not to run and gossip to everybody. Right now it seems like it is the end of the world. And like I said in my last letter about wishing for stuff, well, sometimes you got to watch what you wish for.

I hope this war ends soon and that we will get to be together. Say hello to your parents.

All my Love,
Paul

CHAPTER FIFTEEN

Pearl folded the letter neatly and slid it gently into the envelope, she'd forgotten how many times she'd read his last letter, not to mention the others he had sent. "I haven't heard from Paul in a long time. I'm worried."

"It's only been three weeks," Lottie stretched her legs to rest on the wooden crate, "It usually takes a couple weeks anyway, doesn't it sweetie?"

"The last one I got from him was written on the thirty first of last month."

"It's only the twentieth, or is it the twenty-first."

"I've written him twice since then. It seems I should have heard by now." Pushing herself up from the rocking chair, Pearl leaned to pick up the empty glass of lemonade. "Want some more?"

"No thanks, sweetie. Now, don't you worry, I'm sure you'll get a letter any day. Lottie wiped her brow with the yellow bandana she held in her hand, "Sure has been hot this summer."

"Yeah, it has been a long hot summer."

"I can imagine how uncomfortable it is for you now. I remember when I carried you; it was hot just like it is now." She reached her hand out to grasp her daughter's as she moved past her to the door.

"In a way I hope the baby comes when it's supposed to, Momma."

Lottie sighed and rubbed the side of her neck, "That could be any day." She took a sip of her lemonade and gazed out toward the sound. "It'll be getting cooler soon. Anyway, whenever it comes, we'll be ready."

Returning to the porch with her glass of lemonade, Pearl stooped slowly to sit in the chair, then pulled another letter from her smock pocket. "I told you I got a letter from Ellie. Didn't I? "

"No. What's she got to say? Did she have a boy or a girl?"

"Little girl?"

"She says she's coming up to visit her mother and father in a couple of weeks."

"She ain't driving with that new born baby, is she?"

"Heavens no! She's taking the train."

Lottie shook her head disapprovingly, "That baby's too young to be moving it around. She needs to just stay put."

"Well, you know Ellie. She's going to do what she wants."

"It's so hard for me to imagine Ellie with a child," Lottie sighed, "What did she name the baby?"

"You remember when she came last spring and told us about the argument with her in-laws over the baby's name?"

"Um hum."

"Well, she named the baby Monroe."

"Monroe? I thought that was just some kind of a joke when Ellie said that." Lottie clucked her tongue.

Pearl grinned and raised her brows, "Guess they won the argument."

"Looks like it."

"She said they near about had a fit for her to name it that, so she went ahead and did it."

Leaning her head back in laughter, Lottie slapped her thigh, "That's got to be something, somebody telling *Ellie* what to do."

"I'd like to have seen that," Pearl's hand bounced on her belly as she tittered. "I didn't think anybody would ever tell Ellie what to do and get away with it."

"She'll make them pay." Lottie slid her eyes to catch Pearl's.

Nodding her head in agreement, Pearl chuckled. "They got no idea what's in store for them."

"My lord, Pearl! You look like you're going to pop. And you say that baby's not due till when?"

"I'm not due till around the end of October." Pearl looked up at Ellie from her bed.

"You're not fooling me Miss Pearly White," Ellie slid a chair next to the bed and confidently jutted out her chin."That baby's coming sooner than that."

Pearl's eyes grew wide, "What do you mean?" She could feel her face pale.

"You and my sweet little cousin were *making hay* before y'all got married." Ellie drew her face closer to Pearl's. "Weren't you?"

A sigh escaped Pearl's lips as they turned upward. "Well, now you know. Don't you?"

"You're just not the goody two shoes you want everybody to think."

"I guess not."

Ellie looked questioningly at Pearl, her brow furrowing as she pondered the circumstances. "The way I figure it was when that soldier boy of yours left, you took all your loneliness out on Paul."

Pearl's lips tightened, "I love Paul."

"I'm sure you do. Knowing you, Pearl, I'm sure you love Paul a whole lot." Ellie moved from the chair to the bed and took Pearl's hand in hers. "It's nice when somebody loves you. Isn't it?"

Pearl searched Ellie's eyes, not quite sure what to make of the comment. Had Ellie changed? Had her heart opened? Or was this just another one of her ploys? As children they had been close, but as Ellie reached her teenage years, she had drifted away to a place that Pearl had not understood.

Nodding her head slowly in reply to Ellie's question, she recalled the night the two had sneaked away and rode their bikes down the dusty road to the church. Pearl could see Ellie now, in her mind's eye, turning cartwheels up the aisle to the altar. Pearl had stayed back in the shadows near the last pew, watching as her friend made slow erotic movements to a tune she was humming. Her arms moved slowly, rhythmically in the air as she hunched her back and thrust her hips. *Come on Pearl, dance!* But she stayed near the last pew, watching as her friend continued what seemed to be an unorthodox ceremony.

Was it that Ellie had simply matured before she did? Pearl smiled, remembering how Ellie padded her bra with Kleenex tissues when they were younger.

"What are you smiling about, goody two shoes?"

"Oh, I was just remembering how you used to stuff your bra with Kleenex when you were a kid."

Ellie shot her a puzzled look. "What's that got to do with anything?"

"Nothing," Pearl giggled, "just remembering."

Cupping her hands beneath her breasts and bouncing them, Ellie flipped her long hair to the side. "Don't need to do that anymore."

"You look happy,"

"I am... mostly," Ellie shrugged and sighed.

"Mostly? I guess I should have suspected that you couldn't be happy with having a beautiful baby daughter, and living in *Florida,* where it never gets cold. What in the world do you have to complain about?"

Ellie shrugged her shoulders and sucked at her thumbnail, "I didn't bring Monroe."

"What?" Where is she?"

"With the Bridges."

"What's up Ellie?"

"Long story." Ellie propped herself against the window sill.

"I'm listening."

"I tell you, goody two shoes, those people are simply a whole different breed down there."

"And how's that? You can't control them? Is that it?"

A grin crossed Ellie's lips as she placed a cigarette between them and inhaled deeply. "I don't want to say *that,* but they're hard to figure out. Sometimes I don't think they like me."

"Ha! Not like you? Why Ellie, what makes you say that?"

Sliding a glance toward her friend, Ellie raised her chin and blew a smoke ring toward the ceiling. "Sometimes when I enter a room they all stop talking or I get the feeling that they just started a *new* conversation. And then, as far as Monroe is concerned, it's as if they're done with me. Like – *the bitch had her pup, so we don't need her anymore.*"

A scowl crossed Pearl's face. *Even she doesn't deserve that.* She thought. "What are you going to do?"

"Just give me some time, I'll figure it out." Ellie flipped her cigarette out the open window and moved closer to

Pearl. "There's something else I want to tell you, something worse."

"What's worse than what you've just told me?"

"It's...well...something really bad, Pearl. And I don't want you to hate me for it."

Rolling her eyes, Pearl wondered what Ellie could have done now.

Ellie caught Pearl's gaze and held it for a moment. They were both silent as Ellie stood. "Jay's alive."

It was as if the wind had been knocked out of her and she gasped as she reached for Ellie's hand. "What? How do you know?"

"Here comes the part where you might hate me."

"Just tell me. Or is this another of your little games?"

Ellie released Pearl's hand and dragged the chair to the bed side. "You remember when I came up last spring?"

"Yeah. And you said you had an argument with Chuck's parents over the baby's name."

"That's true. I did have an argument with them about that and a couple other things too. But that wasn't the whole truth about why I was so quiet - so confused - that night at the party."

"Confused? Ellie Rosell, confused? Since the argument with your in-laws was true, then pray tell me, what wasn't true, what were you confused about?" Scowling at Ellie, suspecting another lie or even worse, Pearl propped herself up straighter in the bed. "Just tell me. Is Jay alive and how do you know, or do you just *think* he is?"

"Let me finish."

Pearl folded her arms across her belly.

"I was driving down the road from the banks and just thought I'd get the mail for you."

"How kind of you."

"And there was a letter in there with a return address of Donna, Texas and it was addressed to you."

Pearl felt the flush of her cheeks, though it seemed as if her body had been drained. She felt weak, then outraged that she had never been allowed to read the letter. "You bitch!"

"What's going on in here?" Lottie pushed open the bedroom door.

"Momma, Jay's alive."

"What in the world are you doing?" Lottie moved quickly toward Ellie and grabbed her by the shoulders.

"I'm sorry," Ellie looked meekly into Lottie's eyes.

"No you're not. You've got to stir the pot. Don't you? You can't stand to see things go smoothly."

"Look, Miss Lottie, I'm just trying to tell Pearl about the letter she got from Jay's mom."

"What letter?" Lottie searched Pearl's eyes. "What is she talking about?"

"She stole a letter from our mailbox last spring."
"And this is the first we hear of it?" She jerked Ellie's shoulders, shaking her violently.

"Let go of me!" Ellie pushed Lottie away and stood by the window. "What in the world is wrong with you people?"

"Wrong with us? You stole a private letter." Lottie smoothed her hair and tried to calm herself. "Okay, okay, enough of this yelling. Where is this letter? Don't you have it?"

Ellie reached into her purse, drew out an envelope and handed it to Pearl. She scanned it once quickly, then read again more slowly. Pressing it to her chest, tears rolled down her cheeks. "Oh, Momma…," she gazed in her mother's knowing eyes, her warning eyes that begged for her to keep silent.

"Okay, you disgusting …." Lottie paused to catch herself from cursing, "I hope you're proud of yourself."

"Like I was saying…I thought I'd get the mail for you so you wouldn't have to walk to the mailbox and I found this letter post marked from Texas. Now, I know this sounds bad, but, I was only thinking of Pearl."

"How were you thinking of me?"

"You thought Jay was never coming back, that's why you got all *lovey dovey* with Paul and got pregnant and had to marry him. What kind of friend would I have been to give you that letter? It would have messed everything up for you and Paul. That's why I was so quiet at your little *party.* I was trying to figure out what to do about it."

Silence filled the room as Lottie and Pearl held a knowing gaze between themselves.

CHAPTER SIXTEEN

"Frank Aaron Rosell was born at 7:04 A.M. October 25 at the home of Jess and Lottie Scaggins. His weight was six pounds, twelve ounces. Mother, Pearl Lorraine Rosell and son are doing well. Boatswains mate Paul Aaron Rosell is serving in the United States Navy," Lottie read the newspaper announcement aloud, then added, "Nearly a month – almost to the day. I don't think anyone looking at him now would realize he was born a month earlier. "Do you dear?"

"We were lucky."

Lottie snipped the announcement from the newspaper and taped it to the new baby book she had ordered from the Sears catalogue. "I need a lock of his hair." She watched as Pearl stroked the dark hair of her nursing son.

"Hand me the scissors."

"No, I'll do it. You just be very still." Lottie clipped a wisp of hair from the back of baby Frank's head. "It was a chore to keep Josie out of here these last few weeks."

Acknowledging the comment, Pearl smiled up at her mother. Then gently holding the infant's head, she switched him to her left breast. "It doesn't hurt," she laughed. "Everyone said it would hurt to nurse."

"Wait till he gets teeth."

"Stifling a laugh, Pearl touched her fingertips to the infant's nose, then drew them along his forehead and down along the jaw line. "It's hard to tell who he looks like."

"You're lucky they both had blue eyes."

"But Jay's were much darker, still – Frankie does have his dark hair."

Lottie raised an eyebrow and looked up from the baby book, "Remember? Grandma has dark hair too. Frankie got it from me."

Pearl wiped a line of milk drool from Frankie's cheek, "You're right." Soft breathy sounds flowed from Frankie's open mouth. His tiny hands released their hold on Pearl's swollen breast. "He's sleeping now," Pearl smiled as she whispered.

"I'll take him for you," Lottie bent to gather the infant in her arms. Smiling as she placed him in the cradle, she ran her hand along the smooth scrolling of the wooden bassinette. "Your grandpa is so handy with a saw."

"Daddy did make a beautiful cradle and you... "Thank you, Momma."

"No trouble my dear."

"No, I mean thank you for all you and Daddy have done for me. I don't know what I would have done if I would have stayed with Paul's parents."

"Paul made the right decision….I think he foresaw what a help your father and I could be in the birthing of the baby. It wasn't so bad. Was it sweetie?" Lottie stoked her daughter's hair away from her face. "It really wasn't much more difficult than birthing a colt. And your labor was short. A push or two and *pop* out Frankie came." Lottie tittered. "Not like you. I was in labor twelve hours with you."

"It was the best decision to move here. I'm so glad that Clarence wasn't around when Frankie was born."

"Yep. And do you think you would have seen any of those checks if you would have stayed with Paul's folks?"

"I'm sure ol' Clarence would have found a way to get them."

"You're right about that."

"You and Daddy have helped me … and look at all I've done. I've made a mess of things."

"Shhh," Lottie pressed her finger to her lips, and motioned for Pearl to follow her through the breezeway and into the kitchen. "It's coffee time," She said, plugging in the percolator.

Pearl reached for the steaming cup set before her, "I guess Ellie did a good thing without knowing it."

Lottie nodded, "Yes."

"But even if I would have gotten the letter at that time it wouldn't have changed what I had to do."

196

Nodding her head in agreement, Lottie settled herself in the chair opposite Pearl. "No, it wouldn't have. There's still no guarantee that he'll come back home alive, sweetie. I'm sure you know that. And even if he does, you just remember that Frankie belongs to Paul."

"I know. But knowing he's alive makes it harder to forget him. It makes me look even more into little Frankie's face for Jay's reflection."

"Don't do that." Lottie shook her head, "At least now, you know Jay's alive, or at least there is hope that he is alive. He now can have a life of his own."

"You make a lot of sense, Momma. I guess I really didn't know how good I had it before."

"Before what?"

"Before I fell in love. It complicated things. Didn't it?"

"I guess I should have talked with you more about *love*, about the physical part."

"That's not your fault, Momma. I let it happen. I wanted it to happen."

Lottie's lips curled at the edges as she remembered the passion she first felt with Jess. "Believe it or not, I know what that feels like...to want that closeness, to not be able to deny it, to not be able to say no."

"But if I just hadn't gone with him in the barn."

"It's like you're hypnotized. Your mind doesn't work right... yes, you shouldn't have gone into the barn with Jay and you should have said no. But I understand why you did. Listen, remember when you were a little girl and I was making divinity on the stove and it smelled so sweet and good, so you stuck your finger in it."

"Uh huh."

"Well, there you go. You got burned. And you never stuck your finger into boiling hot divinity again. Did you?"

"No." Pearl laughed.

"And you aren't the only one around here that had an *early* baby. There's lots of folks around here whose babies came *early*. That had to get married."

"But it's Jay's"

"Everyone thinks its Paul's, even Ellie. Don't you see? No one outside this family will ever know the truth. And the whole community will accept you just like they've accepted every other woman around." Rising from her chair, Lottie walked toward the kitchen door, "I'm going to walk up the road and check the mail. Maybe today a letter will come from Paul."

Pearl walked back into the living room and stood next to the handmade cradle her father had made. Frankie slept soundly, his small hands lay to the sides of his face; he smiled a silent smile as he twitched in his sleep. *What is he dreaming about?* Reaching to caress his cheek, Pearl knelt beside the cradle, "my dearest sweet Frankie, I will always protect you."

Lottie wrapped her jacket close around her body as she walked to the mailbox. She looked skyward and watched the falling leaves floating through the air. "Getting cool early this year," She said to herself. Slowing her steps, her thoughts wandered to long ago. She recalled the day it happened.

She had been so tired. She'd stayed up the entire night before and all through the next day keeping watch on her baby son, Billy, who seemed to have a cold; his nose ran a little and he had a slight fever. "Nothing to worry about," She'd told herself.

Jess had gone fishing in Georgia, wasn't due back for two more days and though he'd left plenty of fire wood, she had begun running low. The cold snap just wasn't expected. She cut more wood for the fireplace and even set Billy's crib in the living room to make sure he stayed warm, then she crawled back to bed, pulling the covers snuggly over herself and falling into a deep sleep.

The next morning she woke with a start. Noticing the vapor escaping her lips, she realized how cold it must be. Rushing to the living room, where surely the embers from the fire would have kept the room warm, she reached for her son. The room was ice cold. The baby had kicked the blanket away. Gurgling noises rattled from his parted lips. Bundling him, she ran from the house and climbed into the Model A. Nothing. It would not start. Holding Billy close to her chest she walked the mile and a half to Amos Howard's store.

Josie was there with her son Phil. It seemed she was always there, fetching something so she could get out of the house.

"I need the doctor," Lottie remembered screaming, then without words spoken Josie motioned for her to get in her car, but by the time they reached the doctor the child was dead..

She blamed Jess, and for a solid month couldn't bear the sight of him. His crying and despondent behavior got on her nerves. How dare he even think to feel the pain she felt. She hated where she lived, so far from a doctor. She hated the Model A for not starting and she hated God for taking her only child from her. Twice He had taken babies before their birth. WHAT HAD SHE DONE THAT WARRENTED SUCH TERRIBLE THINGS? The questions never faded; rather they grew as the emptiness settled deeper in her bones. Even her friends, who came to visit with explanations of it being God's will, gave no solace. How could they even begin to understand the loss of her one and only child?

"Get out of bed and quit feeling sorry for yourself." Her father growled a response to her questions and explanations. A Bible lay in his lap; she knew a flask was hidden in one of his pockets as well.

"You always told me that everything has a reason. That God has a plan and that there is a reason for everything. I can't figure this out. What am I supposed to have learned from God taking my child, my children - away from me?"

"Who do you think you are to presume that you could even understand what it is all about? A mere human trying to understand ...God? Men smarter than you and I have been doing that for centuries. And in my opinion they must think *they are better than the rest of us to think they know." His furrowed brow gave way to sadness she had never seen before in her father. "Are you the first to lose a child? The first to hate everything around you? The first to be mad at God?" His eyes softened and filled with the love she was so familiar with. "Gal, don't try to figure it out, it won't solve anything – won't bring that baby back. Just love what God gave you." He touched his finger tips to hers, "This is the hand that you have been dealt. You can't change the cards so do what you can with them -Love all that you see, all that you touch and hear...all the wonderful gifts that God has dealt you. There **is** a reason for everything, but it will unfold as you go along in life. Things will come around, you'll see."*

As Lottie reached to open the mailbox lid, she blinked back a tear. The ache in her heart had never gone away. It was simply stored in a special place. She ached too for her daughter and grandchild. And even for Jay and Paul. "Such is life." Yes, her father's words made sense; they made sense more and more with each passing year, with each passing day.

The mailbox was empty. *No news is good news.* Then Lottie shook her arms about and breathed in the cool crisp air. "Poppa always said to quit complaining and play the hand you are dealt."

As she wrapped her jacket tightly against her once more, she headed back down the cart path to her home. She knew that if Paul had been killed someone from the Army would have brought a telegram. *It must be something else .*As she sifted through the possibilities she heard the rumble of an automobile motor. *God, I hope it's not the Army.* As Lottie turned toward the sound, Josie called out, "Got a telegram! Guess they got it mixed up, sent all the mail to me."

She stopped and stepped out of the truck, running toward Lottie as she waved a telegram high in the air. "He ain't dead! He's alright!" Josie rushed to Lottie and wrapped her arms around her. "My baby's coming home!"

"It says he's been wounded in battle and is being treated for his wounds! Oh, my baby's comin' home!"

Lottie held the paper and read the words. "Oh, thank God, thank God!"

"I know it was addressed to Pearl, his wife, but I just had to open it! Oh, I'm sorry – I hope it's all right."

"Of course it is Josie," Her happiness was catchy and Lottie jumped up and down too.

"I was just coming to bring it over to Pearl, and guess what else." Pulling two letters from her dress pocket, Josie grabbed hold of Lottie's hand. "We got letters too! Come on; let's get this over to your gal. I know she's dying to see this."

Pearl sat in the rocking chair by the cradle and rocked slowly as she watched her mother and Josie bound up the porch steps. "What are you two so all wound up about?"

"Look at what I got here," Lottie held up a telegram and handed it to Pearl, who read it slowly to herself, "He's been wounded . . . and is in the hospital."

"I'm sorry I opened your telegram, Pearl. But I just had to know. But we got letters. Paul sent us both a letter," Josie wiggled her body in joy. "I done read mine – you go head and read yours."

October 19, 1942

My Dearest Pearl,

It has been a long time since I wrote you last and I have received all the letters you sent me. It was so nice to read all of them. They have helped me get through the tough times that I've had of late.

I want you not to worry about what I am about to say, but the good news is that I will be back home soon. Here goes: my ship was attacked on September second. We had seen some action before that, but nothing so bad. To make a long story short, I was hit by shrapnel and have been in the hospital for quite a while. It looks like I'm going to be fit as a fiddle, still got all the main parts, but I have damage to one of my lungs. The doctor says smoking is not a good idea now.

The other good news is that I will be receiving checks from the government for a long time, since what happened to me is considered a disability. But I tell you, I feel fit as a fiddle and I don't think that only having half of my right lung is going to make a difference in our plans to start our own farm. At least now I won't smoke up the profits. Ha Ha.

I guess by now you have had the baby. I can't wait to find out what our child is, a boy or a girl. Please write and let me know. Whatever, Frankie or Josie, I promise to love it forever, as I love you.

This is a short letter and hopefully I will be home before you get it. Remember how slow the mail is.

All my love,

Paul.

CHAPTER SEVENTEEN

"Hold on to Frankie, now," Paul reached to touch Pearl's hand as he held onto the tiller of the outboard. "It's a little choppy out here this afternoon."

Pearl nodded to her husband and pulled Frank closer as he sat on her lap. "Frank Aaron, now you be still," she gently scolded, then turned to Paul, "Wind's picked up a bit."

Paul nodded, though he could not hear her above the roar of the motor.

They had spent the better part of the day on one of the little isles digging for clams. Two buckets full sat in the bottom of the skiff along with a blanket and picnic basket.

Searching the distance, Paul tried to spy the dock he'd built. It reached out into the water a good thirty feet and was a fine place to fish from on days when he didn't feel like taking out the boat.

Forty-five acres of land that abutted the Scaggins home was now his and Pearl's and with the help of a few friends, Paul had raised a small tobacco barn. Pearl kept a garden in the far corner of their homestead, where Jess and Paul had built a small two bedroom house. He'd designed the living room in a way that allowed sun to come in at all times of the day. The kitchen was across the breezeway and located in the back of the house where Paul had added a large screened in porch with a chair swing and picnic table. The bedrooms were small with a bathroom between them and with doors that opened into the other. He had promised that by the time Pearl gave birth to her next child a third bedroom and another bathroom would be in place.

Nodding to himself as he spied the dock he pushed the tiller the slightest bit to make his way toward it.

Pearl watched him - how his eyes searched the marsh. He looked handsome with his blond hair blowing away from his brow. "You hold on to Frankie, I'll tie the boat up," she spoke lovingly as she leaned in for her husband to hear her above the drone of the outboard. As they neared the dock, Pearl leapt from the small boat, grabbing the lines to wrap around the cleats.

Paul handed the buckets of clams to Pearl and stepped from the boat with Frankie clinging to his neck. "Looks like your momma is coming for a visit," he nodded toward Lottie; her arms flung wide as she stooped to greet her grandchild.

"There's my boy," the toddler reached for her, giggling. "He sure is getting big."

"You're telling me. We spent more time chasing him up and down that little island than we did clamming." Paul smiled and tousled the child's dark locks.

"Why don't you two go get cleaned up and I'll take care of him," Lottie stooped to release Frankie who immediately took off running from tree to tree, peaking from behind each.

"I don't know how she does it. I'm plum tuckered out from chasing him all over the isle."

"She's getting on up there, isn't she?"

"Last month she turned fifty seven."

"Her and your daddy sure are in good shape for their ages. My mom and pop can't hold a candle to them and they're ten years younger."

Pearl felt the familiar tingle in her belly as she noticed her husband bicep's flex when he picked up the buckets. Together they walked slowly toward the house, hearing Frankie's laughter in the background as he teased his grandmother in a game of catch me.

Setting the buckets beneath the pump, Paul jerked the handle several times until a steady stream of water rushed out. He splashed a few handfuls to his face. "A nice warm shower would be nice."

"Sure would," Pearl kicked her sneakers off and set them by the porch door. "I'll get the shower ready," She flounced a make believe skirt and rolled her shoulder.

Paul unbuttoned his shirt and unsnapped his dungarees. Pearl was waiting in the shower for him; she rubbed her hands over her slightly swollen belly and smiled. As her husband stepped in, her hands reached to caress his broad shoulders.

"Umm." Moving her damp hair to the side, Paul bent to kiss her neck. "You're right frisky today."

"Got a problem with that?"

"And what if I did?"

Glancing down, Pearl smiled, "I don't think there is one." She drew him close, hungry for his touch.

Their kisses tasted salty as water washed the briny residue from their bodies. Pearl's hands reached around her husband to pull him closer.

"See you ladies in a couple hours," waving good-by, Paul opened the door to the car and slowly drove down the lane."

"His mom's been kind of sick, lately." Pearl answered Lottie's unspoken question.

"Lottie nodded her head," I've heard."

"She won't go to the doctor and hid last time Paul brought one out to her. Says she hates 'em," Leaning back in the porch swing, Pearl motioned for her mother to join her. "I guess Frankie went right to sleep. Didn't he?"

"After a whole day of running around on the beach and then coming home and playing hide and seek with Grandma, I guess anybody would be tired," Lottie settled herself in the swing.

"How long has his mom been sick?"

"Couple months."

"That old man of hers would make anybody sick. He works her like a dog and then treats her like one too."

"I wish Miss Josie would let somebody help her."

"Honey, that woman's tired of living."

Pearl nodded her head. "That's what Paul says. He says she never had the guts to leave old Clarence and that now, this is her only way."

"So Paul's taking care of her."

"Yeah, Clarence sure ain't going to do anything. He still expects her to cook for him. That's what we went clamming for. Miss Josie loves clam chowder and Paul's going to spend the evening making her favorite dish."

"That's a good man, your husband."

"I know." Pearl blushed as she thought of the love making earlier.

"You feel better after your shower?" Lottie threw her head back in laughter.

"Momma, you're so bad. Now, stop it."

Lottie patted her daughter's hand. "It's what makes the world go round, sweetie."

Searching the backyard and resting her eyes on the pile of lumber set by the lean to, Lottie changed the subject. "You're getting fancy on us."

"What do you mean?"

"You're going to have two bathrooms, just like Ellie."

"I think if I asked Paul to, he'd even build me a garage."

"You want one?"

"Naw," she scrunched her nose, "It's just that I know he would do anything for me that he could."

"That's a good feeling. Isn't it?

Pearl nodded her head in agreement, "He works really hard...when he can."

"How's he been doing lately?"

Pearl nodded her head, "pretty good. He's got days when he's just as strong as can be and then there are other days when he has to rest every thirty minutes or so."

"That's understandable."

"The days when he's not feeling so good, is when his daggone daddy's here. I swear that man is the meanest bag of worms I've ever seen."

"You'd think he'd be the one sick instead of Josie, with all the whiskey he's poured down his throat... or at least be in jail for selling it...he's just too mean to die."

"Momma, now you taught me better than that. It's not right to wish bad on somebody." Pearl's tone was sarcastic and she giggled as she and her mother pushed the porch floor with their toes to make the swing sway farther.

"Paul quit smoking?"

"Yes, but he's dipping."

"Icky. I never could stand that stuff. How in the world can you kiss that mouth?"

Pearl laughed loudly, "It's not so bad, and he doesn't do it all the time, only when he's working. He knows I don't like it."

As Lottie stretched her arm around her daughter, Pearl rested her head on her mother's shoulder. "Sweetie, that Paul is a good man. Don't be too hard on him."

"I know, I sure am lucky...I just wish Clarence would leave him alone. He comes over here and starts trying to tell him how to work the tobacco - how high to turn up the furnace, how to pick off suckers, anything. But he won't even lift a finger to help, not even to pull the suckers off the stalks."

"He's always been lazy," Lottie sighed as she rocked back and forth.

"And he's always trying to tell Paul how much money he should be getting for it. I swear, I really think Paul would even quit dipping if his daddy didn't come over here. Pearl lowered her voice to mimic Clarence's gravely tone, 'what kinda business man is it that don't even use his own product,' He's always saying stuff like that.

"Humph," Lottie smirked.

"And then every time Paul has to take a rest cause of his lung, that old you know what starts in on him about being lazy."

"You've talked to Paul about ignoring what he says, haven't you?"

"Yes. And he knows, but still, that's his pa and it bothers him."

"He ought to tell him to go on home to his own place."

"Ha, Ha, Ha, that'll be the day. Paul still won't stand up to that old man. I wish he would."

"Lottie returned a sympathetic glance.

"One day Paul had to come home early to rest and Mr. Clarence came right on in the house and plopped his hinny down by the radio, just like it was his own place. Well, I tried to be as polite as I could be, Momma. Told him that I had lots of things to do and *sorry* but I just couldn't wait on him and that maybe Miss Josie might have supper waiting on the table at *his* house."

"What'd he say?"

"Not a darn thing. Just looked at me like I was a stump and started fiddling with the radio dial."

"You let me come over here one day when he comes around. I'll make sure he understands his place," Lottie snapped her fingers, "I'll have him out of here before you can whistle Dixie."

"I bet you would, Momma. I do believe he's scared of you," Tittering, Pearl gazed at her mother's hair, now almost completely gray.

"There's not that much to him, sweetie. He's an old blow hard, full of hot air."

"Too bad Miss Josie hasn't been able to stand up to him."

"I know she's tried – she's got the scars to prove it." Lottie tapped her front teeth.

"Pearl nodded sadly. "Ellie sure does put him in his place."

"You remember that night we had the party and Ellie was there?"

A puzzled look crossed Pearl's face.

"You know, the night she was so quiet."

"Oh yeah. She sure did tell him off *that* night."

"Everybody can stand up to Clarence except his own wife."

Both women sat in silence for a moment, pondering the sad life of Josie, both knowing that it was a hopeless situation. Pearl reached into the pocket of her dress, "That reminds me. I got a letter from Ellie. Looks like she's paying us a visit here sometime soon. Hope she brings Monroe. I have yet to see that child."

"In the time it takes for *Mrs. Cassie Lou Bridge* to shell a mess of beans, I could drive to Tampa and back."

"Maybe she just likes taking her time."

"Humph," Ellie tossed her hair to the side. "Mrs. Cassie Lou Bridge is going to take her time doing everything, especially if it involves those claws she's got at the end of her fingers. I mean, the nails are at least an inch long. And just look at my nails!" Her bottom lip puckered as she held out her hands. "I had to shell a whole bushel just the other day."

"Oh jeez, Ellie, you've always had pretty hands, they don't look so bad."

"I just can't get my nails to grow long." Her brown eyes pleading, Ellie scooted closer to her friend. "Would you do them for me?"

Pearl rose from the sofa to search her bedroom for her clippers, file and polish.

213

"I don't know what I'd do without you Miss Pearly. You're the only one that puts up with my bullshit."

Settling herself next to Ellie, Pearl reached for her hand, noticing a new emerald ring on Ellie's pinkie finger. "Well, have you ever thought of being a little more patient with people?"

Ellie shrugged her shoulders, "I don't know. It's just that after a while they start getting on my nerves." Her eyes once again searched Pearl's. "I've tried, honestly, I have. But … well… they're just so different down there."

"You've said that before, but I thought you said you'd handle that. Don't you like Florida?"

"I do, I do… the weather is great. But it's so hard living with those people. It's always about the citrus." Ellie's voice sharpened as she crinkled her brow. "Got to prune the trees, got to plant the trees, got to chop down the old trees, got to fertilize them…and they want me to help with all that stuff." She continued as she wriggled in her seat. "And then in the winter. My God! You'd think it was the end of the world if you don't go out and fire the pots."

"What's that?"

"Every once in a while there will be a cold snap and we have to go sit by the fire pots by the trees."

"I'm sure they don't want to lose their crop. Did you ever think of that?"

"But why should I have to go out and do it. That's what they got hired help for. Mrs. Cassie doesn't do it."

"Why not?"

"She says she's earned her *retirement* – but that I need to learn about the family business. I understand it. I can *see* what they're doing, doesn't mean I have to *do* it."

Pearl placed the one hand down and reached for the other. "Ellie, you sure are something." Grinning, she shook her head, "You just never learned how to work for a living. Did you?"

"Mother says that's what husbands are for. We're supposed to have babies and make the house a home." Batting her lashes rapidly, and grinning, Ellie laughed.

"You're supposed to be your husband's companion." Pearl shifted her eyes upward and smiled. "I help Paul every chance I have."

"Isn't he sick or something?"

"He has good days and bad. But I like to help with the fishing and tobacco."

"See, that's the difference between you and me. I don't like that stuff."

"Tsk," *It's no use, she'll never change,* Pearl thought as she changed the subject. "So where is little Monroe? Did you leave her with your parents?"

"Nope."

"She's with the Bridges?"

"Um hum."

Pearl shook her head, listening quietly as Ellie explained.

"They wanted her to stay with them and I figured it would be a good rest for me."

Pearl pulled her lips in and sighed; setting the file aside she opened the bottle of polish.

"They really like spending time with her. Mr. Ned takes her out with him when he checks the citrus and Miss Cassie loves taking her shopping." Pausing as she shifted in her seat, Ellie sighed and shrugged. "I'm just so tired of arguing with the Bridges, I just came by myself."

"That's nice." Pearl applied a coat of polish to Ellie's thumb.

"Do you think it was wrong for me to do that, Pearl?"

"She's your child. I can't tell you what to do with her."

"But I know you. When you do that thing with your mouth, it's because you disapprove of something. So tell me. What's so wrong about me leaving Monroe with her grandparents?"

"There's nothing wrong with it, but I would have liked to see how she's grown. I've never even met my best friend's little girl...and I can't believe that Ellie Rosell can't win an argument... that's not like you."

"Those people are a whole other breed of dog, Pearl. They don't fight fair."

Pearl gazed up from polishing, "What do you mean, 'they don't fight fair'?

Shrugging once again, Ellie brushed her hair away with one hand to expose a diamond earring dangling from her lobe. "And besides, Frankie would be too rough with her."

A startled expression crossed Pearl's face, "So they buy you off...and what do you mean, Frankie would be too rough with her.?"

"Nothing. It's just that I want Monroe to grow up refined. You know, I've always got her the prettiest dresses with crinolines and lace. She's not ever going to have to work like I did.

"What? Ellie, your parents never had you do any hard work. What are you talking about?"

Withdrawing her hand quickly and smearing the bright pink polish, Ellie pursed her lips, "I worked. I helped mother dust and helped her cook...and I used to help with the seine fishing."

"Helped with the fishing, my butt – you *never* did that, Ellie! I guess that's why your poor little fingernails aren't long and pretty," chiding, Pearl grabbed Ellie's hand back and wiped the smear away with a cotton ball. "Ah, poor Ellie. Had to dust and cook and now those mean people down in Florida are making her shell beans, you poor thing."

Ellie rolled her eyes and smirked, "We just weren't...you know, poor. I didn't *have* to do stuff like you did. We always had a man or two hired to help father."

"You are who you are, Ellie." Still holding Ellie's fingers in her hand, Pearl examined her friend: her eyebrows were neatly plucked to match exactly, her long dark hair hung perfectly in soft curls, exposing the new diamond earrings between the loose strands. "You'll never change." Pearl

217

smiled as she tightened the cap on the polish bottle. "That's what I like about you."

"What is that?"

"You're predictable. I always know what to expect. There are no surprises."

"I could say the same thing about you."

"Night and day."

"Thanks for the manicure," Ellie nodded to Pearl's last remark. "Hey, why don't you ask your mom to watch Frankie and we'll go to Wilmington? You need to get out and have some fun."

Cocking her head to the side, Pearl gazed at her friend pensively, and grabbed her purse. "Why not? I deserve a day out too."

"The distance from Dade City to Tampa is about the same as from here to Wilmington." Ellie turned the rearview mirror to check her image.

"Doesn't Dade City have a movie theatre?"

"Yeah." Searching her handbag, Ellie retrieved a tube of bright pink lipstick and began applying it. "But it's rinky dinky. I like the ones in Tampa better."

"The postcards you send sure look pretty. It must be really nice in Florida."

"Yeah," Ellie shrugged, and leaned back against the car seat, scanning Pearl's profile. "You're a pretty girl...just need a little make-up and you'd be a knock out. The guys would be all over you."

"The only *guy* I want all over me is Paul."

"Humph. Have it your way."

Pearl turned to her friend, "Ellie, are you telling me that you have gone out with other men while Chuck's away?"

"Well, not exactly."

"Either you have or you haven't."

"I don't go out with them. I meet guys and we just have a drink and I get them to pay my way into the movie, nothing wrong with that."

"And where is Monroe all this time?" Pearl raised a questioning eyebrow.

"The Bridge's."

"So they know all about this, huh?"

"They don't seem to mind."

"You better watch yourself, gal. When they tell Chuck about you going out all the time, he may not like it."

"And what do you think he's doing over there in Germany with all those frauleins?"

"He's at war."

Ellie rolled her eyes. "Jeez, you're still living in a fairy tale land. Aren't you?"

"I guess it's not for me to judge you, Ellie. Besides, we have no idea what kind of hell our men have to go through. Paul's told me a little about when his ship was hit. It was horrible."

As she nodded her head in agreement, Ellie reached again into her handbag for her pack of Pall Mall. "I know, I've heard. I *do* talk with these guys. They've told me about the war. They're pretty blunt about things, *everything*" She took a long drag from her cigarette. "And yes, I know they're just looking for a pretty girl like me to spend some time with and get their minds off all of that war stuff. Nothing ever happens...I'm a good girl."

"So you're a good girl."

"Yep. Never let them get past a little kiss."

After a long silence, Pearl snapped her finger, "Give me one of those."

"I didn't know you smoke?"

"I don't."

Ellie pulled a cigarette from the pack, "Living dangerously, are you?" Lighting it from her own, she took a short drag then handed the lit cigarette to Pearl.

As she placed it to her lips, Pearl took a short puff. "Yucky," she hacked.

"You'll get used to it."

"So, how's it going with the Bridges? They treat you any better now?"

Tossing her hair to the side, Ellie sighed and shook her head no. "Ned Bridge is a royal bag of worms, and Miss Cassie Lou isn't much better."

"That bad, huh?"

"That marriage isn't a whole lot different than Uncle Clarence's and Aunt Josie's...except instead of doling out broken teeth, this one doles out jewelry. It's all about keeping the wife's mouth shut."

"I noticed a few new bobbles on you too."

"Nothing like Miss Cassie, she's got rings on all her fingers up to her knuckles." She turned to raise an eyebrow and roll her eyes, "She's learned to play that old man, but she's miserable in the process – doesn't dare contradict him, looks the other way when he asks the waitress to sit on his lap."

"Maybe you should learn to do that."

"Shoot me if I get that bad, Pearl. Promise."

"Kinda looks like you're on your way," Throwing the half smoked cigarette out the window, Pearl slid her eyes toward her friend and asked about Monroe.

Ellie grew silent and fumbled with her hair, "That old man has so much money he doesn't care what anybody thinks. He's going to – *they're* going to make me pay," A gasp escaped Ellie's lips as she grasped the steering wheel with both hands. "He said it to my face – that I wasn't fit to be Monroe's mother."

CHAPTER EIGHTEEN
1945

"This little girl looks just like her daddy," Lottie picked up her granddaughter and held her close, patting her back. "Come on now, give grandma a little burp."

"You're sure you'll be all right." Pearl folded her apron and laid it on the kitchen table. "You've got the number to Paul's Aunt's house?"

Nodding her head, Lottie cradled little Josie in her arms. "Yes Sweetie, I've got everything I need. As soon as you and Paul leave, I'll take the kids over to my house. Now, you don't worry about a thing."

Pearl reached to caress her baby's soft cheek, "She does look just like Paul."

"Who do I look like, Mommy?" Frankie asked between spoonfuls of oatmeal.

"You look more like your momma," Lottie gazed at her daughter, "But when Grandma was young, she had dark hair just like you do."

"What are y'all talking about?" Paul asked as he entered from the porch.

"Nothing important," Pearl reached to kiss her husband's cheek.

"Nothing important," Paul chuckled then placed a small kiss on her lips. "Okay. I won't ask. But the car is all packed and ready. Are *you* ready?"

"Just about, let me give the kids a kiss good-bye."

Pearl placed her cheek next to little Josie's, "I love you, baby," then bent to cradle Frankie's head in her hands. He looked at her from the highchair, "Mommy, where are you going?"

"Daddy and I have to drive to Mississippi to see Aunt Amy. We won't be gone but a few days and so you be really good for Grandma and Grandpa - help her with your little sister. Okay?"

"Yes ma'am." Frankie's dark blue eyes tugged at Pearl's.

Paul kissed the boy on the forehead and tugged at his oatmeal caked chin with his fingers, "You be a good boy."

"You kids be careful driving." Lottie laid little Josie in the bassinette and wheeled it near the living room entrance.

"Thanks Momma."

"Yes, thanks." As he leaned to peck his mother-in-law's cheek, Paul slipped a five dollar bill into her apron pocket.

Lottie pressed his hand as he withdrew it, "no need."

"For all you and Jess have done for us, yes there is."

"We'll, be back in a few days, Momma." Pearl hugged her mother tightly and kissed her. "You got everything you need for Josie. Don't you?"

Lottie nodded.

"Frankie goes to the potty really well," She smiled and winked at her son. "He's such a good boy."

"He's a big boy now and I know he'll be really good while you and Daddy go bye-bye." Tousling Frank's hair, Lottie winked at her daughter.

"If you need anything just come on back over here and get it. Okay?"

"Yes, sweetie." Lottie placed her hands on Pearl's shoulders and turned her toward the door. "I got everything I need, and if I don't, I got your Aunt Amy's telephone number." She nodded toward Paul. "Now, you two better get on the road."

Paul opened the trunk of the car and laid the suitcase next to the box of knick knacks and keepsakes that had been his mother's.

"Bye," Standing at the screen door, Lottie waved to the couple as they slowly drove down the path to highway 210.

"It's been a long time since I've seen Aunt Amy." Paul rested his arm on the back of the car seat.

"It's too bad she couldn't come for the funeral."

Paul nodded. "I don't really think it was her so much as Uncle Eli. He and Dad always fought when they got together."

"Everybody fights with your daddy."

"Humph." Nodding in agreement, Paul reached for the bag of tobacco on the dashboard.

"Where in Mississippi is Decatur?"

"Eastern middle part. Not too far from Alabama."

"Have you been there before?"

"Just once, we all went out for a visit … but that was a long time ago."

"Did you like it?"

"I liked the drive out there. I remember driving through the mountains. They're really pretty, Pearl. But the roads… they're skinny."

Pearl's eyes opened wide.

"Yep, one small turn to the right, and it's over the side you go." He squeezed her arm and winked.

"Stop it, you're scaring me. Promise me that you'll drive slowly and be careful."

Paul kissed her cheek, "Don't worry baby, I ain't going to let anything happen to my girl."

They drove for a little more than an hour in silence, taking in the scenery as they drove through Wilmington, then Whiteville and toward Laurinburg. Pearl yawned and leaned her head against Paul's shoulder.

"Your mom looked real nice at the funeral."

"Um hum."

"Just about everybody came."

"Yep, lots of people loved my mom."

"She was a good woman, Paul. I know you're really going to miss her."

"She's at peace." Paul's eyes were fixed on the highway before him. The image of a woman standing staunchly before his father came to view. Unintelligible words seemed to blow from the man's mouth as he ridiculed the small frail woman. Never flinching, her eyes gazed sternly into his, but she obeyed him.

"This looks like the place. The mail box says the Bless family... hasn't changed much from when I was here last." As Paul walked toward the front door it opened and a rotund woman with blondish hair bounded out.

"Lord a mighty. Look at you!" Aunt Amy rushed to Paul, throwing her fleshy arms about him. "You done growed into a man."

Her cushiony flesh pushed against him, the smells of fried foods and sweets emanating from her body. "Let me look at you," she pushed him to arm's length and smiled; her bulbous cheeks shined glossy pink and her eyes twinkled bright blue.

Paul looked into her brilliant and chubby face, *"This is my mom plus fifty pounds."*

"Hi Aunt Amy." Paul hugged her back. "You're just as pretty as ever."

Blushing, Aunt Amy patted her tummy, "I guess you noticed I put on a few pounds since the last time you seen me."

"You're still pretty...always had a pretty face."

"Love ya boy, I just love ya." Amy pulled him close again against her pillow-like body. "That gal you got with you, would that be your beautiful young wife?"

"Yes, ma'am." Motioning for Pearl to come closer, he reached out to hold her hand. "Pearl, this is my Aunt Amy, Mom's sister."

"Pleased to meet you, Aunt Amy," Pearl reached out her hand.

"Ain't no shakin' hands here, honey. You come and give your Aunt Amy a hug; she crushed Pearl into her pillowy softness."

Giggling as the woman held her closely, Pearl returned the hug.

"Where's them young'ins of yours?" Amy peered about the car, searching for the two children her sister Josie had written about.

"We didn't want to put them through the long drive, Aunt Amy. Especially the baby, she's only a few months old."

"You're right. A long trip like this wouldn't be the smart thing to do with a little baby," Amy nodded her head in approval. "You kids come on in now. I know you need some rest and some *good* food after that long drive. How long it take y'all anyways?"

"Paul drove straight through."

"Wasn't bad, took about eighteen hours." Paul yawned, reminding himself that he hadn't slept for nearly two days.

"Boy, you get yourself in that house," Amy scolded playfully as she stooped to pick up their suitcase. "Y'all come on in and make yourselves at home."

"I'll put your suitcase in the spare room. Got it all fixed up and ready for y'all." Within seconds Amy returned. "Y'all relax; sit right down on the couch. It's a comfy one...and don't be afraid to rest your feet up on the coffee table. That's what it's there for. Now, you two just take it easy for a little and I'll go in the kitchen. I was just getting ready to fry up some chicken, since I knew y'all would be coming in sometime today."

"Don't worry about us too much Aunt Amy, in fact I think I might go lay down in the bedroom for a little bit." Paul rose from the couch. He yawned again. "Guess I am kind of tired."

Amy reached her arms around him for another hug, "Paulie, it's so good of you to come visit, I really appreciate it...bringin' those things your momma wanted me to have." She kissed his cheek, and then wiped a tear with the hem of her apron.

"Why don't you come on in the kitchen with me, honey?" Amy touched Pearl's shoulder as she walked. "Come on. Let him sleep for awhile. I imagine you napped a little on the way. Huh?"

"Yes ma'am. I'm not tired at all." She rose to follow Amy into the kitchen.

Amy boldly eyed Pearl, checking, it seemed, every inch from head to toe. "I can tell right off the bat that you ain't one to put on airs...and you're pretty to boot."

"Thank you Aunt Amy. I don't think I did too bad myself."

"Yeah, Paul's always been a nice looking boy. I'm sure as heck glad you and he got away from that Clarence. It's just too bad that my sister didn't leave. She should have left him long ago."

Pearl nodded as she seated herself at the small kitchen table. "We tried to get her to come live with us, but she wouldn't budge. I never understood why."

As she rolled the chicken in flour, Amy nodded, then shook her head, "Well, honey, she come from a long line of women who *obeyed* their husbands. It's how she was raised. How we were all raised.... And there's something to be said for that. A man should have the last word in a good argument." She laughed as she gently placed the chicken in the frying pan. "But she just got plum unlucky with that Clarence, in fact, poor ol' Josie seemed to be unlucky her whole life. Even when we was kids. She was always the one the dog bit or the one getting' caught. Back then it was funny, but ..." She raised her wrist to wipe her eyes, and glanced a playful wink toward Pearl. "So can you tell me a little about my sister's life? Hadn't seen her in such a long time... I know she wasn't a happy woman...living with that *man.* But with you around I suppose things were a little

229

lighter on her, at least, that's what she'd write me about
you. That you and them kids were the light of her life.
Always trying to help her out and taking her places when
Clarence wasn't around."

Pearl could see that Amy was struggling with her words;
holding back sobs. She rose to stand by her and help with
the frying chicken. Silently they cooked all the pieces then
draped the pan of chicken with a tea towel.

"I'll just save this for later when Paul wakes up. If we get
hungry I got a little something around here we can nibble
on."

Pearl smiled and nodded," I'm fine now...your sister, Miss
Josie, was the nicest woman I ever met, Aunt Amy. She just
got beat down, and beat down, by Mr. Clarence."

Setting two coffee mugs on the table, Amy then set the
percolator down. "Help yourself, sweetie."

The coffee smelled strong as she poured it into her cup
and reached for the cream and sugar. "Why didn't she leave
him?"

"We was raised to stay with your man through better or
worse," Raising her cup to her lips Amy shook her head
woefully. "I tried, I really tried to get her to bring those boys
out here and live with us."

"Paul says they came out here about fourteen years ago."

"That's right. They *all* came. Even that old, excuse my
French, son of a bitch. She planned to stay right here with
those boys...tell Clarence to go on home without her. He
and Eli got into a knock down drag out fight – right here in

the kitchen. I'm telling ya, there was blood all over the place and broken chairs and dishes too."

"What happened?"

"You know what happened. They went home." Amy rose and walked to the kitchen counter. "Want a cookie?" She reached into the ceramic jar.

Pearl nodded. "I mean, if there was such a fight...?"

"Eli won, you ain't seen my Eli. He makes two of that skinny old weasel, Clarence. And that, excuse my French, son of a bitch, was ready to leave with his tail 'tween his legs. He got in that old piece of junk he drives and was ready to head down the drive and that young'in – Paul come runnin' out the door screamin' for his daddy."

"Paul?"

"Yessiree, that boy loved his daddy – worshipped him. Don't ask me why. He always treated him like cow dung."

"Still does."

"Yep, for some reason Paul and Josie was drawn to that man... like bees to honey, and not even likin' it. Now Phil, that boy was ready for Clarence to be out of his life. But then he was quite a few years older than Paul and he knew what his daddy *really* was. Well, Paul said he was going back with his daddy and Josie just couldn't let her baby go, so she took Phil and they all went on back to North Carolina. I tell ya, Phil was mad as hell at Paul for makin' his momma go back." Amy popped another cookie in her mouth, "A couple years later Paul wrote me and wanted to know if his mom and he could come on out here and try it again. But by that time, Phil had flown the coop and Clarence wasn't about to fall for the old trick of *visitin' Aunt Amy* again….I reckon my big sister just give up. That's all, just plum give up."

"When we lived with them he was always bossing her and telling her to shut up. Sometimes I just wanted to really tell him what I thought of him."

"It wouldn't have made no difference, honey. He had you over a barrel with you being Paul's wife. He would of tried to pit your husband against you – I'm telling you that man is a weasel and will lie and connive to get whatever he wants."

"My friend Ellie has a father-in-law like that. It's his way or the highway."

"Sweetie, there are people like that. They just aren't like the rest of us." As she leaned against the counter, Aunt Amy reached her hand into the cookie jar once again and winked, "I think they're defective, you know, like some people are born with six toes or born without nipples – I have a friend like that – well, I think people like Clarence and your friend's father-in-law were born missing whatever makes them really human."

Aunt Amy's scowl turned to a smile as she cocked her head to the side, "I think my better half just drove up."

"And who is this pretty little peach sittin' at my kitchen table?" Pearl turned toward the booming voice. A giant of a man, wearing a Stetson hat, stood at the kitchen door way, his shoulders seemed to nearly fill the width of it. As he removed his hat, a shock of thick red hair streaked with white, billowed about his face.

"Well hey, Dumplin'," Amy rose to greet her husband with a peck on the lips. "This here is Paul's bride. Ain't she a pretty one?"

Eli wrapped his arms around Pearl and squeezed. He towered over her. "Little lady, it sure is good to finally meet ya. You're all poor Josie used to write about … how proud she was to have you for her daughter. Now, where's them babies?"

"They didn't bring them Eli. It's such a long drive and the middle of August, you know, it's hot as an oven out there."

"Um. Alright. Makes sense. But you be sure next time y'all come for a visit to bring them out to meet their Uncle Eli."

"Yes sir. I'd love for them to meet y'all."

"We're good folks out here. Hard workin' and we treat ya right. Not like that worthless, good for nothin'…"

"Okay, Eli, we done run that man in the ground enough."

Smiling, Eli grabbed a cookie from the jar then pulled a chair out from the table to join the women. "Glad y'all could make it. I'd have gone on over there to Paul's but I guess Amy has filled ya in on why me and, excuse my French, jackass, don't get along."

Pearl stifled a giggle, "I don't blame you sir. He is a hard man to be around. I'm just glad me and Paul could come here and meet y'all. You sure do have a pretty place."

"We worked hard for it and we get by, little by little. Go to church on Sunday and thank the Lord for what we got. Can't do much better than that." Eli winked at Pearl. "Now, can ya?"

"Sleep good, son?" Eli Bless pushed his robust frame from the couch to greet his nephew as he walked from the bedroom.

"Uncle Eli!" Paul reached out his hand. "I didn't know you'd come home. What time is it?

"You slept the rest of yesterday and all through the night." Amy handed him a mug of coffee and walked into the kitchen, "I'm makin' you some bacon and eggs. How ya like 'em?"

"Scrambled will be just fine, thank you. I'm sorry I missed that dinner you were fixing yesterday."

"We got leftovers."

Following his wife to the kitchen, Eli poured himself another cup of coffee, "You're coming with me this morning. Gotta make my rounds. Check on my chickens and cows. Then maybe I'll take you on over to Roscoe's later for lunch, he makes the best pulled pork sandwiches this side of the Mississippi. Suit you?"

"Sounds good to me Uncle Eli."

Eli drove slowly around the circle drive of his brick home - gravel crunching beneath the tires of his International truck.

Dogwood trees graced the entrance and exit of the drive with Impatiens of varying colors bordering the front of the Bless yard. "Y'all sure have a pretty home. Pearl's mom does a lot with flowers and shrubs too at her place."

"That's my Amy; she's always loved growin' things. As for me, if I touch it, it for sure is goin' to die." Eli chuckled about his shortcoming. Shifting into third gear, he turned toward Paul. "Son, you tell me the truth. Why didn't your pa ever take Josie to the doctor?"

"I wasn't living at home anymore. So I wouldn't know exactly what he ever said to her. Once I came back from the war I moved right in with Pearl's family until I got my home built. And that didn't take more than a few weeks with Mr. Jess helping me, along with a few others. I tell you, that's when you find out who your friends are, when you're down and out. As for Dad, I never heard it come out of his mouth. Never heard *him* ask her. But I asked her and every time she'd say she just didn't want to see one. Finally I took to her Wilmington myself despite her grumbling, but it was too late. The cancer had spread all over her body."

"So, he never even bothered to take her. You know if he wanted to he could have. He could make your Mom do just about anything."

"She said something to me one day when she was lying in bed. It made sense and now that I think about it I guess she got the last punch in."

"What was that?"

235

"She said, 'makes him madder than Hell that he can't make me get up and wait on him. Makes him madder than Hell that I'm going to die and there's not a single solitary thing he can do about it.' That's what she said. She was tickled pink over her finally being able to control him. And the more I thought about what she said the more I realized that this wasn't just her way out of the hell hole he'd made her live in, but it was her way of really giving it to him. He had too much pride to just grab her up and take her to the doctor... never did do an unselfish thing for her in his whole life. Never got her flowers, never took her out on the town, never did a caring thing for her. And now, you should see the old bag of worms, like Pearl calls him. He's walking around the house like a whipped puppy. He goes out to his still and messes around there all day and drinks half his profits up and then the rest of the time he sits at that empty house and listens to the radio."

"Your mom wrote that he was always coming around and bothering you, calling it both y'all's tobacco business."

Paul grinned and shook his head, "I believe it. He'd come over when me and Mom would be out there pulling off the suckers and just watch. And then when it was time to crop the tobacco he might pull off a few leaves from the stalk, but when it came to looping it he'd mess up... he'd give up and call over to Pearl, bossing her around...tell her to do it."

"She do it?"

Paul snickered loudly, "Ha, you should have heard her. Made me so proud. She'd just be so polite and say something like, 'Why yassa Massa Clarence. Anything you says Massa Clarence.' Boy it would burn him up and he'd just walk off cussing under his breath. But since Mom died he hasn't been back. I think now that if he did, I'd run him off or at least let him know where his place is. He doesn't scare me no more. He's just a sorry old man."

"Sorry you got such a sorry pa, son. Wish I could change things for ya."

"It's just the way it is, Uncle Eli. He ran off my brother and now, as far as I'm concerned, he killed Mom."

As they drove around the farm, Eli showed off his calves and bulls. Paul could feel the pride emanate from his uncle as he boasted of the price he'd been receiving for them. Rolling hills and winding roads led through the five hundred acres of wooded land and pastures.

Eli listened as Paul told of his small tobacco farm in North Carolina, and how he hoped one day to be as successful as him. "Just how do you do it all, Uncle Eli?"

"For one thing, Amy and I never had kids. That's one expense we never had to contend with. Not that we didn't want any, understand. Amy especially wanted to have children, but I guess it just was never meant to be. But other than that, every time I got a little money in my pocket, I didn't spend it. I saved up and bought more land or more cattle. And then the chicken business just seemed to take off on its own. That's Amy's pride and joy. She raises them Rhode Island Reds. Says they're the best layin' hens she's ever seen and like me, when she gets a dollar she saves fifty cents of it to put back in the chickens. She's done pretty good with them. In fact, that was her that paid for the little duck pond in the backyard."

Eli turned down onto a black top road; the ride smoothed immediately. "Roscoe's place is just down the road a piece. We'll stop on in there and have a bite for lunch. I'm tellin' ya they got the best pulled pork sandwiches around."

"You know how I like mine, Roscoe. Slice of cheese, slice of tomato and a heap of cole slaw on it."

"Fix me one like his," Paul called out to the stocky man behind the counter.

"This here is my nephew Paul from out in North Carolina, Roscoe. He and his pretty little bride drove all the way out here."

"North Carolina, huh? That's a good piece away. How long it take you to get here"

"About eighteen hours. Close to it." Paul sipped from his Coke-a-Cola bottle. "It wasn't a bad drive, just a long one."

"What part of North Carolina? Sliding the grilled pork from the steel spatula to the buns and adding the extras, Roscoe turned to face the men. His dark hair was flecked with grey and his blue eyes reflected a tired but earnest look.

"A little north of Wilmington - near a town called Holly Ridge."

"Isn't that where that Camp Davis is?"

Paul took a bite from the sandwich, "Um hum," he mumbled as he chewed.

"Well, I'll be. My nephew, my older brother's son, was stationed out there. Sure is a small world. How 'bout that."

"I think half the Army's been through Camp Davis. But what's his name? I might have heard of him."

"Jay, J. Frank Bishop. First name's John. But everybody took to just calling him Jay. Jay Bishop. Ever hear of him?"

Frank. Jay Frank. Yes he knew him. Frank…Frankie.

Paul's body tightened, his gaze fell to his plate. Quickly regaining his composure, he raised his head to study Roscoe. Yes, he could see the family resemblance; the dark hair the dark steely blue eyes and the broad forehead. *Jay Frank's Uncle Roscoe. Small world,* "humph," Paul took another bite of his sandwich. "Can't say I have. Lots of folks come through there, don't stay too long."

"Said he was all set to marry some little gal from around there and he got sent over to Germany. Thought he was dead for a while, but come to find out he spent the war in one of those prisoner of war camps."

"So he's back now?"

"Yeah, saw him a couple weeks ago. Me and Katy drove down to Texas to help welcome him home. Kind of banged up though. Got caught trying to escape and the Nazi bastards busted his knees. Beat the hell out of him. He's got a scar over his left eye and walks with a limp now. He says he doesn't know how much more he could have taken, and was glad the war in Germany is over. Sure does look right

239

puny now. Hope they end this mess we got with the Japs real soon.

"I don't think it'll be too long for we beat the hell out of them too." Eli motioned for Roscoe to make another sandwich. "You ready for another one of these babies, Paul?"

"No sir, I think I'm full enough."

CHAPTER NINETEEN

"Ever since we came home from Mississippi he's been acting strange. He says it's because of his lung, Momma, but I think it's something else."

"He did lose his mother, Pearl. You know, it all could have hit him at once. Maybe it didn't sink in until he saw his aunt. She does look a lot like Josie."

"And I know he's been drinking."

"With the war ending and all, and some of his friends who didn't make it back, he could be going through a lot, sweetie. You know, Enid Abbott lost two brothers in the war."

Pearl shook her head, "I know. Do you suppose Paul's feeling badly about the Abbott brother's not coming home when he did. He got hurt too but really didn't see a lot of the war. That could be bothering him."

"He saw enough of it." Lottie looked up from peeling potatoes. "He been hanging around his dad?"

"Not much. But I know he's gone over there a couple of times."

241

"Sweetie, you need to sit down with Paul and find out just what the problem is. You can't let it go on. Something's eating at him and you need to find out what it is."

A light breeze coming in from the north rustled the tobacco leaves about as they lay scatted in piles under the broad awnings of the barn. Jess rapidly tied a large brown leaf, looping it with others, and hung it alongside a cluster of finished poles on the tier. He was quiet as he busied himself; he liked the work. It reminded him of his youth and helping his own father when they cropped tobacco; the banter was incessant as they discussed fishing or local gossip. Paul and he were much like that when they worked the tobacco, but for the last several days Paul had been uncharacteristically quiet. He had even snapped replies to some of the crew. He didn't need Lottie to tell him about Pearl's concern. He knew already that something serious was on Paul's mind.

"Your Aunt Amy and Uncle Eli doing okay out there in Mississippi?"

"Seem to be. They sure do have a pretty place out there; fancied the yard up and all since last time I saw it." Paul turned toward a small group of men sipping sodas, "Hey! I ain't paying you to loaf out here. Now, I better not see no more of this stuff or I'll fire the lot of you!"

Jess was quiet and didn't bother to ask Paul anymore questions. He gazed at his son-in-law, watching him grumble

242

beneath his breath; his furrowed brow belied his anger. Slowly it seemed to subside and Paul's demeanor lightened, "I know you have a bunch of sisters…Miss Lottie have any brothers or sisters in her family? Pearl mentioned something about an Uncle Frank some time ago. She got a brother Frank?"

Jess shook his head no, "you must be thinking of Uncle *Hank*. Now, my sister Clara married a man named Hank Lewis out of Cookeville, Tennessee. But ain't got no Franks in the family, except for your little Frankie. He's getting right big. Before long we can bring him out here and put him to work," Jess chuckled as he continued looping the tobacco leaves to the poles.

There was silence once again and an angry look of discontent settled on Paul's face. He walked to the water barrel and ladled water to his lips, wiping his mouth with his sleeved arm, "Rough day today. Can't seem to catch my breath." He sat down on a soft drink crate, settling his hands on his thighs, gazing out into the fields.

"You'll be fine. That water's warm, why don't you grab a Pepsi out of the cooler and relax for a bit. It's just about break time anyways." Jess joined Paul, grabbing another crate and placing it just close enough to the wall of the barn to lean back against it. "Won't be long now we can go on down to Georgia and seine fish. You coming aren't you?"

"Suppose so. It always brings in good money. Now that the war is over I'm just wondering when we're going to get the banks back. Sure would be nice to be able to go over there and fish."

"Yeah, now that most of the men are gone from Camp Davis, you'd think they'd let us on over there, but who knows what they got in mind. I hear they're doing something with rockets. Hell, some kind of space thing. Something to do with shooting rockets to the moon."

"I heard something like that. Jeez, it's all a bunch of baloney. "

Jess leaned back against the building and wiped the sweat from his brow with his handkerchief. "Well son, I guess they're going to do what they're going to do. Ain't much we can do about it. May as well just relax." He turned to his son-in-law, "That's what I've learned to do, anyway. Just can't fight progress." Jess chugged the Pepsi till it was empty. "Wait 'til you're my age, you'll learn to let things just go on as they may and concentrate on the good stuff."

"Maybe you're right. Just some things don't seem fair. No matter how hard I try, it seems lies keep staring me in the face."

"Want to talk about it, son?"

"Naw, guess I just got to learn to live with some things."

"Your mom dying was hard on you, Paul. We all know that. And you never did get a fair shake with Clarence. But, like I say, you concentrate on the good things. You have a good wife that loves you. A son, and no matter what anybody can say, that boy is more yours than … well, you know what I mean. You've been the best daddy to that boy.

244

No one could ever say a bad word about it. And then there's that little baby girl of yours. Son, you got a lot to be thankful for."

Paul lowered his head and nodded, "Yes sir. I know I've got a lot to be thankful for. I keep telling myself that. I guess I have to do like you say and concentrate on the good stuff. But sometimes that's hard to do." Paul rolled the Pepsi bottle between his hands and gazed out to the fields again.

"Your mom was a good woman. Wasn't right what happened to her." Clarence lifted the bottle to his lips and chugged. "No sirree, that woman was the salt of the earth."

Each word Clarence uttered riled Paul to the point of wanting to spit in his face. This was as close to hatred as he had ever come. *What world is Dad living in,* he thought to himself, *he did nothing but treat her like a dog her whole life.* Watching his father as his gnarled hand grasped the bottle neck, he noticed the scarred knuckles, the stubble on his unshaven face, the food stained shirt and the stench from the man's body - it repulsed him. *This is my father.* He looked at him now as if he were some kind of insect – a cockroach. *How could I be part of that? Frankie isn't even part of me.* It didn't make sense.

"She *was* a good woman," Clarence reached to pat Paul on the shoulder, Paul withdrew. "What?" Clarence straightened in the chair and lifted his chin. "You too good for me now? Over there with them Scaggins people."

"Ain't got nothing to do with it." Rising from his chair, Paul looked loathingly at Clarence. "When's the last time you took a bath?"

"Humph,"

"When's the last time you washed your clothes, or even changed them?"

"Who the hell do you think you are, talking to me that way? I oughta...." Clarence pushed himself from the chair, and grabbed the table edge to steady himself.

"Look at you, ha! You deserve to live like this. You're nothing but dirt anyway." As he turned to leave, Paul swatted at the bottle of whiskey, knocking it over.

"You're still my son, boy. Don't you forget it! You owe me!"

Paul rushed down the steps and headed toward the shed. He reached behind the loose boards of the tack room and grabbed a bottle of his father's liquor.

CHAPTER TWENTY

"Wow, that's a big bird. You didn't drive all the way to Wilmington to get that did you?" Jess asked as he rolled up his shirt sleeves and straightened the knife and fork by his plate.

"Got it at Boom Town in Holly Ridge," Lottie smiled as she settled the platter in front of Jess to carve.

"I tell you now, that store's got just about anything and everything you could want in there." Jess picked up the carving knife and fork and eyed the turkey for the best place to begin cutting.

Paul watched as Jess pierced the crisp brown skin. "Looks mighty good Miss Lottie."

She placed a bowl of marshmallow covered yams and the gravy boat on the table, "Thank you Paul. Pearl, once you get Josie in the highchair, come help me get the rest while Jess finishes up carving that bird."

Once the table was completely set with all the fixings for Thanksgiving, Lottie removed her apron and sat at the far end of the dining table, facing her husband. "Okay, everyone hold hands for the blessing. You say it Jess."

"Our heavenly father, bless our family and keep us safe from the harms that surround us every day. Keep our faith strong in each other and in you. And bless this food that we are about to eat. Amen."

"Amen."

Pearl watched Paul as he took bites of different kinds of foods on his plate. After eating about half, he toyed with the rest. In the months since they'd returned from Mississippi she'd seen him lose weight and his complexion turn sallow. Though the weather had turned cooler and the season for planting had passed, he spent most days outside the home.

She knew he was not going to his father's house, she checked. But she had spied him in one of the far fields one day as she was walking to Clarence's. He was leaning against a tree, seemingly staring into space. A bottle of liquor sat next to him, but as she continued watching, she noticed he barely drank from it.

He did not go seine fishing during the season, telling Jess he did not feel well enough for the drive to Georgia. On occasion he would join her father to gather oysters, but it was rare.

The doctor said there was no change in his condition. That the lung looked as healthy as it could be, and that his one good lung looked fine. There was something bothering Paul that Pearl could not figure out. And despite her reworded efforts to garner information from him, Paul remained steadfast in his response that everything was fine.

Jess and Lottie even went to Clarence and bombarded him with questions of what he had said to Paul to cause him such grief. "Are you trying to get him to help you with that darn still of yours? Are you blaming him for the sorry condition you've got yourself in? Just what is it that you've done?"

Clarence blustered as usual. "That boy ain't hardly been around since his mom died...told me to stay the hell away from him. You better believe that won't be hard to do. He don't even come over here and help me with nothing. And you can see how the place looks. Jess and Lottie ignored the filth that had accumulated and Clarence's implication that Paul was obligated to help clean it. "He's wrote me off just like his brother, Phil. Ain't neither one of them worth a plug nickel....but I seen him sneak over here and steal a bottle of my whiskey." Clarence confessed that only a bottle or two had come up missing in the last few months. "That boy never could drink much," He puffed out his chest in pride, "not like his old man can."

"Now if his mom was here, she'd get him straightened out. That woman was the salt of the earth."

"You dog, you mangy old dog. You treated poor old Josie like trash. You never lifted a finger to help her, never gave her a damn thing, only the back of your hand. I know what you are, just plum no good. Paul makes ten of you. And Josie, she's at peace, finally." Lottie moved close to

Clarence, the stench of urine and whiskey was stomach churning. Tilting her head as she held her breath Lottie raised her hand to slap him. The gaze in his eyes was blank and she lowered her hand, "You're worthless."

Clarence's mouth pursed as his ears burned red. "Y'all get on out of here, now. Ain't got nothing more to say to you. If that boy's having troubles, ain't no fault of mine. Wouldn't bother me a bit if I never seen him again. Now git."

Pearl walked through the shin high growth of bushes, pulling her thin wool coat around her closely. Her hair was covered in a cotton scarf to protect her ears from the wind. It was a typical February, gray and chilly. After five months of feeling her husband slip farther and farther away from her she decided to follow him to the field where she knew he spent hours of his days. Watching Paul as he rested against the same tree with his half empty bottle of whisky, and the same forlorn stare, she approached him, a picnic basket in one hand and a blanket in the other.

"It's kind of cold out here today, but I thought that as long as you're going to spend time in this field, I may as well come join you."

Paul looked up and glanced at the bottle by his side.

"It's okay, I know you been nursing that same bottle for weeks."

"Can't fool you, can I?"

With the blanket spread on the ground, Pearl knelt and removed her scarf, then opened the basket. "Got some fried chicken and some potato salad." She waited for his response as he gazed in her eyes questioningly. "Come on now, you got to eat."

"Maybe. So you been following me out here, huh?"

Pearl nodded.

"You think I've gotten lazy? No good like my dad?"

"No...I think you're trying to get the pieces together about losing your mom."

Paul shook his head, "No.".

"No? Then what is it, Paul?"

He looked blankly at her, shoulders slumping, he turned away.

"I won't quit asking. Now, at first when your mom died and you seemed so blue, I figured it was normal and then you just lost interest in everything. You haven't touched me in months. What did I do, Paul?

The look in his eyes was the most sorrowful she had ever seen. She reached her hand out to stroke his hair. "Are you getting sick...you know, your lung."

Looking down, Paul shook his head no.

"I don't know anymore. I know I can't possibly know what it's like to lose your mother, or to have half a lung. I've talked with the doctor and he says you should be doing fine, that getting tired more often is normal, but there's something else, Paul. I just don't know what to do anymore.

Please. Tell me what is wrong. Have you stopped loving me?"

"Humph." Paul pushed the cork into the bottle of whiskey, "I'll never stop loving you."

"Then what is it. I've asked you time and time again and you always say it's nothing. It *is* something. And I can't bear seeing you like this anymore. It's killing me. And the kids, Frankie and Josie, you hardly spend any time with them.

"Frankie," laying down a drumstick, he repeated the name. "Frankie."

"Yes, Frank Aaron Bishop, your son. Our son," She paused for a moment to search his eyes. "Is that it? You're upset *now*. I don't understand. Why *now?*"

Paul leaned against the tree and closed his eyes.

"Paul, you knew. That's *why* you married me."

"I married you because I loved you. I've always loved you, since we were little kids. When we used to go to the banks and you'd wear that yellow bathing suit and we would run into the water and get all wet, then race up the dunes and roll down to get all sandy, then run back into the water to wash the sand off."

"We kept doing it over and over." Pearl laughed, "That was so much fun."

"Since then I loved you. I watched you grow. Watched you bloom. And watched you fall in love."

Pearl drew close to him and wrapped her arms around his neck, trying to move her body as close to his as possible. "God, Paul. I love you too. You're my whole world. I don't know what I'd do without you. Please...is it Frankie? Did he do something? Say something? Does anybody know? I've never told a soul."

"It's come down on me like a wave, just washing away everything that made sense. I don't know what to think anymore. I know it's not Frankie's fault. But..."

"What do you mean?" Not his fault."

Backing away from her, Paul's eyes searched Pearl's ambiguously. "I don't know what to think or believe anymore. I never once felt badly about the boy. Not once felt like he wasn't mine." A scowl crossed his face as his eyes darkened. "You lied."

"About what? I don't know what you mean."

"His name."

It all fell into place. He knew who she'd named the boy after. *But it doesn't mean anything anymore.* She felt her body chill as if the wind blew straight through her thin coat. Her face felt hot. Words wanted to come but she didn't know how to start.

"I don't know what to believe, Pearl. Did you wish I would die and he would come back?"

She gasped in disbelief. All she could do was shake her head as tears welled in her eyes.

"You have no Uncle Frank. That was a lie."

Pearl lowered her head, her shoulders felt like weights. Weakness overcame her body as she slumped forward, shaking as she sobbed.

"Every time I say his name, I see Jay's face...I see the lie. You know he's alive. You know he made it back from the war and that prison camp in Germany."

"I'm so sorry." Pearl covered her face with her hands as tears poured down her cheeks.

"I believed you. I believed you loved me - that all the other stuff was over. That *he* was gone. Even if he lived, he was gone; out of our lives. But now, every day, the lie - the lies. Every day I'm bringing him back each time I say our son's name...*his* son's name."

"We'll change it." Pleading sobs trembled from her lips as she reached to touch him.

"Change it?"

Nodding her head as she wiped her swollen face with her hands, Pearl gasped for air between sobs.

"He's too old for that. Don't you think he knows his name? Tell me Pearl. Did you think I was stupid? Did you think I'd never find out? The only thing that makes sense is that you thought I'd die in the war and that *he* would come back."

"I don't know. I wasn't thinking back then. I just..."

"Why didn't you tell me when the boy was real small, just a baby? Maybe we could have changed the name then."

"I was afraid to. I didn't want to hurt you."

"Haven't I always been there for you? Haven't I always tried to understand? You didn't trust me. Or maybe you were still hoping. Did you know he was in a prisoner of war camp?"

Pearl nodded her head.

"Good God, another lie. You never told me you knew that."

"It didn't matter then." As her sobs diminished, Pearl searched for acceptance in his eyes; in his responses.

"I find that hard to believe."

"Paul, of course I didn't want Jay to die. Of course I didn't want anything bad to happen to him. But when you were gone… the letters, they meant so much to me. And then living with your parents, I came to understand you more too. And then Ellie…"

"Ellie?" Anger filled his voice, "Why did you tell Ellie?"

"I didn't tell her anything. She thinks Frankie is yours. She took Jay's letter, or rather his mother's letter, the one she wrote to me about him being alive and in a prison camp. I didn't know about it for months." Pearl's eyes begged understanding, "She told me right before Frankie was born…Paul, I never wrote back. It was over."

"But you knew before I came home that he was alive…."

"But I didn't contact his mother. She would have written him that I was waiting for him. Don't you see? I didn't write back because I wanted you. *Pearl's* hands reached to cup Paul's face, *"I want you."*

As he turned toward her, Pearl could feel his body relax, though his eyes still welled with pain. The anger was gone from his voice as trembling words fell from his lips, "I don't know. I feel so numb, like I've lost my son. Like I've lost you. I don't know what to think anymore."

"I remember you saying once how nice it was to name someone after another person. How it keeps that person alive. I guess that was what I was trying to do with Frankie. I didn't want Jay to die. I didn't want him out of my life. But, how do I explain it? I don't know. But that love, the love that you and I have is so much more than what it was between Jay and I. Don't you think that I questioned too what I had done. That if you ever found out, how it would hurt you. I prayed you would never find out and by not writing back to Mrs. Bishop, I hoped it would end that part of my life. Now, when I look at Frankie and I see Jay, I think of that handsome young man who treated a naïve girl with kindness, sweetness and tenderness. I think Jay was a good man. I think you do too. I don't look at Frankie and long for Jay. I look at my son and think that he has the best of two wonderful men. I think of what a good father he has, *you,* what an understanding, kind man you are... I'm ashamed that I never said this to you. Because I know that's how you feel too...that Jay was a good man, or at least how you used to feel. I hope I haven't ruined things. I hope you will forgive me. I never wanted to hurt you."

Kissing her temples, Paul smoothed the damp hair from the sides of her face. "You mean everything to me," he whispered, pulling her closely. Pearl moved even closer, wrapping her legs around him. Slowly he pushed her to the ground; nuzzling her neck. The chilled wind blew dried brown leaves about the blanket as the lovers tangled, drawing warm breaths from one another.

CHAPTER TWENTY-ONE
1949

Jess reached into the cooler and grabbed a cold Pepsi, popped the top against the bottle opener on the post and chugged nearly half. A smile crossed his lips as he placed the bottle down and thought of the future. Yes, he and Lottie had always dreamed of having a restaurant, but now it was actually going to happen – and at his age. As he picked up the spool of twine, he felt the tingling of his left hand. He'd felt a tingling in his hands before and attributed it to old age and arthritis. He fumbled with the twine, wrapping it first around his third finger, then looking at the large brown leaf in his left hand, gasped. *What*, he thought to himself, the pain was excruciating. He watched as the leaf fell from his hand to the ground as the crushing pain against his chest grew and he slumped to the ground. Numbness seemed to consume him and he gazed about, wondering if this was to be his last day on earth.

"Jess! Paul hollered as he raced toward his father-in-law. "God, Jess! What's the matter?"

Whispered words, barely audible came from his lips, "feels like a mule sat on my chest." His brow, now beaded with sweet, crinkled in disbelief as he reached out his trembling right arm.

It did not take long for Paul to grab him up in his arms and carry the man to his truck. He pulled away from the barn, leaving dust trails as he shifted into a higher gear.

The drive to Cape Fear Hospital was nearly twenty-five miles. There was no time to stop and tell Lottie or Pearl as he glanced through the fields toward the Scaggins home. .

In the years since the end of the war Jess had busied himself helping Paul with the tobacco. In fact, it had even been his idea to sell his cattle and plow under his own crops and plant it, joining his and Paul's land into one large tobacco field. They called their business JP Tobacco Sales. They were doing well.

Jess bought a new car, and gave his home a brand new paint job. Paul bought a new truck and together the men invested in a new tractor. One Thanksgiving the families piled the kids in the car and drove out to see Eli and Amy who fawned lavishly on the children and even followed them back to North Carolina for a long visit.

The tobacco business didn't make the families rich, but it made them a bit more comfortable to where they could afford a monthly trip to Wilmington to see a movie and to allow the women trips to the beauty salon. There was a sense of security; a feeling of accomplishment that came with working tobacco and life seemed not more pleasant, but less stressful for the working Scaggins and Rosell families.

By 1949 the missile base on the banks had dismantled and moved to the east coast of Florida. The narrow little island was released from all military control and once again people came there to fish and picnic as they had nearly a decade ago.

Seine fishing was still, to many families, a livelihood. And families and friends seemed to pick up right where they had left off in 1940.

Of course, everyone liked the pontoon bridge left behind by the military. It surely made it a lot easier to get over to the banks. But the bridge was not the only improvement made by the military – there was now a good road from the banks to Holly Ridge – and the buildings left behind by them would become useful homes and businesses to many. Men and some women took civil service jobs at nearby Camp Lejeune, making them more financially secure than their fathers before them who had relied solely on farming and fishing. Not long after all military left, a grocery store opened up in one of the vacated military buildings on the banks to accommodate the families moving to the island.

Jess had declared that the Scaggins family was not about to be left out of the development rush and so talk of opening a little restaurant at the banks become quite serious. It was no longer just a dream, now it was a true possibility. Already Jess and Paul had talked to Carl Burns about buying a little piece of property.

"It's got to be oceanfront. We've got to have a big plate glass window for people to look out of – so they can see the ocean while they dine," Pearl was adamant about this one particular thing.

Lottie emphasized the importance of building a patio outside where people could enjoy the ocean air. They all agreed that they needed a dance floor and place for musicians to play. This was going to be the island hot spot.

As for a name, many were suggested: JP's, Lottie's Oyster Roast, Jess's Oyster Roast, Pearl's Place and Paul's Place. Finally, as the family stood atop the dunes discussing just what to call their new business they noticed a large flock of sea gulls gathered around a carcass.

"Looks like some poor dolphin's been washed ashore. There's gotta be fifty gulls dining on 'im, "Jess chuckled. "Looks like they're having a mighty good meal there, ya think if the gulls flock to come here ..."

"Great place to eat," Paul said jokingly. They all looked at one another, nodding their heads simultaneously.

"Well, I guess it's settled then, Lottie shrugged, "The Sea Gull will be the name."

"But we ain't having dolphin on the menu," Jess laughed.

"I think it's a great name," Pearl ran down the dune, Frankie and little Josie following closely behind. Jess, Lottie and Paul slowly made their ways down also, and the group

stood with their backs to the ocean, gazing upward to
where their new restaurant would sit high upon the dunes.

"I was beginning to think it wasn't going to happen – that
it was only a dream," As Jess pushed gently against the bed
to straighten himself, he half smiled. "That's what dreams
coming true will do to you, take your breath away."

"Sweetie, you're just too stubborn to die now. You got a
good twenty years left in you," Lottie pulled her lips tight;
"you ain't leaving me now." She bent down to kiss her
husband's forehead.

Jess stayed in the hospital for two weeks before he came
home. Against the doctor's wishes he insisted that he could
recuperate at home just as well as in the hospital.

"After all, it was just a little heart attack. And I'm not
missing the building of my restaurant."

It was an exciting time as construction on the restaurant
began. Paul worked late into the evenings with Clarence
even coming by to lend a helping hand. He'd become quiet
and worked with his head held low, barely daring to look at
anyone. But he did come to work, and was usually at the

site before anyone else. Enid Abbott lent a hand as well, and a new man by the name of Bart Ralston, worked on all the plumbing fixtures. An ex GI, originally from New Jersey, he'd settled at the banks.

Clarence chipped in with painting and moving heavy equipment. All was not forgiven of Clarence, but it seemed that an effort was being made by all parties to get along and let bygones be bygones. He worked silently, speaking rarely unless spoken to. Unlike the old days, it seemed he never had a bad word to say about anything. He had become more compliant and much more humble since Josie's death. Since then he'd found himself not only friendless but with few patrons for his moonshine business. It had all but dried up, though he kept one small still in the woods near his home for those who didn't want to drive to the next wet county for their booze.

Paul commented often on how glad he was that the mouthy drunk had finally found his place, that he was no longer cock of the walk.

"As long as he keeps his mouth shut and doesn't start telling me how to do everything and bragging about all he thinks he's done, he can stick around. I don't give a damn," Paul commented to Jess, still uneasy about his father's presence.

"I guess I found a way to get out of all the hard work," Jess commented, propping himself up against the pillows. Once, the family drove Jess to the site where all the construction was going on. He nodded his head, then shook his head, then nodded again. "Okay. I've seen it. You can take me back home."

While Jess lay at home recuperating, it was Clarence who helped with the tobacco and who helped put the finishing touches on the restaurant. Paul waited for his father to begin scolding and demeaning him. He listened with pricked ears at every sound, practically wishing that Clarence would utter some derogatory phrase – giving him a reason to chase him off. But none ever came. It was as if he were a stranger coming off the highway, grateful for any work that would simply offer a plate of food in return.

"Boy, things sure have changed over here." Jess stepped from the backseat of the car as Frankie and Josie tumbled out after him. It was his first trip back to the banks after his heart attack. He stood in wonder at the nearly completed restaurant nestled in the dunes, "You near about got the Gull finished. Now all you need is a couple coats of paint..." Jess turned toward his wife, "And what color have you women decided *we* are going to paint her.?"

"Yella," both Lottie and Pearl chimed.

"Yellow? Why not pink or purple?" Jess added sarcastically, "What's wrong with white? Reflects the sun...cooler in the summer...easier to touch up," he nodded his head."

Lottie rolled her eyes at her husband, "Yellow...yellow...yellow. Got that?"

Paul echoed her words, "Got that, Jess? We're painting her yellow."

As he opened the door to the building, the group walked in and looked about at the tables and booths that had already been arranged, and then they walked out onto the patio and down the stairway to the beach.

Pointing northward toward the building set high in the dunes, Pearl leaned against Paul as they walked. "That was the officer's club. Remember? And over there behind it were the horse stables." She picked up the shoes the children had thrown on the sand and called for them to be careful. "Don't wander out of my sight!" "Seems like such a long time ago when the Army was here." She turned her attention to Jess.

"Yep, they left a lot of buildings... Rawl says some man's thinking of buying one of the barracks and making it into apartments." He snuggled close against Lottie, "we ought to buy up one of the old fire stations and make it our summer house," he laughed gently as he squeezed her shoulder.

"I'm not leaving my home, Mr. Scaggins. I'm too old to be starting all over again."

"There's land for sale all over the place, Lottie. They say they're going to *develop* it. More and more families are moving here every day." Jess grasped his wife's hand as they walked toward the dunes.

"Develop it? In to what?"

"A vacation destination, that's what I read in the Wilmington Morning Star. Said the banks are now called

Topsail Island and that this here part of it leading from Sears Landing is called Surf City."

Jess nodded his head, "Sounds okay. I know there's always been a lot of good surf fishing here. Not a bad name."

"Ron Butler moved over here and he's the one owns the grocery store. He and his wife Janie run it – open every day. Open on Sunday after twelve thirty. Going to be bustling like Myrtle Beach before long."

"You're going to take it easy from now on. No more lifting wood beams and banging nails. Hear me?" Lottie's eyebrow arched as she sternly gazed into Jess's eyes."

"Yes ma'am." Clicking his heels, Jess saluted his wife.

"No kidding Jess. All we need on the place is a good coat of paint. We've got just about everything else in place and if nothing goes wrong we'll have her opened by May."

"You are going to let me supervise, aren't you?"

"You can do more than that!" Lottie nudged Jess, "There's nothing wrong with you cleaning up and helping make meals...doctor said you could do some things, just don't overdo it."

"No strenuous labor." Pearl added, "We won't make you work evening rush hour."

"So you think there'll be an evening rush hour?"

Nodding his head, Paul spoke seriously, "You bet, this place is really going to grow. Rawl said they're building two fishing piers. One where the officer's club is and another there," he pointed in the opposite direction.

"It's going to really grow, Daddy."

"I hope not too much," Jess sighed.

As they walked slowly along the beach, Pearl moved to walk beside her father and search the shore for shells along with Frankie and Josie. Lottie and Paul walked ahead at a quicker pace toward the old officer's club.

"It's been really hard on him, not being able to get out and work with you at the barn or coming over here and help build The Gull," A wave washed gently across Lottie's feet and they sank as she waded into the reaching water to retrieve a whelk. "I guess we're just getting old. I'm not as quick as I used to be either."

Wrapping his arm around her shoulder, Paul turned his head to look at Jess and Pearl as they helped the children pick shells from the shore. "He's always been such a help to me Lottie. It's hard to see him not able to do the things he loves."

"He's got good days and bad days. Just like everybody else, I guess. But he seems to be getting stronger. I know his momma, by the time she was his age, was bed ridden. Within a year she'd died. I wished he wouldn't get like her, but you know what Jess has always said about wishing."

Holding out both hands, palms upward, Paul laughed as he recited what he had heard Jess say many times before, "You *can wish in one hand and shit in the other and see which one fills up the fastest.*"

"Humph," A grin crossed her lips as she nodded her head, "He was at the hospital for two weeks and spent over a month laid up at home. He says it seems like the whole world just passed him on by. It eats him up to think that he can't do the things he used to. I'm just so afraid he's going to start feeling like he can go back to working like he used to and then, well...."

"We're here for you, Lottie. Whenever you need us just call. I know Pearl goes over to your house nearly every day, but, just the same. We're here for you."

"You sure are lucky," Eying the cotton dress Pearl had put on, then tugging at his own jeans, Paul pulled Pearl close and pushed her gently to the bed.

"What are you doing? The kids are right outside the door." She grabbed a handful of his blond hair and tugged gently. "Come on now, if we're going, we better get moving."

"I still say it's not fair that you get to wear a dress when it's hot and I'm stuck with these," He tugged once again at his pants.

"You can always borrow one of mine, you know. I can feel the breeze all the way up," Pearl flounced the skirt of her dress and tossed her short locks across her face.

Paul rolled his eyes, "I think I'm going down to Boom Town and buy me a pair of those Bermuda shorts."

"Why don't you just cut your pants off around the knees? Everybody else does it."

267

"Where's the scissors?" Sliding the jeans from his body while Pearl reached into the bedside table, Paul reached his hand beneath her skirt to caress her thigh.

"Paul! Stop it! The kids." She laughed as she sat next to him on the bed and snipped along a make believe line above the knee of the pants leg.

"There you go," Tossing the cut offs to her husband, Pearl moved quickly toward the doorway,
"Hurry up now, the kids are waiting outside."

The rear of the car bounced hard against the pontoon bridge as they drove onto it. Paul looked in his rearview mirror, hoping not to see his tailpipe lying on the planks. Pearl looked straight ahead at the new buildings that were now in place at the top of the dunes. They stood like a gateway to the Atlantic. Pop Jones's Pavilion, the most recent to open, offered cold drinks and potato chips along with an assortment of beach toys, umbrellas and rafts. Beneath the building were showers and lockers where swimmers could clean up after a day on the beach. Across the way was the Sandpiper, it did not offer quite the assortment of beach paraphernalia, but they served hamburgers and hot dogs. Paul parked in front of Pop's and the family walked the stairs to the dunes. Already a few umbrellas were perched in the sand; a few swimmers had ventured into the still cool water.

Paul pushed the rented umbrella deep into the sand and opened it, Pearl spread out the blanket; placing shells at the corners to keep the breeze from blowing the blanket about. "Okay, here's a pail and shovel for you Jo and one for you too, Frankie."

As the children dug into the gritty sand, Paul instructed from the blanket just how to go about making a sandcastle. Pearl half listened, grinning to herself as she opened to the page of the book she'd been reading.

"Can't wait to see you in that new swim suit you got." Paul laid his head in Pearl's lap and closed his eyes against the sun.

Pearl smoothed his windblown hair away from his eyes, "Uh huh," she said as she continued to read.

"You look soooo sexy. It's a two piece isn't it?"

"Yes," Cooing softly as she turned the page, Pearl slid a seductive glance toward her husband. "Maybe in a couple of weeks I'll put it on, the water's still a little cold for me." As Pearl turned another page of her book she continued, "Sure was nice of Momma and Daddy to work the Gull so we could have a day off...it's been a long time since I've had a picnic on the beach."

"Not much going on today. But you just wait until after Memorial Day and when the kids get out of school. I bet you it takes off like a rocket." Paul propped himself up on his elbows, turning to Pearl, "Didn't I tell you this place was going to be something. It isn't even summer yet and we have all kinds of business."

"All those fishermen want a place to eat."

"Their wives and kids want a nice place to go into and get out of the sun...you know, if we do well this summer I think we ought to get a couple of those air conditioners to put in the windows. "

"But that will block the view of the ocean."

"Yeah... maybe we can ..."

Pearl could see the wheels turning in Paul's head. He was thinking, planning. She loved to watch as he dreamed. It excited her. He always came up with the best ideas, like the sprinkler system he had designed for Lottie's flower garden. It seemed there was no end to his dreams to better his surroundings. He had even mentioned buying one of the old barracks and renovating for apartments.

Before the tobacco farm, Paul had seemed so compliant, but once he got started making good money for his labor it seemed he couldn't stop. His lung condition did keep him from long hours of manual labor, but it didn't keep him from other tasks that were less strenuous. He hired hands and even began relying on Clarence to manage part of the tobacco business. Paul's interest now was on the Gull. He talked about expanding, building an arcade next to the restaurant or buying the space across the road to put in a miniature golf course. Pearl was proud of her husband and eager to share his dreams.

As he lay his head down once again on her lap, Pearl shook her head in disbelief as she heard her husband's gentle snoring. Not even the clanging and banging of construction on the fishing pier, not fifty yards away, could keep him awake. *Yes, it is all changing* Pearl thought to herself as she smiled. So much had changed in the last ten years. She liked it and she liked her life. It was nice having the little bridge to drive across, even though it sometimes broke down. And it was nice to have a grocery store and restaurant at the banks, even though she had packed her own basket today. She liked the idea of having a restaurant. It had been fun to pick out the yellow checkered table cloths with Lottie. They had hung netting from the walls with glass buoys and shells decorating it. Japanese lanterns hung throughout the place; she'd seen them at the Paradise Club in Holly Ridge during the war. It had been such a fancy place where big time singers performed. For her small restaurant, that would have been too much, she loved the local combos playing at the Gull. It was perfect for the island. It wasn't fancy, but it was like she had always envisioned a beach restaurant to be. She swelled with pride thinking of all the hard work she and Paul had put into it. The long wooden bar he had made was the most exotic thing in the Gull. Having taken a few of Jess's ideas about scrolling and beveled edges, the bar was definitely one of a kind. It sat in the far left part of the building, tucked away and was to be used mainly in the winter months when oysters were in season. The juke box was essential of the restaurant too, since everyone liked music. It was placed near the patio door where music could be heard outside when the door was kept open in the summer months.

271

Pop's Pavilion held a square dance every Saturday night, so the Gull had dances once a month on Fridays. They even tried a few bands that played the new music – rock and roll. It was fun to dance to. Even Paul enjoyed it and they danced something she had seen a few times by folks at the Lumina in Wrightsville – the Bop.

She liked the idea of an oceanfront restaurant where she could watch the waves come to shore, where she could watch her children play, and where she could watch the tourists that most certainly would flock to Surf City in the coming years. Pearl gazed down at her sleeping husband; his light complexioned skin was already turning pink. She roused him to wake, "Sweetie, you're going to get a sun burn. You should have worn your hat."

"Huh?" Rising, Paul leaned to kiss his wife's shaded face. "No, I should have stayed in the shade like you ... where's the kids?" He searched the shore, then nodded as he spotted Jo and Frank patting the sides of a sandcastle, drizzling wet sand along the sides to make it stay in place. They had even begun digging a moat.

Pearl opened the basket and called for the children to come eat their lunch. Afterwards, she suggested they take a little walk northward toward the old officer's club.

From the stone patio of the club Jay stood watching as the family neared. He couldn't make out just yet the faces, but the walk of the woman seemed familiar. Her dress held tight against her body. Pearl came to his mind.

The two children ran to and fro, from the dunes to the water, splashing one another. He could hear their laughter now, and the faces of the man and woman became clear as well.

"Who's that?" Paul nodded toward the club and the man standing there."He's been watching us for quite a while."

Shrugging her shoulders, Pearl raised her hand to her eyes to shade them. *It could not be. This man looked so much older than the Jay she remembered.* She watched as he made his way down the staircase and walked slowly toward them. She noticed a slight limp. A smile came upon her lips as he neared.

"Hello!" Jay looked at the couple, from one to the other, but his gaze settled on Pearl.

"Jay," Paul reached his hand to shake Jay's hand. "Good to see you."

Pearl reached her hand out as well. "Yes, it is good to see you." She noticed the deep scar above his eye; it nearly split his eyebrow in half. He seemed smaller than she remembered him, but he still was handsome. His dark blue eyes glimpsed hers intermittently, searchingly as he spoke to Paul.

"And these?" Motioning toward the children, he stooped to reach out to the little girl. "What's your name?"

Jo held tight to Paul's leg and peeped out from behind, eyeing Jay with curiosity.

"This is Jo – Josie," Paul could feel his heart beat, "And this is Frankie," He reached out to the boy and pulled him close, "shake hands with Mr. Jay. He's an old friend of your mother's and mine."

"Nice to meet you," Holding out his hand, Jay forced a smile to his face. "I knew your momma and daddy a long time ago. We used to come over here, just where we are now."

As he rose, Jay could feel his breath come in short gasps, he felt the earth shake beneath him. "Guess I'm out of breath from all that walking." He nodded toward his weak leg and half smiled. "I can't do things like I used to."

"Let's sit down," Paul's voice sounded stern as he nodded toward the old officer's club. "I could use a rest myself." As he motioned toward the shore Paul tousled Frankie's wavy locks, "You two go on now and find me some shark's teeth." He leaned against the concrete bulwark and folded his arms. "I'm glad you made it back... heard you had a rough time of it over there."

"Yeah, those camps aren't all they're cracked up to be," Jay chuckled as he straightened his leg for comfort.

Pearl searched Jay's face as the two men spoke, looking for some recognition of the past. *Where had it gone? Where were the bright sparkling eyes that had shown so lovingly on her?* Was this dark haired handsome man with the sad eyes a reflection of someone a young girl dreamed? She nodded, recognizing Paul's defensive stance; it conjured her own defense for the man she loved now, Paul.

274

Jay half listened as Pearl talked about the tobacco farm and she and Paul's restaurant, about Miss Josie's passing and Jess's poor health.

Trying to keep up with all the information that seemed to fly from Pearl's and Paul's lips, Jay's mind sped in circles as he studied their faces, he searched for the girl he had left in 1942. Was this her? And Paul, the docile and quiet young man had filled out. His eyes held a confidence and his stance a sense of security. Jay said the only thing he could think of as he heard Paul speaking.

"And how is that impertinent cousin of yours, Ellie?"

"Oh, she's the same old Ellie." Paul shook his head and laughed.

"You know she married that boy from Florida."

"Really?" Jay could feel his heart beat loudly. "She still living there?"

"For now," Pearl giggled. "Last I heard she was getting a separation from Chuck…you never know with her."

"Old Smellie Ellie. Never could see her married. She have any kids?"

"A little girl, Monroe." Pearl responded, and lowered her head, instantly lifting it high to gaze directly into Jay's eyes. He held her gaze for a moment then turned to Paul.

"Can't imagine Ellie having kids either."

"Well, you know she's coming for a visit in a few days. Maybe you can catch up on how she's doing. That is if you are going to be around for a while. I know she'd love to see you.

Jay's mind raced back and forth as he searched Pearl's face for familiar emotions. He wanted to remind Pearl of the days before the war, the love he had...still had for her. How it had kept him going throughout his long tormenting period in the Nazi camp. But it was evident- the trust and love between she and Paul was almost palpable. The way they touched one another when referring to the other's ideas for designing the restaurant, the way Paul gazed at her when she turned to speak to *him,* tilting her head flirtatiously to smile at her husband. He could feel the strong ties between the two - almost taste the love ...he cried out in his mind, silently masking the devastating feeling of loss.

Lost in that place, Jay woke to a high pitched squeal as Frankie cried out, "Daddy, Daddy, I found the biggest shark's tooth ever," Jay turned as the others did, excited for the boy and his new find. *The dark hair, deep blue eyes...are they mine? The name?* Fleeting glimpses of the day he had told Pearl of his middle name speed through his mind. He looked again at the boy. Yes, he could see Pearl in the features – high cheek bones, the shape of the boy's lips. But... there was something... And it struck him with near certainty.... *This is my son....*

Kneeling down in the sand, Jay reached to tousle the boy's dark hair – he looked up at Paul and Pearl. Yes, it was confirmed by the look in their eyes.

"Son...Frankie...that's a mighty fine tooth," Jay smiled at the boy, "My, you're so big, I bet you put your Momma to task every day. Don't you?"

Frankie put the black tooth in Jay's hand, "You can keep it, you're nice. He can keep it, can't he Daddy?" Frankie looked up to his parents, "Mommy?"

"I tell you what," Jay struggled to stand up as Paul reached out his hand to help him, "That's such an impressive tooth, that I think you should give it to your mom and dad for safe keeping.

The three adults stood speechless, the sound of the waves washing to shore making the silence almost deafening.

Pearl grasped the outstretched hand of her son and lowered her head. She took a breath and looked both men in the face.

"I know Momma would love to see you, Jay. Won't you come for dinner?"

Jay heard himself, "That would be great, thanks."

CHAPTER TWENTY-TWO

Jess pushed his empty plate away and leaned back in the chair. He did not like the idea that Jay had been invited to stay for dinner. He didn't like that the young man had even come back into their lives. Frankie resembled him in so many ways that he was certain that if Jay stayed around for very long someone would see the resemblance. Jess eyed Jay slowly . . . he had changed. Of course, nearly ten years had aged him and it was obvious that he had physical scars from the war, but there was something more. He didn't have the confidence he once had. His eyes didn't hold the same eagerness.

Jess felt no bitterness toward Jay, but the difference between the old Jay and this one was that the old Jay would not have come; he would have been too polite.

"So, I hear you were in a prisoner of war camp. How have you been getting along since then?" Jess asked.

A wave of nostalgia swept across Jay. Jess had offered only a nod and handshake when he first stepped onto the screened porch. It wasn't like he had remembered such coolness. Before the war Jess had been like a father to him.

Jay answered him reservedly, "Yes sir, I was in a couple of camps, they kept moving me around, especially at first….and now… well sir, I've been doing okay. Been staying with my parents, but soon I plan to get me a little place of my own.

"Um hum," Jess looked sternly at the man.

It was not hard for Jay to know what was on his mind, it was obvious – Jess did not want him there. The pain of seeing Pearl so in love with Paul and their strong undeniable bond as a family had been such a painful realization. Yet he had no remorse; he was happy for their happiness. Jay felt Jess's gaze on him and a flashback of the times they worked the cattle together, fished together, and the encouraging words Jess had spoken about Pearl swept over him, but it left as quickly as it had appeared and he felt his heart sink in his chest. It was somehow the final blow. With Jess's disapproval, there was certainly no hope for a future with or near the Scaggins family.

Rising from the table, Jess's eyes searched the room, then came back to Jay's, "bring my dessert out here on the porch, sweetie," He nodded toward Lottie.

Lottie sliced a large piece of pie and strode toward the breezeway, returning in moments, mouthing an "I'm sorry," as she shrugged her shoulders. Jess's overt display of disapproval left an uncomfortable feeling with the rest of the family. Lottie especially felt embarrassed and apologized to Jay for her husband's behavior," Oh Jay, he just hasn't been the same since he had his heart attack."

"He had a heart attack?" Sliding his chair away from the table, his face became a composite of disbelief. "I had no idea. When did this happen?"

"Paul was there at the tobacco barn when it happened. He took Daddy right to the hospital." Pearl reached to caress her husband's shoulder. She was so very proud of him. But she too felt badly for Jay, though quite understood her father's reaction to his presence. Ambivalent feelings raced through her head. Why had she asked him to dinner? *Curiosity,* she thought. *The feeling, what used to be, is just not there. It's gone.*

She had often wondered how she would react if she ever saw Jay again. She had not expected this. She had considered she might swoon in his presence as she had recalled their love long ago. That time felt like a dream and now she knew it was all behind her –puppy love, they called it – she told herself this, then felt the ache in her heart. No it was not puppy love, it had been real love. Frankie was the proof of that. But it was not as real as her love for Paul.

The realization that she was finally over Jay - that she was truly in love with her husband hit Pearl like a rogue wave and a smile came to her lips. Pearl could hardly contain her happiness. It was truly over and oh how happy she was that Paul was her husband. Yes, Jay had been wonderful. He had been a love she would never forget. But watching him - looking at him now... she only wished him happiness. She felt her face smiling and noticed the puzzled look on Jay's face, "Oh, Daddy's been out of the hospital for quite a while now, about four...nearly five months."

"The doctor says he's got some good years ahead of him if he'll just take it easy and lay off all the pork he's been eating – he tries to sneak some at the restaurant, but we watch him closely."

Jay smiled as he recalled the chatter, long ago, of someday building a restaurant on the beach. "So, y'all finally got your dream. I remember how you used to sit around and talk about having a business."

"It's wonderful," Pearl's eyes lit up. Paul built most of it and we finally opened it up a few months ago."

"We're not doing too badly, considering." Paul leaned in, explaining the details of how the building was constructed. Pearl and Lottie added details of how they had decorated the Gull. Their enthusiasm was obvious as they described the tables and booths, dance floor and menu items.

With his arms folded behind his head, Paul leaned back in his chair and grinned. Though he felt a sort of pity for Jay, the bravado in his voice was noticeable; it surprised him. "Yep, it's all come together like we planned...like *they* planned." He chuckled, watching Jay's noticeable reaction. *Why do I still have this feeling of rivalry? I've got everything he ever wanted*, Paul thought.

Changing the subject back to Jess's condition, Paul explained how Jess sometimes felt lost when he wasn't able to participate in the harder chores around the place. "But I think he'll get used to it."

Jay looked toward the porch, "Maybe I should go out and talk to him. I just…"

" Oh, just let him be out there…he'll pout for a while and then come on back in here," Lottie settled herself at the kitchen chair and leaned in to speak," Now, What have you been doing down in Texas since the war ended?" Lottie handed Jay a large slice of pie.

"Well, ma'am…Miss Lottie, it took me a while to get back into the swing of things, if that's what you call it. I near about lost my leg and that took a while too… you know, getting used to not being able to do things like I used to."

"While he was in the Navy, Paul's ship got bombed."

Paul shot a disappointed glance toward Lottie.

"I'm sorry dear," she rubbed his shoulder gently. "I know you don't like talking about it, but… all this *did* happen."

"It's all right, tell me about it." Jay eyes sternly searched Paul's.

"We got hit by six Jap planes. They came flying in and started bombing the hell out of us. Just out of nowhere, it seemed like. I was one of the lucky ones."

"You catch one?"

"Paul lost half of his left lung, some shrapnel hit him."

"I've got good days and bad days – like you. Most are good though. It's just that some days I really can't do too much…have to take a break every half hour or so. But I ain't complaining. I got it a lot better than most." He felt pity for

Jay, with a gimp leg and scarred face and no doubt a torn heart. *Why had he come back?*

Jay nodded in agreement as he started to rise. "I'm glad you made it back, Paul. You always were a good man, but I guess I ought to be getting on back, now."

"No need for you to go. You're welcome to stay a while longer," Paul reached, motioning for Jay to remain seated, "You can't leave before Ellie gets here; she's coming up from Florida in a couple days. You know how she is and if she found out she'd missed you, there'd be no living with her."

"Ah, who could forget smelly Ellie," thoughts of the days before the war filled Jay's mind. "They need to invent a repellent for that one."

Pearl chuckled nervously. *Just why does Paul want Jay to stay around.* She glanced to her mother who seemed relaxed with the whole situation. Jay's arrival did not appear to bother her in the least.

"Stay for a few days. You're not in any hurry to get back are you? We got a spare room here at the house," Lottie leaned in to whisper, "And I could use the help with him," she nodded toward Jess who sat motionless in the rocking chair gazing toward the sound.

"You sure?"

As she smoothed her dress beneath her, Lottie sat closely next to Jay, "We all might be able to heal some old wounds. Huh?"

The slam of the car door startled Jay as he rose from the sofa where he had been resting. Without having to see her, he knew it was Ellie. The wind seemed to pick up and the wind chimes on the porch tinkled wildly. *She always did cause a commotion when she came around.*

"Hey!" Ellie bounded up the steps to the porch, "I'm here!" She entered the living room where Jay stood with his hands firmly on his hips.

"Well, I'll be. If it ain't my favorite stink." Jay rolled his eyes, "come on over here Smelly Ellie. He held his arms wide to receive her with a warm hug. "You look just as pretty as I remembered and from what I hear, just as ornery as ever."

"You better believe it, bub." She tossed her dark hair to the side and released herself from the embrace, then stepped back to look him over, "You don't look so bad yourself. Even that scar makes you look kind of dashing."

"That was the exact reason why I got it too, just to make myself look dashing to women." As he smiled he moved toward the breezeway. "Lottie's in the kitchen fixing up some lunch. I'm sure she'll be glad to see you."

"Ha, that'll be the day." Ellie smirked, "I just stopped at Pearl's and she said you were here for a visit. So how's that going?"

"It's interesting," Jay leaned against the window sill of the breezeway. "Everyone's been awfully kind to me, but I hate to see Jess the way he is. I never imagined anything could get to that man."

As Ellie lowered her eyes and sighed, "Yeah, I hate to see it too. *He* was always real nice to me."

Holding a plate in each hand, Lottie stood at the breezeway, "y'all going to stand there all day?" Scowling at Ellie, Lottie reached a plate toward her, "I heard you drive up like a whirlwind, Miss Ellie. Just how fast do you think you were driving…in my yard?" She motioned for Jay to take a plate, "Chicken salad sandwiches. Hope you like them." She walked down the steps, leading the way toward the picnic table. "Come on out here, it's pretty outside today, nice breeze blowing." Lottie poured ice tea in the glasses. "So, how are things with you, Ellie? I hear you're getting a divorce."

"Not a divorce, we're just separating for a while." She looked at Jay, raised her eyebrows and sighed.

"Is he running around on you?"

"Miss Lottie!

"Are you running around on him?"

Jay watched the two women. Both strong willed. Both used to saying what they pleased. It seemed as if the years had only made them more comfortable with their dislike for one another.

"Miss Lottie, how can you ask me such a thing?"

"It's just that you've always been so *friendly,* Ellie. I don't know what to think."

"If I have been *friendly* with other men, it's none of your business, for one thing. But that is not the reason we are separating."

Shrugging her shoulders, Lottie cast a questioning glance her way. "Pray, do tell."

Ellie pushed the half eaten sandwich away, "Look, I know you've never liked me."

"You've always got a plan, Ellie. It seems the wheels in your head are always turning with something to benefit you."

"I'm leaving," As Ellie rose, Jay grabbed her arm.

"Hey! You just got here. Sit down. You two are talking like I'm not even here and I came all the way from Texas just to see you."

"Sorry Jay, but I should have known better than to come over here. We always end up with some kind of argument...unless Pearl's here. And besides, you just always seemed like family anyway."

"I guess this much hasn't changed. You two arguing is very reminiscent of the past."

"Ooh...reminiscent...big word." Ellie licked her finger and poked Jay on the shoulder, "Sssssssssssssss, too hot to handle."

Lottie rolled her eyes.

"I don't understand this *thing* that has always gone on between y'all...not liking one another, and I don't care what it is. But your daughter..." he nodded toward Lottie, "seems to think that the world would quit revolving if anything happened to either of you. Now sit down and quit sniping at one another."

Sliding her leg across the bench of the table, Ellie settled herself then looked directly into Lottie's eyes, "Yeah, Miss Lottie. Why have you always hated me so much?"

"I never hated you Ellie. I disliked your arrogance. I saw for years how you put my baby down, said cruel things to her. You're a mother. How does it make you feel when someone says something mean to Monroe? Or do you even care. You never bring her with you when you visit. How can you bear to be away from her for so long?"

Ellie lifted her head, tears filled her eyes, but her firm jaw indicated that none would fall. "I'm not good enough for *them*. From the day she was born they've pushed me out - treated me like I was nothing. Whatever I do with Monroe is always wrong. They correct me; make me feel stupid in front of Monroe. When I wanted to nurse her, Mrs. Bridge made fun of me – the whole family did... until I agreed to give her a bottle. *That's* why I came up here so soon after she was born. They didn't want me around. Took her right out of my lap and stuck that damn bottle in her mouth."

Lottie looked sternly at Ellie, "Why don't you stand up to them?"

"Fat chance that does any good. I may as well be one of their poodles with the rhinestone collars." She moved behind the oak tree near the table, turning her back to dab at her swollen eyes. "Then they're always taking her off, buying her things...and leaving me out of it. It's like I provided a child for their son and now they're done with me. I may as well not exist. They've taken my child away from me." She turned her head to dab a laced kerchief at her eyes.

"Why don't you just leave? Bring Monroe with you and leave all that behind."

"Take her away from her father? That family would have the law all over me. You don't know how powerful they are in Pasco County… and in the state. And now, it's too late. She wants to be with them, prefers it. She ignores me when I try to discipline her and goes running to Mrs. Bridge."

"Let her go."

Both Ellie and Lottie looked astonished when they heard Jay's words.

"Let her go," Jay repeated, "If Chuck is not backing you up. *Does* he support you?"

Ellie shook her head no, "He never says a word. Never says anything in my defense. And when I do say something to him about the way his mother cuts me out of everything he just says that Monroe is her only grandchild. That I should let the old biddy spoil her."

"It's not going to change, Ellie… it'll only get worse. Then you'll end up hating everyone. Leave. Your daughter will be well taken care of and she won't end up hating you."

"What makes you think you know everything about this?" Lottie's accusatory tone shocked Ellie.

Jay sat unruffled as he lit a cigarette, "I just know." His eyes drew toward Lottie's.

"Let me have one of those," Ellie leaned into Jay's cupped hands that held the lighted match.

"I know," Jay repeated, his eyes still gazing into Lottie's; she lowered hers. "I've seen enough to know that you can't fight against a bigger foe you have to either go along or retreat." He paused for a moment as the women listened intently.

"If you go along Ellie, let them continue belittling you in front of Monroe, you become everything they say you are, but if you retreat, you're not there to be diminished – they can't hurt you. And when Monroe grows up and learns the ways of the world, you may have a chance to get her back. Anyway, that's my advice." Jay leaned back, then flippantly added, "But, on the other hand, Ellie. You've always been a strong and formidable person. Maybe you can handle the Bridges. Maybe you could go back there and tell them the way it's going to be … that Monroe is your daughter and not theirs." He grinned at her, "Can you do that?"

"What goes around, comes around Ellie," Lottie slid a stern glance toward her."

"And just what is that supposed to mean?

"The way you treat people in your life always comes back to you. The selfishness – think about it."

"So you think that since I've been so selfish in my life that now I'm getting what I deserve. Is that it?"

"I think it comes back to *everybody*. The Bridge family will eventually pay for their selfishness. We all pay for our sins…one way or another."

Ellie rubbed her furrowed brow, "I have a head ache – all this talk about sinning and selfishness. I wish I was like you Lottie – I wish I could see the future."

Lottie rolled her eyes.

"I can't imagine leaving my little girl. But oh, how I want to tear into those people. Every day they tear me down-right in front of her, over the silliest stuff, like how I chew my food, or what I decide to wear. Just the other day I told Monroe she couldn't have this little cat she saw at the pet store in Tampa. Well, Miss Cassie Lou Bridge – *Meme*, took her right in that shop and bought it for her. You should have seen the look Monroe gave me when she came out of there. Chuck didn't do a damn thing, shrugged his shoulders, that's all."

"You got a problem, that's for sure. You can stay there and be just as sweet and nice and kind as you can be…. Or you can try to stand up to them . . . or you can leave. Which one will it be? Asked Jay.

"There's no way on earth Ellie's going to hold her tongue," Lottie shook her head.

Tossing the cigarette butt to the ground, Ellie stretched her foot out to crush it. "I came up here to think. I wanted Monroe to come, but after Mrs. Bridge got a hold of her it was no use."

Lottie rose and gathered the plates, "I'll take care of this. And Ellie, you have a lot of thinking to do."

Jay sighed as he heard the water from the kitchen run and the clink of dishes. As he pushed himself up to rise from the table he reached out his hand, "Come on Smellie, let's take a walk."

"Never did like you calling me that."

"Who would?" Jay smiled broadly as winked at her. "Have you spoken to Pearl about this?"

"Um hum. Pearl is such a good friend. Makes me wish I hadn't been so mean to her growing up. But we're just two different kinds of people, Jay."

"No Joke."

Sliding him an exaggerated glare, Ellie continued. "Don't tell her this, but I always thought she was so smart, so level headed. I'm not. I know that. I'm flighty and fickle."

"I think you know yourself pretty good," Jay chuckled, "But you always speak your mind. That's what baffles me about why you don't put those Bridges in their place."

"Oh, believe me. I have a couple of times. But they play dirty...a lot dirtier than I can. They've got loads of money and power in that part of the country and believe me what they want to happen, happens. Took me a couple of years to realize that I needed to keep my mouth shut...hold my tongue."

"Looks like you held that tongue pretty tight," Jay glanced at the gold charm bracelet on her wrist.

"I've got a few bobbles out of keeping my mouth shut, but ..." She jerked the bracelet from her wrist throwing it as far as she could toward the sound. "I'm tired of it. I'm tired of keeping my mouth shut, tired of being second fiddle...third fiddle."

"You being third fiddle? That must have been hard," Jay chuckled again.

"No fooling, Jay. It is pure hell being around those people. Chuck does not stand up in my defense at all. And whatever his mother and father say, he does. We had plans at first to buy this little house up around Mulberry, about thirty miles away. Well, they put an end to that. We live about a mile away from them and every day, *every day* they come over to our house, just pop in unannounced, wanting to take us out to dinner, take us to the movies, or some other kind of treat. It's all about the money." Ellie cocked her head to the side and grinned. "Don't get me wrong, I like money, but hell, that's all they think about. It comes before everything. The right thing to do...according to them...is what gets you the most money - never seen anything like it."

"I'm surprised Ellie, I thought you were one of the world's greatest lovers of money," Jay's snide tone obviously took her aback as she fell quiet and moved a bit away from his side.

"Sorry, but as I remember you always did like to have expensive things."

"I still do. But there is such a thing as manners. There are some things you just don't do. Believe me, there is *nothing* that family won't do for a buck."

"What does Pearl say about all this?"

"She suggested she and Paul drive down there some time and pretend that we're going to take a scenic trip to the Everglades and just not come back."

"Sounds like a plan. Do you think Paul would go for it too? I mean, will Paul support something like this that Pearl would cook up? "

"Paul would do anything for her, but it wouldn't work. That family's got strings, I'm telling you. They know the sheriff really well and there are pictures in that house of Mr. and Mrs. Bridge with the last three governors."

"Did Pearl have any other suggestions?"

"Not really. I know she would love to have us up here, though."

"Has Pearl ever seen Monroe?"

"No," Ellie shook her head and crossed her arms.

"I guess you and Pearl write a lot of letters and talk about things."

"Tsk," Ellie clicked her tongue. She noticed the eagerness in his eyes, "That's the third time you've asked about Pearl, Jay, if you want to talk about her just say so."

Pausing to rub his brow, Jay tried to calm himself.

Ellie turned to him, touching his arm, "Jay, that girl is the most happy person I've ever seen. Paul would swim across that ocean for her if he had to, and she'd do the same for him."

"They looked happy. I can see it in their faces - the trust and closeness." Jay hung his head low against his chest.

293

"She's all I ever thought about and now, it's all just slipped away."

"Why did you come back here?"

"Just one last time. I just wanted to make sure before…"

"Before what?"

"Well, there's this girl back home in Texas. She'd make a good wife; loves me like the sun…"

"You love her?"

"Yeah…but there was something about Pearl and me. Something you just don't forget. I figured after all this time that she, more than likely, would be married, but you never know. My mom told me she wrote to her a few years back and told her that she never heard back from her, so we all figured it was over. Mom was pretty adamant about me not hounding her. Especially after Dad died, I think she just wanted to keep me home…didn't want to lose me either. But I just couldn't forget about Pearl. I wanted to make sure. I didn't want to have any doubts."

"What's your girl's name?"

"Feona."

"Pretty name."

"Pretty girl."

"Jay, you go to her. You have a happy life and forget about Pearl. She and Paul fit together so well. And that boy, Frankie . . ."

"I didn't know, honest. There was just no way I could have known."

"So you figured it out, huh?"

"I thought so...first time I saw him, and that dark hair. He's got my eyes too. And then the way Paul was so protective over him...I suspected. And the way Jess acted the other night at the dinner table. He was just as cold to me as could be."

"Well, you're messing with his little Pearly White, goody two shoes. What did you expect? He doesn't want to see anything go wrong with her life. And I will tell you Jay, I'm envious as hell. She's got everything anybody could want. Wish I had it so good. You don't need to be messing things up.

"I'm not," Jay lowered his head and drew his shoulders in, "I wouldn't hurt her or that little boy for all the gold in the world...wouldn't hurt Paul either."

"Like you told me, leave him. Leave it alone. It won't help anybody if that boy knows about you. And if you like I'll keep you current with his life...send you a picture now and then."

"That would be nice." Jay paused, he could feel the salty breeze on his skin - he felt another tie with the past fade away.   "Did she ever talk to you about me being the boy's father?"

Ellie leaned her head back, laughing, "She doesn't even know I know. As a matter of fact, I wasn't sure until Frankie was about six months old and that dark curly hair of his cropped out of his head. Before that I just thought that she and Paul were fooling around right after you left. You know she was puny acting after you took off. I figured she turned to him in a *moment of weakness.* I imagine Miss Lottie birthed that baby."

Jay bit his lip, imagining a birth and Miss Lottie – Pearl and no doctor. "She's an amazing woman."

"You talking about Pearl or Lottie?

"Both."

"You're right. I always was envious of this family." Leaning against Jay's shoulder, Ellie grinned, "They really are good people."

"Are you becoming a woman with a conscious? First I find out that you actually have scruples, and now I understand that you're not using this information about Frankie to taunt Pearl."

I guess that despite all the Bridge's meanness and outright cruelty, I've learned a couple of things..."

"Yeah. What?"

"What real friends are."

As he nodded his head in agreement, Jay wrapped his arm around Ellie's shoulder. "Seems some people are just cut out to have all the blessings."

"Yeah, sometimes I wonder if it's all in the name.

"Pearl." Jay's eyes pleaded sadly with Ellie's, she could see the heartbreak in them. The crack in his voice echoed it as well. She reached out to smooth his unruly hair.

That evening after the children had been put to bed, Pearl and Paul, Jess and Lottie, and Jay gathered to discuss

Frankie. There was no mention of the relationship between Pearl and Jay, the night they made love, or any discussion about Jay's interment in the prisoner of war camp. It was mainly understood among all that the past was the past and that there was no reason to question it or bring it up. It was what it was.

Before any questions could be raised about whether Jay would be a part of Frankie's life, he suggested that it would be best if the boy never knew who he was. "Maybe every few years or so I'll visit, if curiosity gets the better of me. But I think it's best if I stay away. Paul is his rightful daddy. But if you ever need anything, anything at all – please let me know."

Jay also shared his plans to marry Feona and how he hoped to get on with his life and how he only wished he could be half as happy as Paul and Pearl.

That night as he lay in Pearl's old room at the Scaggins home, he cried. He cried for his lost love, his lost son and his lost life. He vowed that he would never do anything to disrupt Frankie's life, never to meddle.

As Pearl and Paul held each other in their bed, they did not sleep, but gazed into each other's eyes, fully aware that they were truly blessed.

CHAPTER TWENTY-THREE

The Sea Gull Restaurant was situated about a quarter mile north of the old Officer's club and sat comfortably in the dunes overlooking the Atlantic. Just as Pearl wanted, the tables cloths were yellow checkered; she'd made them herself. The sugar bowls, salt and pepper shakers and napkin holders were situated in the center of each table and booth. Four booths lined the far wall and a juke box stood in the corner close to the bar and patio door.

As discussed, Paul hired extra help for the farm and started fishing more to provide fresh catch for the restaurant. Clarence went with him often. Bent with age, he had become quiet and remorseful in his loneliness. He no longer worked his still and spent most of his time puttering around the tobacco barn or fishing with his son. On Paul's bad days, when he tired quickly, Clarence pulled his weight and then some, praising his son for giving up half a lung for his country.

Business was good at the Sea Gull the first year it was open. Folks from Holly Ridge, Sloop Point, Verona and even

Jacksonville found the ocean front restaurant to be cozy and accommodating. The food was simple yet delicious – "If you cook seafood too long or with too much breading you cook the good right out of it" – so Lottie had said time and again. She helped in the kitchen, preparing and cooking the food, and often Jess sat on the patio wrapping silverware or filling salt and pepper shakers. On occasion he joined in the banter with the customers, recalling the days when Surf City was known simply as the banks.

The second year the Sea Gull was open for business, it boomed. Weekends were crowded and Pearl hired extra help to wash dishes and wait on tables.

Ellie came up from Florida to live permanently after what she called a nasty divorce. "I swear I tried for nearly two years; I've been kissing ass – both cheeks," her eyes widened as she stressed the last words. "It just got worse and worse and finally I went to a lawyer in Tampa - the best one, mind you. I told him how Chuck and the family were treating me and how he was running around on me every chance he got."

"He was?" Pearl questioned, thinking that perhaps it had been Ellie who had done the running around.

"I never, *never* cheated on that man. Now you know I flirt like the dickens. You know that if it wears pants I'm going to flirt with it. But I never, *never* had sexual relations with anyone."

Pearl nodded in agreement, then catching Ellie's gaze, recanted, "No, sure you didn't."

"I felt like the red headed stepchild when we'd go out to dinner or visit someone. They barely talked to me or they interrupted me when I did try to join in the conversation. They went to the mountains this past winter and left me home in that big house all alone – said they knew how I hated the mountains and didn't see why I was so upset about the whole thing. But you can be sure they took Monroe."

"Without even asking you?"

"Oh, it was *assumed* that I wouldn't mind, that it would be heartless to deny Monroe a trip to the mountains just because I didn't like them."

This was the first time Pearl had ever seen Ellie cry. "My own little girl doesn't even want to be around me...God I love her so much Pearl. I just don't understand why they have done all this." Wiping the tears from her eyes Ellie straightened her shoulders and thrust her chin forward. "He got custody, you know."

"I'm so sorry," Pearl consoled her friend, "In time things will turn around, you'll see."

Ellie dabbed at her eyes again, "I hope you're right."

"Couldn't your lawyer do anything?"

"Ha!" Throwing her head back in laughter, Ellie's eyes darkened with anger. "Those sons of bitches. When I went to the lawyer, he said he'd try to help me. Paid him two hundred dollars, then when I went back a week later for our appointment his secretary comes out and hands me an envelope... seems he decided he couldn't take the case after all, didn't think he really could help. Well, I know what happened. I told you that family pulls strings all over the state. Well, when they realized who I was, or whose family I belonged to, they contacted Chuck."

"So, I went to another lawyer, forked out another two hundred dollars, told him about the way things were and the running around, and the same damn thing happened... a week later I get a letter almost identical to the one the first lawyer gave me."

"That's not right. Isn't that against the law?"

"Sure it is. But the Bridges own the law down there. I didn't stand a chance. And then when we finally went to court over it, he has some guy I met at one of those little parties they're always throwing, say that I had an affair with him. They had pictures of us dancing together and a picture of us kissing."

"You kissed him?"

"Pearl, I said I never had sexual relations with anyone, not that I never kissed anyone. And as I recall he was pretty pushy about the whole thing. He seemed in a hurry to take me out by the groves."

"Well, I guess they *did* get you then."

"He said we'd been seeing each other for months and then he described me right down to the mole near my tee tee. You know the one. You used to tease me about it when we were kids. That's when you started calling me *smelly Ellie*, said that little black mole was a sign that my cooter was rotting." Ellie pulled her shorts down and showed the mole to Pearl, "remember?"

Pearl smiled as she nodded. "I guess I was mean to you too in some ways."

"Hell, we were kids. That's what kids do."

As she lit a cigarette and leaned her chair against the wall, Ellie continued describing the events of her divorce. "Well, I do have visitation. I get Monroe every other Christmas, and every other Thanksgiving. I get her two months during the summer and I'm allowed to visit *at their home* every other month."

"I'm surprised they're even giving you that."

"Me too, but I figured they always have such big parties on the holidays, that what I'll be doing is babysitting. And then, every summer we always took a trip out west or flew to the Bahamas. Last year we went to Spain."

"I'm glad you came back home – sorry about Monroe – but I think your hands were tied there." Pearl shook her head in disgust as she wiped a table in preparation for 11 A.M. when she opened the doors for business. "Just see her when you can, and make the best of it. You never know what the future will bring." She looked at Ellie's skimpy outfit and grinned, "You know that what you're wearing doesn't help you any. Did you dress like that in Florida?"

"Sure did. And I've got the legs to pull it off. In fact, I think you should make this the official waitress uniform of the Sea Gull." The white short shorts she wore were snug against her body and the blue and white stripped sailor blouse tugged against her breasts. "It's cute, don't you think?" Ellie questioned as she cocked the white sailor hat to the side.

"I like the outfit, but I think I'll wear my shorts a little longer. Never did have the legs you've got."

"God has blessed me," Flouncing her long hair with her hand, Ellie turned the closed sign to open; "Here they come."

Already a crowd had amassed outside the door, waiting for the little restaurant to open. Bathers with towels wrapped around their waists stepped in and made their way to either a table or booth. Fishermen who had arrived predawn to surf fish were coming in for iced tea and a burger with fries. Within minutes the juke box was playing and the Sea Gull restaurant came alive with sounds of conversation and laughter. Smells of hamburgers sizzling on the grill and seafood frying permeated the air as the hustle and bustle of summertime began.

"Lord my dogs are tired," Ellie kicked off her sneakers and wiggled her toes. "I sure will be glad when Labor Day comes and the tourists go back home."

Ellie popped the top off of two Tru-Ade sodas and set them on the counter, "Me too, I suppose. But it sure has been a good summer."

One customer sat alone at a far booth, nursing a cup of coffee and finishing the last pieces of the peach cobbler Lottie had made.

"Nodding toward the kitchen Pearl whispered, "So, what do you think of the new cook?"

"I haven't had the chance to taste his cooking, but I can tell you that he ain't bad to look at." She cast her eyes toward the kitchen, "hubba hubba."

Roger turned the kitchen light off and made his way toward the women. "Long day," he poured himself a glass of iced tea and sat at the table nearest Ellie and Pearl, taking a long look at Ellie's feet. "It's beyond me why you paint your toes red when you're wearing shoes all day long," As he touched the cold glass to Ellie's foot, she jerked quickly and slid him a teasing glance."

"I wear sandals when I'm not working, fool." She stretched her long legs forward and rotated her ankles till they popped. "Umm, this is the first time I've had a chance to sit down all day." Ellie pointed her toes and swung her legs close to him, "You don't think they look pretty?"

Roger's eyes made their way along the long stretch of her legs, then moved across her torso and finally rested, boldly gazing into her eyes. His lustful stare was met with one of her own, but he ignored her remarks as he gulped from the glass of tea and turned his attention to Pearl, "I bet your mom was a real power house when she was young. She just about out does me in the kitchen."

"Momma always worked right alongside Daddy. I don't think she knows how to stop. And a few hours a day here at the restaurant keeps her active and makes her feel needed."

A broad grin crossed his lips as Roger nodded knowingly, "My mom and dad worked right to the end too. But we didn't have anything like this," He stopped to survey the room and nodded to the last patron as he tossed a dime tip on the table. "But Dad dirtied up the house and Mom cleaned up after him," Roger chuckled. "Sure do miss them."

"Maybe you could get them to move down here," Ellie jumped into the conversation.

"That would be kind of difficult for them to do."

"Why?"

"They're dead."

"Oh." Feeling embarrassed, Ellie rose to take her empty glass to the kitchen.

"I'm sorry to hear that," she called from across the counter, "Any brothers or sister?"

"No."

"So, it's just you."

"Yep," Roger turned his back to Ellie and leaned toward Pearl. "You're an only child too. Aren't you?"

Pearl nodded, she felt uneasy as she shifted her eyes from his. His obvious coolness toward Ellie after a day of overt flirting with her was puzzling.

"You're from Pennsylvania, right?" Ellie called out.

"Sure am...little town called Brownsville...coal mining country. That's what Dad did most of his life."

"Get's cold up there, doesn't it?"

"Our whole winter is like your coldest day here. You have a short winter compared to ours."

Pearl excused herself from the conversation to wipe down the booth where the last customer had been, leaving Ellie and Roger to continue their conversation. He took another long drink from the cold tea and slid a glance toward Pearl as she stretched across the booth table to wipe it clean.

As he rose, Roger reached to caress Ellie's cheek with an extended finger.

She looked boldly into his eyes, "Better get home and get my beauty rest... going to be another mad house tomorrow, I imagine."

"Just make sure you make it clear on those orders whether you want a fish platter or fish sandwich. You screwed up on that twice today."

Ellie's flirtatious tone shifted to one of sarcasm. "I wrote it plain as day, I can't help if you can't read my writing."

Ignoring her remark, Roger passed closely by Pearl, touching her shoulder, "See you in the morning."

"Okay, Momma ought to have everything ready for you when you get in. See you." His touch made her feel uncomfortable. Pearl switched the open sign to off and locked the door. "We may as well head on home too." She motioned for Ellie to follow her through the kitchen. "So,

306

how do you like him? She asked, "I know you think he's handsome, but what I mean, is how to you think he is as a worker?"

As she rolled her eyes in disgust, Ellie sighed, "There's nothing wrong with my writing. He's just trying to make me look bad. Look..." Ellie grabbed an order pad, "I write FS for fish sandwich and FP for fish platter...now you tell me. Can't you tell the difference?"

Pearl nodded. "It's not that big a deal, we can always scrape the side dishes off and put the flounder filet on a bun. You two just need to get it worked out. Maybe you could write out the platter or sandwich until he gets the hang of it."

"I just don't think he likes me that much."

"It isn't for lack of you trying to make him. I guess tonight was an example of what you told me the beginning of the summer... that you flirt with everybody."

Ellie laughed, "Well, not everybody I guess, only if they're good looking. And he, my dear Pearly White, is good looking. He looks like Clark Gable."

"What?"

"Except for the hazel eyes, he looks like Gable. Don't you think?"

"Girl, you kill me. He looks like Clark Gable like I look like Rita Hayworth. But you listen to me... I don't want any trouble. If he's not interested, he's not interested. Don't try too hard."

"I can't help it. You know me, half the fun is in reeling them in."

"If you two *do* start seeing each other, you just make sure he sticks around until after Labor Day. I need a good cook until after the summer season is through."

"Yes Ma'am," Ellie saluted, touching her hand to her sailor cap. "

Lottie arrived early the next morning to prepare the hush puppy mix and cut potatoes for fries. She fluted the edges of an apple pie before setting it in the oven and then brewed the tea for the lunch crowd. It was nearly ten o'clock and the cook would be arriving soon, as would Ellie and Pearl.

She wasn't sure about Roger. He was nice enough, always polite. But there was something about him she simply did not trust. It wasn't that she believed he was stealing from the restaurant, on the contrary, when it came to money he was very honest - insisting on paying for all his meals even though Pearl and Paul had told him that meals were part of his pay.

Watching him from the corner of her eye, she had noticed how he looked at Pearl; how he seemed to move closer to her whenever she was in the kitchen. Yet, he openly played a baiting game with Ellie, as if he understood the kind of woman she was. He teased her during the day as he prepared her orders, but during slow periods ignored her. He openly ogled her, but also admonished her for little mistakes she made. It was as if he was toying with her. At first the little cat and mouse game was fun to watch - Ellie confidently flaunting her body, teasing Roger and he in return flirting merely by ogling and calling her hot stuff, or sweet thing. The fun was short lived though and Lottie grew annoyed, calling it typical Ellie trash.

What Lottie could not get out of her mind were the questions Roger asked periodically – spacing them far enough apart so as not to appear too nosy. She had noticed too how he hovered around Jess when business lulled. He'd walk her husband to the patio and sit with him; she could see them talking. Of course, whenever she questioned Jess about any conversation with Roger, he dismissed any implication that the young man was trying to pry. Lottie suspected that Jess was just happy to have someone to talk to.

Yes, it was his nosy-ness that bothered her and she thought that maybe it was a Yankee trait – being nosy – but whatever it was, it did not feel right. Roger had asked her once how much land they owned, he'd asked about expenses. But most unsettling was when he asked if Pearl was their only child. That in itself was not so odd, it was the way he said it, flatly, as if he were thinking aloud.

"I don't know what you mean, Momma. What questions?
"It just seems like he's trying to pry into our business."

"I think he's just kind of lonely down here – besides, he just got out of the Marine Corps and doesn't have any place to go home to. Remember, he's a Yankee and you know how nosy they are."

"I've met Yankees, and you might be right. They are a queer lot. But Bart Ralston is a Yankee and he's fitting right in. And Pop Jones isn't from around her either; he's not even a southerner."

Pearl shrugged her shoulders, "I don't know. But I do know that he does his job and knows what he's doing. Not many people know how to cook seafood without over doing it."

Lottie nodded, "Could be you're right. Guess I ought to give him a chance. And this being the middle of the summer it might be hard to find another cook as good as him."

Pearl had to admit she felt uneasiness sometimes around him – especially when she'd catch him watching her. Sometimes he stood so close she'd feel his breath and sometimes he rubbed against her. Always there would be an "oh, excuse me," but still, it just didn't feel right. She toyed with the idea that perhaps this young man had a crush on her. Again, she had to admit the thought made her feel attractive again. But acting on such a feeling was certainly out of the question.

From July fourth on the crew at the Gull worked seemingly nonstop. Business boomed, they sold out of hamburgers twice, leaving Lottie to walk to the Superette to buy more hamburger. Jess stayed in the kitchen constantly on weekends brewing tea, since it seemed to disappear as soon as it was made. He sliced lemon wedges and potatoes for frying and washed dishes.

"I thought I was supposed to be in retirement," He jokingly complained one evening as they readied the Gull to close for the night.

"What are you talking about?" Roger questioned, "You and Miss Lottie are the hardest working people around here and you're more than twice our ages."

"We all work hard around here," Paul spoke out, "And I'd like to say that I think everyone has been doing a fine job this summer. I know it took a while to learn each other's ways, but all in all....I'm happy." Paul pulled Pearl up from her chair and wrapped his arms around her. "And you, Sweetie Pie, you're the main reason everything turns out so well." He dipped her low, kissing her long and deep in front of the small crowd.

"Don't those two make you sick?" Ellie jokingly whispered to Roger.

"There's nothing sexier than a woman in love."

Puzzled by his response, Ellie pushed him gently on the arm, "What does that mean? You think Pearl is sexy...sexier than me?"

"Oh no, honey." He responded quickly; his eyes never leaving the loving couple before him. "I just mean that it's nice to see two people so devoted to one another. I hope one day to have just what they have."

The next day after lunch while they prepped for dinner, Ellie pulled her friend aside, "Come out on the patio with me," Her words seemed nearly like an order. Lighting a cigarette, she fumbled with it in the ash tray, rolling it from side to side.

"Well, what's this all about? What's on your mind? Do you need a few days off?

"No." She took a long drag, then blew a smoke ring, breaking it with her finger as it floated in the air. "I think ol' Roger has the hots for you."

Nodding her head in agreement, Pearl sighed, "I suspected as much."

Ellie's mouth pursed, "You know?"

"Well, I know he made me feel strange and I noticed he was always coming around me." Pearl grinned sheepishly... "It's probably just a little crush on the boss lady."

"I can't believe you. You like it!"

"Oh, he'll get over it," Pearl shook her head, "It's nothing."

Resting her elbow against a piling, Ellie pursed her lips, "Feels nice, doesn't it? Someone paying attention to you, but let me remind you Miss Pearly White Goody Two Shoes – if you notice Roger's flirting and I notice it, what makes you think that Paul hasn't noticed it?"

"He hasn't said anything, but you're right. Oh my God, poor Paul. I should have fired Roger before the fourth,"

Pearl placed her hands to her face, "I just never thought...Roger is such a wolf I just didn't take him seriously, he's always ogling the customers and you – well, you know he just wants to get in your pants, Ellie."

"And yours too."

"He's gone after Labor Day, I don't care how good a cook he is or ...."

"Don't get you panties in a knot over this. I just wanted to see if you were interested in him.

Gasping loudly Pearl felt her face redden. "How in the world could you ever think that I would be unfaithful to Paul?"

"I guess you're right, after all, once one has had steak, they rarely go back to hamburger."

"And I'm hamburger?"

Sharply cocking an eyebrow, Ellie retorted, "You know what I mean."

"You better watch yourself, I don't think this one is like the other boys you've flirted with...and why do you want someone like that anyway...he has no money."

"I've learned that money isn't everything. Remember?"

"I think you ought to let Roger go. We can handle the Gull now without him.

"What? Why do you want to let him go? There's only a few more days before the season ends. What's up?" Paul leaned back against the driftwood log, watching the children as they raced up and down the dunes.

"Haven't you noticed how he acts sometimes?" Pearl held his gaze and raised an eyebrow. "Momma thinks he's too nosy."

"He is," The corners of Paul's mouth turned upward, "But I suppose you want to get rid of him because of the flirting."

"Oh. You mean how he flirts with everybody."

"And you," Pulling Pearl to his side, Paul kissed her neck. "I'm not blind."

"So you've noticed."

"Who wouldn't?" Paul pulled her closer and kissed her cheek," You're such a pretty girl, who wouldn't want to flirt with you. But I trust you honey. You'd never stoop to that." He pulled Pearl close, "I don't have to compete, I know you're mine and besides, the summer's almost over and we can let him go then. This winter it will just be the locals and we can handle that."

"Ellie isn't going to like it."

"Ellie doesn't like a lot of things. And I kinda agree with your mom. She's brought a lot of things on herself."

Pearl shrugged her shoulders and squeezed Paul's hand. "The Bridges do sound mighty harsh, Paul."

"There you go again." Holding her gaze, Paul spoke softly, "You always look for the good in people...that's one of the things I love about you." He pulled her close and nuzzled his face into her neck.

"Oh, I forgot to tell you," Paul started as he turned to reach into the cooler for a cola, "When I brought the shrimp in this morning Ellie said she wanted all of us to go out on her houseboat next Wednesday."

"You really want to go?"

I wouldn't mind taking a ride on that new toy of hers. It sounds like fun."

"We'd have to put up with all that *hootchy* between her and Roger."

"I'm not worried about it. Let's go. It'll be fun. Your momma can watch the kids I guess and you can schedule the help to run the restaurant for us. It ought to be slow. You okay with that?"

"Yeah," Pearl agreed though if it were solely up to her she would have declined the invitation. But Paul wanted to go and that was enough to persuade her.

CHAPTER TWENTY-FOUR

Pearl was aware of his eyes on her as she stepped onto the new houseboat. She did not like the feeling and held onto Paul's arm as they stood on the deck. She wished again that she and Paul had not come along. But Paul seemed so enthusiastic; he always had been a little awed by Ellie's toys. Chuck's alimony came in handy when it came to the finer things in life. Pearl reached for the beer Roger handed her and watched he and Paul climb the ladder to the top deck. Ellie sat beside her, sipping her own beer, smoothing her hair back into a ponytail.

The two friends sat in silence watching the gulls and egrets; empty osprey nests topped the waterway markers. Here and there small docks reached out into the water, evidence of the construction that was occurring on the island. "Ooh, I'd love to have a place like that." Ellie cooed as she noticed a long pier that led to a two story home among the water oaks. She grew silent again.

The day was as beautiful a day as any Pearl had ever seen. A light breeze filled the air and gulls called, squawking as they glided about in the cloudless sky. Ellie looked beautiful, her unusual quietness gave Pearl a chance to look at her; wisps of hair curled around her brow, there was not a freckle on her face and the slight upturn of her corners of her lips belied the secret that her eyes held; one she was not ready to tell. Of course, Ellie had dressed as provocatively as possible without giving everything away; her black two piece revealing every curve of her body.

"I know you have something you're dying to tell me. Fess up."

As Ellie threw back her head in laughter, she rose from her chair lean against a bulkhead. "Not going to tell you."

"Suit yourself, but I know it won't be long. You never could keep a secret."

Ellie motioned toward Roger, chattering away as he stood next to Paul. He wore swimming trunks covered by a terry cloth robe. It was obvious he was already a little tipsy by the way he leaned in and spoke too loudly. Paul stood listening, nodding his head. As he caught a glimpse of the women watching, he winked at Pearl. She winked back – then Roger winked. Her eyes flew to Paul's. He laughed and winked again and mouthed the word *okay.*

Pearl overheard Roger's drunken slurred words, "that sure is some wife you have," she rolled her eyes and shook her head, Paul's lips pursed, Pearl shrugged her shoulders and rolled her eyes again.

"You know, Ellie, what in the world do you see in Roger? I hope this little secret you're keeping has nothing to do with him."

"Nope, has to do with those old bags of worms in Florida."

"And?"

"When Monroe went home last week she told the Bridges she wanted to move up here with me."

"Oh, I'm so happy for you."

"Don't be happy yet. It's going to be a fight and it may not happen at all, but at least I know my daughter wants me."

Wrapping their arms around one another the two friends squealed in joy.

"I guess this is turning out to be a beautiful day after all. But I still don't see what you see in Roger."

"He's not that bad, but let me tell you honey, he ain't that good either – know what I mean."

They set the anchor in a spot around twenty yards or so from one of the little intracoastal isles, secure that they were in deep enough water to dive into. It was tricky, however; since with each attempt to set the anchor it seemed too deep, until finally they pulled the boat closer to shore where the anchor could grab hold.

There were a couple other small boats on the water - fishermen out for the day relaxing, and Pearl was happy for

Ellie and so profoundly in love with Paul she could hardly contain her feelings. Maybe it *was* a good idea to come along just to spend some time on the water and enjoy its peacefulness. Paul had fallen asleep below and after rising from a short nap had climbed the ladder to the top deck. He stood, no doubt, admiring the beauty before him. She called up to him, "hungry?" He nodded his head. Pearl then called down to the galley to Ellie to bring her one of the sandwiches she and Roger were supposed to be making. She heard giggles and laughter coming from below and she giggled herself, relieved that Roger was giving his attention to Ellie, not her. Paul waved to her from above, flexing his muscles playfully; he teased his wife as she watched from below.

Suddenly, Roger burst from the galley, laughing as Ellie chased him. He grabbed at Pearl as he passed, throwing her off balance and into him. Still laughing he held her by the shoulders and steadied her, then plunged head first from the stern, diving into the murky water. Pearl turned to watch him surface; from her peripheral vision she saw Paul preparing to dive – she heard him call her name. Gazing up toward his tanned body she smiled, swelling with pride for her man and all they had accomplished in not much over ten short years. Their tobacco business was booming the Gull was a success. Her beautiful children were healthy and happy and Paul, Paul was her rock, her most precious rock, more dear than anyone could imagine. She laughed as he dove from the top of the boat; she heard a loud grunt and laughed at his monkey shines. Pearl walked the few step to the port side of the boat, where Paul should surface, but as she neared it Ellie called, "Hey, look at Paul, how does he do that?"

Pearl saw her husband's body making circles in the water, round and round. "What! Paul! She screamed, knowing something was wrong. Roger reached him just as she jumped into the water. Together they pulled his limp body onto the boat. Ellie called frantically on the C.B. radio for help and when they arrived at Sloop Point an Ambulance from Cape Fear Hospital was waiting to take Paul there.

Paul lived for three hours once he reached the hospital. Cause of death was not listed as a broken neck as Pearl had feared, but his facial bones had crushed into his brain. The isles of the waterway had given way to tides and erosion and though the waterway itself may have still been near to thirty feet deep, the bottom near the isles was closer to four or five feet - the dive was fatal.

The funeral had been larger than she expected. It seemed that nearly the entire areas of Holly Ridge, Surf City and the little communities in between came to pay their respects to one of their own. Amy and Eli came from Mississippi, forlorn and grief stricken, they came to comfort Clarence who had made amends years before. Phil, Paul's brother, appeared from nowhere. How he had found out about his brother's death was a mystery since no one had either seen or heard

320

from him in over fifteen years. He resembled Paul dramatically except for the color of his hair; it was much darker. He had not forgiven his father yet and kept his distance, spending time with Pearl and the Scaggins family instead. The Burns, Abbott, and Butler families along with the Weldon, Rosell, West and Pike families were there with so many other families of the area. Several brought food and comfort.

After several weeks, a respectful period of deep mourning, the knowing families came by often to check on Mrs. Pearl Rosell and her young children, asking her to join them in a trip to the movies in Wilmington or to a pig picking. Knowing grief themselves at different periods in their own lives it was as if they knew the playbook by heart and delivered their love and compassion at what seemed the right times.

Ellie had Rawl West take the houseboat twenty miles off shore and sink it. Her affair with Roger dwindled and within a month of Paul's death they parted ways. "We're still friends though," she insisted. "He likes the job at the Ark Restaurant in Jacksonville and is moving to Verona. But he asks about you all the time."

Pearl's stomach churned when she heard those words and whenever Ellie brought up the subject of Roger, she quickly changed it.

Christmas neared and Monroe made the permanent move to Surf City. Pearl relished the vivacity of the girl - reminding her so of Ellie as a child. She laughed at the thought of another spoiled brat her children would learn to contend with. An oyster roast was thrown in celebration of Monroe's arrival, complete with Will Pike, Enid and his band of guitar and banjo pickers.

Ever so carefully Ellie had watched as Pearl muddled through the phases of loss, wondering if she should write Jay and if so, when would be a good time. As promised she had periodically sent him pictures of Frankie; he responded biannually with a simple thank you note. She respected both he and the Scaggins' desire for privacy.

As she sat in the dunes and gazed at the bell-less yuccas, the gray stems of the hairawn muhly and the colorless landscape of the banks, the emptiness seemed woven deep within her; Pearl felt the chill of loss. It would not go away and then a part of her did not want it to. She wanted to hold on as long as possible - forever.

"Oh, if I could just see him once more, feel him press against me." She could almost smell his scent; the light breeze seemed to carry it, the light musk of his sweat, the salty sweetness of his neck as she buried her face in it. She balled her fists to strike the air around her, "My God I need you Paul! I want you! I want him back God, I want him back! "She struggled to feel him nuzzle her hair as he did in the mornings, *make it so, make it so,* tangling it – gently caressing her throat, then softly massaging her breasts. She saw his smile, the lines at the corners of his eyes, and how his lips laid against his teeth, the stubble of his unshaven face as he entered the kitchen door in the evenings after work. She held her arms out to reach to him, to pull him close. "I want to feel you. I *need* you." She felt his tongue part her lips; she felt the kiss, *the smell.*" She nuzzled the air as she closed her eyes, seeing his image – waiting for it to respond.

Questions filled Pearl's mind constantly. *Was Paul showing off for me? And why? Why did he go to the top deck? Why didn't he think to check the depth? He always warned the kids about diving into water.* The questions ate at her. *I should have talked Paul into getting rid of him weeks ago. I should have talked him into not going...Oh my God, if I could just go back.* "If only I had told him not to *jump.* "I want to go back to the minute before. God! Please!" She screamed aloud. "Let me go back!" Pearl leaned into the dune, the sand caressing her form, a long screeching sound escaped her throat – *If I scream loud enough and long enough will it make it not real*; aching with want, with despair. It was as if there was no time, as if the world was caught in a fog.

"Mommy, Mommy! Are you alright?" Frank and Jo rushed to their mother as they heard the screams. "Are you thinking about Daddy again?" Both children lay next to Pearl in the sand. She drew them even closer then wiped the tears away with the sleeve of her coat.

"Um hum. Mommy thinks about Daddy all the time. I miss him very much." She straightened herself to sitting position. "But I know he's with God now. I know he's looking down at us and telling me not to be so sad." Pearl felt guilty for drawing attention to her sorrow, especially for the children. It was her job to go on with life and be strong for them. But time had escaped her; *I must not do this anymore.* She scolded herself. "I'm okay now," she smiled gently then kissed each child on the cheek. "I promise I will get better. Now, why don't y'all go see if you can find me some shark's teeth?" She patted each behind to shoo them off to the shore.

Ambiguous feelings swirled in her head as she felt the obligation to be strong for her children but keep the memory of Paul alive within her.

Now, in the gray and dreary coldness, the staple of eastern North Carolina winters, Pearl wrestled with the past, the present and the future. Paul had left her in the summer, when all was abloom – full of life. She wore her ache like a shroud, unwilling to take it off. She pulled the light coat snuggly against her swollen belly as his memory washed over her; the child would never know its father.

Watching Frankie and Jo skip backwards from the incoming waves, Pearl closed her eyes, remembering doing the same thing as a child with Ellie and Paul. She pulled her hair back away from her face, the cool salty breeze felt soft on her skin. Closing her eyes, Pearl envisioned the purple heather in bloom, how it swayed with the ocean breeze. She heard the children's laughter and rose to join them.

Made in the USA
Columbia, SC
24 March 2019